# Murder
## in the
# Grave

## A Redmond and Haze
## Mystery Book 5

## By Irina Shapiro

# Copyright

# Contents

# Prologue

The day dawned bright and humid, the sun blazing in a cloudless sky and the temperature rising with every passing hour. The worst kind of day for a funeral, Arthur Weeks reflected as he entered the cemetery and walked toward the grave he'd dug yesterday. It was bad enough to bury someone in pouring rain or biting cold, but to stand beside an open grave in black, often woolen mourning attire while the sun beat down mercilessly on one's head and shoulders was as near to hell as Arthur could imagine. He would take a crisp autumn day over the heat of summer any day.

There was no need for Arthur to check on the grave, but he liked to make sure everything was ready for the burial, nonetheless. He was a conscientious man who took his responsibilities seriously. The graveyard at St. Martin's was neat and tidy, the weeds pulled, the flowers watered, and the grass cut. Arthur often spoke to the dead as he went about his duties, calling them by name, especially since he'd known so many of them in life. He told them about his days and the happenings in the village, desperate for someone to talk to since his wife had joined the ranks of his deceased friends nearly five years ago now.

Approaching the grave, Arthur frowned in consternation. When he'd finished digging the grave, the sides had been straight, the corners sharp, and the mound of earth piled on the side had been a neat brown hillock just waiting to be returned to its proper place once the coffin had been lowered into the ground. This morning, the hillock was considerably smaller and one of the sides of the grave looked ragged, as if someone had stood at the very edge and rocked back and forth, undoing all his hard work. Striding toward the grave, Arthur yanked the shovel he'd left nearby and was just about to fix the edge to make sure it looked right and proper when something struck him as odd.

The grave wasn't deep enough. Arthur peered in, unsure what to do. Had he made a mistake in his measurements? Was there time to dig another two feet before the funeral? He was already dressed in his best suit, his only suit, and he didn't want to be covered in dirt when the mourners arrived. Nevertheless, the grave had to be six feet deep, and it was his responsibility to ensure that everything was up to snuff.

Arthur removed his coat, hung it over a nearby headstone, and jumped into the grave, ready to rectify his mistake.

He was about to drive the shovel into the rich earth when his gaze fell on something long and pale sticking out of the ground. A root? Arthur bent down and grabbed the offending piece of wood, ready to yank it from the soil. He let out a shrill cry when he found himself holding on to a cold, stiff finger that was still attached to a hand. Being made of sterner stuff than most, Arthur took a moment to collect himself, then used his hands to clear away the dirt from the person's face. Wide blue eyes met Arthur's gaze, a grimace of pain etched into the man's bloodied face. Arthur took a step back, his heart hammering in his breast.

"Dear God," he whispered as he looked heavenward, hoping for guidance. He'd seen many a dead body in his sixty-five years, but he'd never seen anything like this.

# Chapter 1

## Tuesday, August 6, 1867

Jason Redmond came awake in the best way possible to find his new wife leaning over him, her lips brushing against his as her nightdress offered a tantalizing glimpse of her lovely breasts. He wrapped his arms around her and returned her kiss, ready and willing to perform his husbandly duties until his bride was satisfied. His plans were unexpectedly thwarted when Katherine suddenly pulled away, her hand flying to her mouth as she jumped out of bed and ran for the newly installed water closet, slamming the door behind her.

*So, it's like that, is it?* Jason thought, smiling happily despite his disappointment at having to forgo making love to his bride.

Katherine emerged a few minutes later, looking pale and ill. "I'm sorry," she moaned. "I must have eaten something that didn't agree with me last night."

Jason came toward her and took her in his arms, holding her close.

"Do you feel unwell?" Katherine asked, studying his face. She looked heartbreakingly vulnerable without her spectacles and with her hair tumbling down her back, a different person to the calm, composed Katherine, whose hair was always modestly arranged, and her glasses perched on her pert nose, magnifying her dark eyes.

"I'm well, Katie. In fact, I'm better than well," Jason said, taking her face in his hands.

"Are you?" Katherine said, looking at him earnestly. "Well, that's something, I suppose."

"Do you feel any better?" Jason asked as the color began to return to her face.

"A little. Perhaps a cup of tea will set me to rights. I think it was that creamed veal Mrs. Dodson made last night. It really was too rich."

"Katie—"

"I'll tell her not to make it again," Katherine said, the look of determination returning now that she felt marginally better. "I really do prefer lighter fare, especially so close to bedtime." Katherine gently removed Jason's hands and glanced at the window. "I suppose I had better get dressed. It looks to be a fine day outside. I promised I'd visit Father this morning."

"Katie—" Jason tried again.

"Yes, I know I was at the vicarage only a few days ago, but he does get lonely. He likes me to read over his sermons, and it's my turn to arrange the church flowers."

"Katie—"

"Yes, my dear?" Katherine asked, focusing on him once again.

"You haven't had your courses since we were in Rome," Jason pointed out gently.

"Haven't I?" she asked, blushing prettily. This was not the kind of thing she felt comfortable discussing, even though he was a doctor and knew all about the female body, at least in theory.

"And this is the third time this week you've felt unwell," Jason continued.

Her mouth dropped open and her eyes widened in shock, the true meaning of his words finally sinking in. "Oh, my word!" she exclaimed, grabbing his hand. "Do you think...?"

"I think it's a very good possibility given how often we—" He never got to finish the sentence.

There was an urgent knock on the door, followed by Dodson, who colored with embarrassment when he saw Katherine in a state of undress.

"I beg your pardon, my lord, my lady. You're wanted, sir. Urgently."

"What happened?" Jason asked, wishing more than anything that whatever it was hadn't happened today of all days, or had at least waited for an hour or two so that he could spend some time with Katie. She was sure to have questions or, at the very least, require his support at such a momentous juncture in their lives.

"There's a body, sir. In a grave. Constable Pullman is downstairs," Dodson added, his disapproval evident.

Dodson didn't enjoy having the police invade Redmond Hall every time there was a suspicious death, and didn't bother to hide his opinion that no nobleman should involve himself in solving crimes, and worse yet, perform autopsies on the deceased in the basement mortuary of the Brentwood police station. But Jason Redmond was no ordinary nobleman, nor had he been raised in England, where duty and a sense of propriety would have been hammered into him since birth. Despite his proud lineage, Jason had been born and raised in America, had trained as a surgeon, and had fought in the American Civil War, the scars of that conflict still fresh on his heart, if no longer on his body. He had resigned himself to claiming his inheritance but wasn't prepared to give up medicine or the need to feel useful and intellectually stimulated. He loved a challenge, eager to solve the puzzle using nothing but his wits and gut instinct. And as long as Katherine took no issue with his desire to assist the police, he would continue to do so.

"Tell Constable Pullman I'll be right down," Jason said. "Katie, will you be all right on your own for a few hours?" he asked, feeling like a cad for leaving her.

"Of course I'll be all right," Katherine said as she reached for her spectacles and slid them onto her nose, her gaze now more focused. "Jason, are you pleased?" she asked, her voice small and unsure.

"I'm thrilled to bits," Jason said, and pulled her to him, giving her a sound kiss. "And I will show you just how happy I am when I return. In the meantime, have a light breakfast and go for a walk before it gets too hot."

"Doctor's orders?" Katherine asked, her earnest expression bringing out his every protective instinct.

"Husband's orders," Jason replied, stroking her cheek. "I wish I didn't have to leave you. I'm sorry."

"You don't have anything to apologize for, and I wouldn't have you any other way. Now, go. A body won't keep long in this heat."

"I love you, darlin'," Jason said, putting on an exaggerated American accent that always made her laugh.

"I love you too, Yank," Katherine replied, flashing him an impish grin.

# Chapter 2

Jason jumped down from the police wagon driven by Constable Pullman and followed him into the graveyard, where Inspector Daniel Haze was waiting impatiently, his hands clasped behind his back, his face tight with displeasure. Ned Hollingsworth, the police photographer, was leaning against a gravestone, a cheroot dangling from the side of his mouth, his expression radiating irritation as he awaited his opportunity to photograph the victim. His camera was already set up, the tripod positioned several feet from the open grave in order to get a closeup once the body was lifted out. The police called him when there was a particularly puzzling or gruesome case that required photographic evidence, and Ned, a weasel of a man, had a sideline of selling copies of crime-scene photos to the newspapers, which was probably more profitable.

Inspector Haze seemed to relax marginally when he spotted Jason and raised his hand in greeting, clearly relieved to be able to get on with the morning's work. Ned Hollingsworth tipped his hat and continued to smoke.

"Jason, thank you for coming so quickly," Daniel said as Jason approached the open grave and stared down into its depths, his eyebrows lifting in astonishment at the sight that greeted him. It was gruesome, and unexpectedly disturbing because the victim appeared to be staring directly at him, his blue gaze full of accusation, his face crusted with blood, and the split skull already crawling with maggots.

Jason looked away. "Have you examined the surrounding area?" he asked Daniel.

"I have. The side of the grave had been disturbed. I believe the victim had been standing at the edge, or close to it, just before falling backward, probably driven over by the force of the blow. The killer used some of the dug-up soil to cover the corpse. Had the gravedigger not come by this morning to check on his work, the coffin would have been lowered into the grave, and the body would never have been discovered."

"Were there no footprints?" Jason asked.

"I think there must have been, but they were obliterated when the soil was disturbed. There's blood on the shovel, which belongs to Mr. Weeks and has been here since he dug the grave yesterday. Would you like to examine the corpse inside the grave, or would you like it lifted out?" Daniel asked.

"I want the body shifted onto a wooden panel and lifted out carefully, so as to preserve as much of the original setting as possible."

"Understood," Daniel said. "Constable Pullman, please assist Mr. Weeks in retrieving the body."

Constable Pullman groaned but didn't argue, knowing it to be useless. Someone had to do the grunt work, and it was usually him. He removed his helmet and set it on one of the neighboring graves, then turned to the gravedigger, who'd already brought a narrow wooden panel that might have been part of an old door, and two lengths of thick rope.

"How shall we go about this?" Constable Pullman asked, his reluctance to get into the grave obvious.

"I will go down there, shift the body onto the plank, then run the rope beneath the wood. Then we will use the ropes to lift 'im. You needn't go down there, Constable," Arthur Weeks said.

"Well, go on, then," Constable Pullman said, his relief palpable.

Arthur Weeks lowered himself into the grave and went about arranging the body while the four men looked on, each ready to do his bit. It took less than ten minutes to lift the body out of the grave, at which point everyone stood aside to allow Ned Hollingsworth to take his photographs. Once finished, he closed the lens, detached the camera from the tripod and set it on the ground, then folded the tripod and stuffed it under his arm before picking up the camera and striding off, his presence no longer required. He would return to Brentwood with Constable Pullman and retire to his darkroom, where he would develop the photographs and deliver them to the station, probably no later than by noon tomorrow.

"Do you think he was dead when he went in?" Daniel asked as Jason bent over the body.

"I hope so, but I can't be certain until I perform a postmortem," Jason replied. "He was struck on the head with something hard and sharp, most likely the shovel you found," Jason said, examining the head wound that had nearly cleaved the man's skull as if it were a ripe melon. Rigor mortis had already begun to set in, and the presence of maggots confirmed Jason's suspicion that the man had been in that hole for at least twelve hours.

"He doesn't appear to have any other injuries, but there's dirt under his fingernails," Jason said, lifting the man's hand to show Daniel.

Daniel nodded. "Let's get him to the mortuary. I don't think there's anything more we can do here. Constable, get him into the wagon," Daniel instructed.

"Yes, sir."

Constable Pullman and Arthur Weeks hefted the wooden panel and carried the body to the police wagon, which was parked just beyond the lychgate. Ned Hollingsworth was already perched on the bench.

"I'd like to complete the postmortem within the next few hours. I need to get home," Jason added anxiously.

"Is everything all right?" Daniel asked, truly looking at Jason for the first time. "You seem a bit distracted."

"Everything is fine. It's just that Katherine wasn't feeling well this morning. I want to check on her."

"The postmortem can wait until tomorrow," Daniel suggested with some reluctance.

"I'd rather do it now. It's too hot to leave the body lying around for too long. I'll have answers for you by this afternoon," Jason said, and tipped his hat. "We'll talk later."

He strode toward the wagon and climbed into the back, grateful that the victim's body had been covered with a length of filthy sackcloth. At the very least, it would keep the flies away. Jason leaned against the side of the wagon and closed his eyes, his mind turning to more pleasant thoughts than the postmortem he was about to perform.

# Chapter 3

Having seen the wagon off, Daniel returned to the graveyard and entered the church, which was marginally cooler, its dim confines a welcome respite from the blazing sunshine outside. The vicar sat in the front pew, his shoulders hunched, his head pulled in like that of a turtle. He was an elderly man with wispy white hair combed over his balding pate and a narrow, wrinkled face with a thin, hooked nose and light blue eyes. His cheeks were damp, either with sweat or tears; Daniel couldn't tell.

"Do you feel up to answering a few questions, Reverend Hodges?" he asked, sitting down next to the old man.

The vicar nodded sadly. "Yes, of course. Anything I can do to help."

"What time was the funeral scheduled for this morning?"

"Eleven o'clock. It was for Mrs. Crowe."

"Did she die of natural causes?" Daniel asked. The cause of Mrs. Crowe's death wasn't relevant, but that could change once he had more information to work with.

"Yes. She was ninety-six and had outlived half her children. I've asked Mr. Weeks to inform the family that the funeral is postponed until further notice."

"Thank you. That was good thinking on your part," Daniel said. "Did you know the deceased?" The vicar had been present at the gravesite when Daniel had arrived nearly two hours ago and had seen the body in all its gruesome glory.

The vicar's shoulders slumped even lower. "Yes. I knew him. It's Sebastian Slade, the curate."

"The curate?" Daniel wondered if he'd heard correctly.

"Yes. Mr. Slade had only just come to Upper Finchley. He'd been here less than a fortnight. I can't begin to imagine why anyone would want to do him harm. He was such a pleasant young man, so unassuming in his manner."

"Is it common to have a curate?" Daniel asked. St. Catherine's in Birch Hill, where Daniel had worshipped since he was a boy, had never had a curate.

"I'm getting on in years, and the duties of a parish priest are becoming onerous," Reverend Hodges explained. "I'm ready to retire, truth be told. Bishop Garner has assigned Mr. Slade to the parish with a view to him possibly taking over once he's completed his training."

"Was he not trained?" Daniel asked. He knew little of the inner workings of the Church.

"Mr. Slade graduated from the seminary just over a year ago. It's customary for a novice clergyman to serve as a curate for four years before becoming a full-fledged incumbent. Usually, the four years are done in the same position, but Mr. Slade had some sort of difficulty at his last posting and was transferred to Upper Finchley, as something of a punishment, I think," the vicar added.

"Why would that be a punishment?"

"Because Mr. Slade was from London and had hoped to find a permanent position at one of the many churches there. He wasn't overly fond of the country. He said so himself."

"I see. And has anything unusual happened since Mr. Slade's arrival? Had he had any arguments with anyone?" Daniel asked.

"No. He was so kind and self-effacing. Everyone liked him."

"Surely someone didn't," Daniel said, the face of the deceased appearing unbidden before Daniel's eyes and making him flinch.

Reverend Hodges shook his head. "I wish I knew who it was."

"Have there been any strangers in the village in the past few days?"

"No. Upper Finchley is not a coaching stop, and The Black Boar does not have rooms to let, so unless someone was staying with a relative or a friend, there'd be nowhere for them to lay their head. And, as far as I know, no one has had any visitors of late."

"I see."

"I do think you should speak to my wife. Edith is way more observant than I am, and she's an excellent judge of character. She's at home now, at the vicarage."

"Thank you. I will. And where would I find Bishop Garner?" Daniel asked before taking his leave.

"The bishop has an office in Chelmsford, but he resides in Brentwood. Number ten, Ingrave Road, if I'm not mistaken. You will keep me informed, won't you, Inspector?" Reverend Hodges asked. His manner had gone from shocked bereavement to stoic resignation during the course of the conversation.

"Of course," Daniel promised, eager to get going. There was nothing more to learn here.

The vicarage had seen better days, much like its occupants. Mrs. Hodges looked careworn and utterly colorless, her gray hair an almost perfect match to her dove-gray gown. She invited Daniel in and offered him tea, but the thought of drinking hot liquid on a day like today made him break out in a sheen of sweat. He was sweltering in his tweed suit and bowler hat.

"If I might have a cup of water, I'd be most grateful," Daniel said, wiping his forehead with his handkerchief.

"Of course. How about a nice glass of lemonade?"

"Yes, please," Daniel replied as he sat down on the worn settee.

Having drained the glass of lemonade without really tasting it, he turned his attention to Mrs. Hodges. "Your husband said that Mr. Slade was a pleasant, self-effacing young man. Do you share that view?"

"Oh, yes. Mr. Slade was a dear, dear man." She dabbed at her eyes and sniffled. "I just don't understand. Who would do such a dreadful thing? He didn't even know anyone here, not well enough to have offended, at any rate."

"Had he met everyone in the parish?" Daniel asked.

"He'd met most people, I should think. He took the service last Sunday since Neville—that's my husband—wasn't feeling well. He was very eloquent."

"Might he have said something that could be deemed offensive?" Daniel tried again.

"Oh, no. Nothing like that."

"Did anyone make any remarks after the service? Perhaps single someone out?"

"Not that I saw. Everyone seemed to have enjoyed the sermon. Mr. Slade was so pleased," Mrs. Hodges said. She looked utterly perplexed.

"And did anything unusual happen before, during, or after the service?" Daniel asked, hope quickly fading that he'd learn something of interest.

"One couple left during the service. Their child was fussing, so they took the poor mite home. I think he was unwell."

"I see. And did Mr. Slade reside here at the vicarage?"

"Oh, no. He lodged with Mrs. Monk. She's been taking in lodgers since her husband passed a few years back."

"Did Mr. Slade have to pay for his own lodgings?" Daniel asked.

"The expense would have been covered by the Church," Mrs. Hodges explained.

"Your husband mentioned that Mr. Slade's first position didn't work out. Did he say anything to you about what happened?"

"He just said there was some unpleasantness. A woman, most like. He was an attractive man," Mrs. Hodges said, dabbing at her eyes again. "What a waste of a young life."

"Yes," Daniel agreed. "It certainly is. Mrs. Hodges, were there any strangers in the village that you know of? Maybe someone had come for Mrs. Crowe's funeral," he suggested.

18

Mrs. Hodges shook her head. "Not that I can think of. Wait, no. There's Beth Lundy. She arrived in the village about a month ago, but she's not really a stranger. Born and bred in the village."

"And where has she come from?"

"She was working as a housekeeper in Chelmsford these forty years, but she finally saw fit to retire. Her sister was widowed last year, so she moved in with her. It's nice to have a bit of companionship in one's twilight years."

"Anyone else?"

"No, definitely not. This is a small village, Inspector. A stranger in our midst is not easily overlooked."

"Thank you, Mrs. Hodges."

"Happy to help," Mrs. Hodges replied, and pushed to her feet, ready to see him out.

Daniel left the vicarage and went to call on Mrs. Monk, who was waiting for him on her front step, eager to say her piece.

Mrs. Monk was considerably younger than Mrs. Hodges. In her late forties, Daniel estimated. She wore a becoming gown in a dusky shade of blue with a cameo brooch pinned to the bodice. Her hair was parted in the middle and wound into a neat bun at the back, but on her, the style didn't look severe, simply practical. Her light blue eyes were red-rimmed, which led Daniel to believe that she already knew the identity of the victim and was moved enough to mourn him.

"Please, come in, Inspector," Mrs. Monk said, opening the door and inviting him to go first. "Will you take a dish of tea?"

"No, thank you, Mrs. Monk. I'm rather warm," Daniel confessed.

"I think this has been one of the hottest summers of my life," she agreed. "A cup of ale, then?"

Despite having just had lemonade, Daniel accepted with alacrity and took the seat Mrs. Monk offered. The house was cozy and tastefully decorated, the furnishings and carpets in good condition, the curtains not yet faded. There were several stuffed birds displayed in glass cases, and needlepoint samplers of inspirational quotes hanging on the walls.

Mrs. Monk brought Daniel a cup of ale and settled in a chair across from him, watching him eagerly as he took a sip.

Daniel set the cup down and took out his notebook. "How well did you know Mr. Slade, Mrs. Monk?"

"As well as you can come to know someone in a fortnight," she replied.

"What was Mr. Slade like?"

"Earnest, polite, and surprisingly kind," Mrs. Monk said, her eyes welling up.

"How was he kind to you?" Daniel asked. Did the man have no flaws to work with?

"I've had a number of lodgers since my husband passed. They were civil and well-mannered men, but not one of them took the time to talk to me, to make me feel like a friend rather than just their skivvy. Mr. Slade was different. He treated me, not like his mother exactly, but more like a beloved aunt. He enjoyed my company," she said softly. "It's been rather a long time since anyone has made me feel like that."

"What did you talk about?"

"Books, music, art. Life," she added.

"And did he mention anyone who might wish to do him harm?"

"No, not at all."

"Did he tell you about his last posting?" Daniel asked.

"No, we didn't talk about that."

"Was there anything, anything at all, that you might describe as suspicious?" Daniel tried, desperate for something to go on.

Mrs. Monk considered the question. "Well, he did seem upset when he came home from church on Sunday. Something was on his mind."

"Did he tell you what?"

"No. He excused himself and went up to his room. Didn't even eat luncheon. He asked for a tray in his room at suppertime and went out early the next morning. Said he had some letters to post and wanted to make sure they went out that very day."

"Do you know whom he'd written to?" Daniel asked.

"I only saw the topmost letter. It was to his sister."

"Do you know the lady's name?" Daniel asked, hoping he'd have something to write down on the blank page.

"Yes. Mrs. Iris Holloway."

"And how many letters were there, Mrs. Monk?"

"There were three or four in total, I think," she replied.

"Did you see or hear Mr. Slade leave the house on Monday evening?"

Mrs. Monk shook her head. "My room is upstairs, but Mr. Slade's room is on the ground floor. If he'd gone out after I had retired for the night, I wouldn't have heard him unless he made a racket."

"And what time do you normally retire, Mrs. Monk?" Daniel asked.

"Around nine. I read for about a half hour, and then it's lights out. I'm a sound sleeper too," she added with an embarrassed smile. "My husband always said the house could burn around my ears and I'd never wake."

"Was the front door locked when you got up on Tuesday morning?"

Mrs. Monk looked thoughtful for a moment. "To be honest, I don't recall. I was in the kitchen preparing breakfast when I heard the commotion. That was after Mr. Weeks had found the body and raised the alarm, you understand. So I ran outside to see what was happening. Now that you mention it, I don't remember unlocking the door, but at the time, I might have thought that Mr. Slade had unlocked it first. I didn't know it was him who had died yet," she added, her eyes misting with tears.

"Mrs. Monk, may I see Mr. Slade's room?" Daniel asked as he stepped into the corridor, followed by the landlady.

"Yes, of course. It's just there," she said, pointing toward a door at the end of the corridor. "It's not locked."

Daniel entered the room and looked around. It was spacious and bright, with a window that overlooked the back garden and a freshly painted window frame and door. Blue-and-white wallpaper patterned with large, leafy flowers and vines matched the blue of the bed's coverlet and the curtains, which looked fairly new, the fabric not yet faded. A slightly worn carpet lay in the middle of the floor. There was a small writing desk facing the window, a matching chair, and a chest of drawers decorated with a crisp doily topped with a vase of wildflowers.

"I spruced up the room a bit after my Elliott died," Mrs. Monk explained. "For the lodgers," she added. Daniel took that to mean that this gave her leave to charge a higher price, but he couldn't say he blamed her. It was a pleasant room where a stranger might feel at home.

Daniel opened the drawers one by one. There were clean cotton drawers, shirts, and socks, and a neatly folded tweed suit and black tie, but not much else. He then turned his attention to the desk. Besides the usual writing implements, there were three books, all theologically themed, and a slim volume of poetry. There were no letters, photographs, or a diary, and no handwritten notes for a sermon.

"Is anything missing, Mrs. Monk?" Daniel asked, wondering if Sebastian Slade might have at least brought a photograph or a few keepsakes, given that he was in Upper Finchley to stay.

"No, that's just how he had it. He brought hardly anything with him. Said he liked to travel light."

"I see," Daniel said, taking one last look at the room. It was highly impersonal and told him little of the man, other than that he liked order and minimalism.

"Thank you," Daniel said, and turned to leave.

"You will find whoever did this, won't you, Inspector?" Mrs. Monk asked. "This terrible crime can't go unpunished."

"I will do everything in my power to apprehend the killer, Mrs. Monk."

She looked at him, her gaze intense, her mouth slightly parted as their eyes met. Daniel wondered if Sebastian Slade might have been more affectionate to his landlady than Mrs. Monk was letting on but decided not to ask, not unless he came upon a reason to suspect that she'd been the one to wield the shovel.

# Chapter 4

By the time Daniel arrived at the Brentwood police station, it was well past two o'clock. He was hungry and tired and wanted nothing more than to go home for a few hours and have a kip. Charlotte had been up half the night, crying, fussing, and kicking her little legs as if she were in pain. Daniel had taken over from Sarah at four-thirty and walked with the baby, singing and cooing to her until her eyelids grew heavy and she finally fell asleep around seven.

Unfortunately, it was less than an hour later that Constable Pullman had arrived at his door with a message from the police station, dispatching Daniel to the graveyard in Upper Finchley, while the constable made his way to Redmond Hall to summon Jason. Daniel hadn't even had time for breakfast, a fact that his stomach reminded him of as it rumbled loudly, eliciting a spiteful comment from Sergeant Flint, who was behind the front desk, enjoying a cup of tea and a bun he must have brought from home.

Before making his way to the mortuary, Daniel stopped to speak to his superior, the recently promoted Chief Inspector Coleridge, and update him on the situation. CI Coleridge sat behind his desk, his normally florid face an unprecedented shade of beet red, his mutton-chop whiskers damp from the heat, and perspiration glistening on his forehead. CI Coleridge laced his fingers across his sizeable paunch and fixed Daniel with a basilisk stare.

"When honest citizens don't feel safe in their beds because someone's bashed a clergyman on the head on hallowed ground, we must act quickly, Haze. This is not some cracksman or kidsman getting what they richly deserve, this is a man of God, for Christ's sake. Have you any leads?"

"Not as of yet, sir."

"Well, get some. And quick," Coleridge exclaimed. He pulled out his handkerchief and mopped his brow, letting out a defeated sigh. "This infernal heat is making me irritable," he said by way of apology. Chief Inspector Coleridge was not an unreasonable man and wouldn't normally expect Daniel to solve a case in an hour. "I have faith in you, Haze. You are a good copper. I know you'll get results. Now, get to it."

*So, no unreasonable expectations, then*, Daniel thought bitterly as he closed the door behind him and descended the stairs to the basement level. He knocked on the door of the mortuary, hoping Jason would step outside rather than invite him in. Daniel wasn't easily frightened, but if he could avoid the sight of a flayed body, he would gladly do so, having witnessed a postmortem in the past and all too aware of what was involved.

"Come in," Jason called, disappointing Daniel's hopes. "I'm just about done," Jason said. He wore a bloodstained leather apron to protect his clothes and a linen kerchief tied around his head, which served to keep the sweat from dripping into his eyes in the hellishly hot room. Jason set aside the scalpel and wiped his hands on a towel before turning to face Daniel.

"What do you think?" Daniel asked.

"I think the victim was still alive when he went in the grave. There's a copious amount of dirt in his lungs, which means he was still breathing when he was buried."

"The blow to the head didn't kill him?" Daniel asked, astounded that Sebastian Slade had not died instantly.

"It probably stunned him, maybe even made him lose consciousness for a time, but the cause of death is asphyxiation."

"Anything else you can tell me?"

"Aside from dirt under his fingernails, which is there because he probably tried to claw his way out, there are no defensive wounds. The blow must have taken him by surprise. Otherwise, he was a healthy man."

"Time of death?"

"I'd say around ten last night. Did you find anything out?" Jason asked as he threaded a needle and prepared to close up the body. Daniel averted his gaze from the gaping chest cavity and focused on Jason's face instead.

25

"By all accounts, Sebastian Slade was a kind, likeable man. He'd been in Upper Finchley for only a fortnight, having been transferred from London. He hadn't known anyone in the village when he arrived and had not had any unpleasant encounters that we know of," Daniel said with a deep sigh. "No strangers were seen in the village in the days leading up to the murder. According to his landlady, Mrs. Monk, Sebastian Slade was upset when he returned from the service on Sunday and remained in his room for the rest of the day, during which time he penned several letters, one of them to his sister. Mrs. Monk seemed warmly disposed toward him, but at this time, I have no evidence to suggest that their relationship was anything more than that of a lodger and his landlady."

"In other words, you have absolutely nothing," Jason said as he pushed the needle into the dead flesh.

"Exactly."

"What will you do next?" Jason asked.

"I will have a huge meal at The Bells—I'm starving—then pay a call on Bishop Garner, who oversees the parish of Upper Finchley. I will find out about Mr. Slade's last posting, which came to an end rather abruptly, and obtain an address for his sister in London. What about you?"

"I will join you for a huge meal at The Bells," Jason said, smiling, "then I will return home to my wife and spend the rest of the day with her."

"Are you sure all is well?" Daniel asked.

Jason was newly married and had returned from his wedding trip only six weeks ago, but Daniel had never known him to rush home. Katherine wasn't the type of woman who expected her husband to spend his every waking hour with her. She had pursuits of her own. She visited the elderly and sick, just as she had done when she'd still lived at the vicarage with her father, the Reverend Talbot. She read, gardened, and spent time with Jason's ward Micah Donovan and his sister Mary, who had a one-year-old son, Liam, fathered by a confederate soldier she'd helped during the Civil War. The child was illegitimate, but Katherine didn't care about such things and took great pleasure in playing with Liam and helping Mary when the poor girl was run off her feet after chasing the rambunctious toddler all day.

A slow grin spread across Jason's handsome face. "I think Katie is with child," he said, his voice catching with emotion.

"My congratulations to you both. You must be incredibly happy."

"I am over the moon," Jason said. "I've longed to be a father for some time now, and given Katherine's age, it's not wise to wait too long to have our first child."

"I'm sorry to have taken you away at such a delicate time."

"It's no problem. I have roughly seven months to coddle her and annoy her with my constant fussing."

"So, you think she's two months gone?"

"About," Jason replied. "I'd say the child is due mid-March."

"Do you wish for a son?" Daniel asked, wondering if Jason had given any thought to securing an heir to his title and estate. Probably not. He wasn't one to worry about such things.

"I would be just as happy with a daughter. Speaking of which, how's Charlotte?"

"She was fussing all night," Daniel said. Charlotte was only three months old, and both Daniel and Sarah tended to give in to mindless panic every time the child so much as sneezed. Having lost their three-year-old son several years ago, they were easily frightened and overprotective, a fact they both readily acknowledged.

"Would you like me to take a look?" Jason asked.

"Would you?" Daniel asked, ridiculously relieved by Jason's offer.

"Of course. I'll stop by your house on the way back to Birch Hill and examine the baby. I'm sure she's fine, Daniel."

"I know, but I worry so," Daniel confessed. He'd never take a child's wellbeing for granted again.

"I know," Jason said softly. "Never hesitate to call me, Daniel. I will come day or night; you know that."

Daniel nodded. The smell in the room and the heat were getting to him, and he felt faint, his mouth suddenly dry.

"You don't look so good," Jason observed. "Wait for me outside. I'll be with you as soon as I clean up."

Daniel stepped outside and breathed a sigh of relief. He didn't know how Jason could be so matter-of-fact when a human body lay splayed in front of him like a butchered carcass, but Jason didn't seem to notice. Once, Sarah had called Jason a man of blood, and Daniel supposed she was right. Having been a soldier and an army surgeon, Jason had seen more blood and death than most people did in a lifetime. He didn't fear either, but the experience had left its mark. Jason Redmond was the most fearless man Daniel had ever known, but also the most compassionate. He was also a damn good detective. Jason had helped Daniel solve several cases in the past, and Daniel counted on him to assist with the investigation into the murder of Sebastian Slade.

Most cases that crossed Daniel's desk were straightforward and easily solved, but Daniel had a feeling this one would be as baffling and complex as any of the cases he'd worked on to date.

# Chapter 5

Bishop Garner's residence was more modest than Daniel would have imagined, the two-story red-brick house identical to its neighbors to the left and right. Tired-looking maroon curtains hung at the windows, and the black paint on the door was faded and cracked. A middle-aged maidservant, who looked as faded as the hall carpet, opened the door and asked Daniel to wait in the narrow foyer while she announced him to the bishop. She returned a few moments later, took his hat, and invited him to follow her into the drawing room, where the bishop sat by the window, an open book on his lap. He was in his fifties, with broad shoulders, thick legs, and a sizeable belly that strained against the buttons of his waistcoat. The bishop was nearly bald except for a ring of gray fuzz that encircled his head just above the ears. Tufts of matching hair formed bushy eyebrows and sprang from his rather large ears. His dark gaze was shrewd and direct.

"Good afternoon, Inspector Haze," Bishop Garner said, looking up at Daniel. "Do sit down." He smiled in a pained manner, a note of irritation discernable in his tone. Daniel didn't think the bishop was the sort of man to enjoy a friendly chat.

Daniel lowered himself into a maroon and silver upholstered wingchair opposite the bishop.

"How can I help you?" Bishop Garner asked.

"Sebastian Slade, the curate at St. Martin's in Upper Finchley, was murdered last night," Daniel said, stating the facts as succinctly as possible so as not to waste time.

"How was he killed?" Bishop Garner asked.

"He was hit over the head with a shovel, pushed into an open grave, and buried alive."

"A terrible business," the bishop said, shaking his head in dismay. "Sebastian was a promising young man. Do you have any suspects, Inspector?"

"Not yet, and the motive for the murder is unclear."

"Perhaps there was no motive, and Mr. Slade was killed by a madman," Bishop Garner suggested. "Might he simply have been in the wrong place at the wrong time?"

"I don't think that's likely," Daniel replied patiently. "Bishop, Reverend Hodges mentioned that Mr. Slade's last position didn't work out. Can you enlighten me as to the circumstances of his departure?"

"Sebastian Slade was a curate at St. Dunstan-in-the-East. That's in London," he added, in case Daniel wasn't familiar with the name. "He violently disagreed with the vicar's fire-and-brimstone rhetoric and implored him to be kinder to people who were already struggling and in need of comfort. Reverend Kent took great offense at Mr. Slade's comments, particularly when he questioned the reverend's treatment of a young woman who'd fallen pregnant out of wedlock and was publicly humiliated and made to leave. Mr. Slade said that no person, no matter their sin, should be evicted from church when they needed God's understanding and love most. Irate, Reverend Kent made a complaint to his bishop, asking that Mr. Slade be removed from his church."

"And Mr. Slade was punished for his impudence by being sent to the sticks?" Daniel asked.

Bishop Garner smiled for the first time. "It wasn't quite like that, Inspector. Bishop Whitehead is a friend of mine. We've known each other since our seminary days. He wrote to me, asking if there might be a suitable position for Mr. Slade, with whom he did not wholly disagree. I thought Reverend Hodges and Mr. Slade would get on well and he might be a suitable candidate to take over the living once Reverend Hodges retired. So, it wasn't so much a punishment as a promising opportunity."

"Did Mr. Slade see it that way?"

"He was reluctant to leave London, but he saw the benefits of accepting the post in Upper Finchley."

"Did he get on with Reverend Hodges as you had hoped?"

"Yes. Reverend Hodges is a mild-mannered, sympathetic man. Their views aligned quite nicely."

"Was Mr. Slade possessed of a quick temper, Bishop?" Daniel asked.

"Not that I know of. He did not argue with Reverend Kent or berate him, as it were. He entreated him to try to understand the plight of his parishioners and set aside his somewhat outdated views."

*Always an effective method in dealing with a superior*, Daniel thought sarcastically. If that didn't land you in some backwater, nothing would.

"Can you think of anyone who might have wished Mr. Slade harm?"

The bishop shook his bald head. "No, I can't. Mr. Slade was an amiable and pious young man. I meet many young clergymen and can honestly tell you that at least half of them are not suited to the vocation they've chosen, but Mr. Slade had the unwavering faith and commitment of someone who, in time, would have made an excellent spiritual leader. His death is a loss to us all."

Daniel nodded. He'd heard enough. "Would you have an address for Mr. Slade's parents?"

"His parents are deceased. He was quite close with his sister. I do have her address, as it happens. Polly," he called out to the maidservant. "Bring me my address book."

The woman returned a few moments later with a leather-bound book that must have had the capacity to store thousands of entries. It was as thick as the Bible and just as well thumbed. Bishop Garner found the entry and read it out to Daniel, who copied the information in his notebook.

"Thank you, Bishop Garner," Daniel said.

"I hope you find whoever did this. And please, inform me when Mr. Slade's body is to be released for burial. I would like to officiate at his funeral."

"I will, sir. Good day."

Daniel stepped out into the street and strode toward the High Street, his heels pounding the parched earth. He was irritated beyond belief. He'd interviewed four people, all of whom had implied that Sebastian Slade was a veritable saint. Daniel didn't believe it for a second. No one was all goodness and light, he thought as he headed back to the station. Sebastian Slade might have chosen to go into the Church, but that didn't mean he didn't have vices or secrets he wished to keep hidden. Someone had nearly cleaved his skull in half and buried him alive. That was a crime of passion if Daniel had ever seen one, and he'd bet his last farthing that Sebastian Slade was not an innocent victim of a raving lunatic. There were random victims of violence, to be sure, but this wasn't the case, Daniel concluded as he approached the police station. Besides, the individuals he'd spoken to hadn't known Sebastian Slade well. The vicar and his wife and Mrs. Monk had only met him a fortnight ago, and Bishop Garner had known the curate more by reputation than through any prolonged personal experience. Perhaps interviewing the people who'd been close to him would reveal a more realistic side to his character and shed some light on what had got him killed.

It was too late in the day to venture to London, so Daniel retrieved his dogcart and headed home, eager to spend some time with Sarah and Charlotte. The thought of his wife and baby daughter always brought a smile to his face, and he was in much better spirits by the time he surrendered the cart to his stable lad and hurried inside.

# Chapter 6

Jason found Katherine, Micah, Mary, and Mr. Sullivan outside in the garden, having tea. Liam was curled in Mary's lap, fast asleep, his thumb in his mouth, while Micah's attention seemed to be fixed on the sky, his expression dreamy. Jason's gaze went directly to Katherine, who smiled happily when he approached the table situated in the shade of the old oak tree. Mr. Sullivan jumped up to offer Jason his seat, but Jason waved him back down.

"Please, don't get up, Mr. Sullivan. I don't want any tea. Katie, would you care to take a stroll?" he asked. "I need to stretch my legs."

"I'd love to." Katherine set down her nearly empty cup, stood, and accepted Jason's proffered arm.

"How are you feeling?" Jason asked her as soon as they were out of earshot of the others.

Katherine's smile was slow and sweet. "I feel much better than I did this morning. This heat is brutal, though. It's as if there's a furnace inside me and the flames are leaping higher and higher." She did look flushed, even though it was marginally cooler than it had been during the afternoon.

"Perhaps you should take a cool bath," Jason suggested.

"That's an excellent idea," Katherine said. "But first, I want to hear about the case. I expected you back earlier," she said without a hint of accusation.

"I stopped in to see Charlotte Haze," Jason said. "She had a difficult night, and Daniel was worried."

"Is she ill?" Katherine asked.

"No," Jason reassured her. "I think she just had a bellyache. She was sleeping peacefully when I looked in."

Katherine nodded. "Sarah and Daniel are anxious, given what happened to Felix."

"Felix's death was a terrible accident, but it has nothing to do with Charlotte. Charlotte is a beautiful, healthy child. Peach-perfect, as my mother used to say. They need to set aside their fears and try to enjoy her."

Katherine grinned up at him. "Easy to say when it's not your child. You'll probably be a worse fusspot than Daniel," she teased. "Now, tell me about the case. I'm dying to hear what happened."

"Katie, I don't think that's a good idea," Jason said. A pregnant woman required a safe and serene environment, not tales that would frighten her and give her nightmares.

"Jason, if you are going to treat me like an invalid for the next seven months, I shall be very cross," Katherine said, giving him her best daughter-of-the-vicar glare. "There's nothing wrong with my mind, nor do I believe that an unpleasant conversation can hurt an unborn child."

Jason chuckled. "So bossy," he said, shaking his head. "What did I get myself into?"

"You got yourself into a partnership. I don't need a father. I already have one, thank you very much."

"All right, all right," Jason replied, amused by her vehemence. "But I will spare you the more gruesome details."

"Fine," Katherine agreed, but he could see she wasn't best pleased.

"A curate has been killed in Upper Finchley. His body was concealed in a grave that had been dug for a funeral that was supposed to have taken place this morning. Had the gravedigger not noticed that the grave didn't appear to be as deep as it should have been, no one would have been the wiser. No strangers have been seen in the village, so it stands to reason that it was one of his parishioners."

"Who would kill a curate, and why?" Katherine asked, clearly intrigued.

"That, my dear, is the million-dollar question."

Katherine's eyebrows lifted in response to the unfamiliar expression, which she would likely store for future use. Jason had noticed her using some of his turns of phrase of late and found it endearing. "Does Daniel have any leads?"

"Not as yet. He went to question the bishop after we parted ways."

"I can never understand how a seemingly decent person can suddenly forgo all reason and give in to such primal urges."

"What makes you think the killer was a decent person?" Jason asked, surprised by the comment.

"You just said it was likely that one of the parishioners was responsible. Had this person had a reputation for violence, the villagers would have pointed Daniel in his direction right away. As they have no idea who killed the unfortunate man, it must be that the killer has done nothing to attract attention to himself all this time; therefore, he was probably a decent person, or posing as one, until something tipped him over the edge."

Jason nodded. "Yes, I suppose that's true. The question is, what was it that had tipped the scales? What could Mr. Slade have done in the two weeks he'd been in Upper Finchley to incite such violence?"

"Whatever he did must have been unexpected," Katherine replied.

"What led you to that conclusion?" Jason asked.

"Unless the killer knew all along that someone would die and there would be an empty grave ready and waiting, it's safe to assume that he acted on the spur of the moment. It was an opportunistic act."

"I'm not sure about that. It's a small village, so the killer would know if someone was to be buried in a few days' time. He would have heard the news and seen the grave being dug. Perhaps he would have used a different method had this opportunity not presented itself."

"I suppose that all depends on whether he'd planned to commit murder. Do you mean to assist Daniel with the investigation?" Katherine asked, her gaze anxious as she looked up at Jason.

"I am."

"You will be careful, Jason." It wasn't a question, more a command.

"I will be very careful," he promised. "You have my word. Now, how about that cool bath?" he asked, eager to distract her from talk of murder. "I'll join you, if you like."

"I like," Katherine said, her cheeks turning an even deeper shade of pink than they were already. She reached for Jason's hand, and they walked back toward the house in companionable silence.

# Chapter 7

## Wednesday, August 7

Daniel was pleased that Jason was able to join him on his trip to London. He valued Jason's input and enjoyed his company immensely, but there was an added benefit to having him along. His very presence, his title, and his American accent tended to throw the individuals Daniel interviewed off balance, their nervousness often making them more forthcoming than they would have been had Daniel interviewed them alone. Few people relished talking to the police, be they of the upper or lower orders. The nobility and gentry viewed the police with disdain and treated them no better than tradesmen, expecting them to use the back door and be grateful for the brief time they were allotted to conduct their inquiries, while the poor feared the rozzers, as they referred to the police, and wanted nothing to do with them, even if they happened to be a victim of a crime and might benefit from the police's efforts on their behalf.

Daniel and Jason didn't discuss the case on the train ride to London, since there had been no new developments to speak of, taking the time instead to enjoy the scenery and read the papers they'd purchased before entering the station. Exiting Charing Cross Station, they hailed a hansom and took it to St. John's Wood, directing the driver to the address provided by Bishop Garner.

The door was opened by a young woman with carrot-red hair and freckles. She wore a starched apron over her black cotton dress and a white cap that did little to contain the frothy curls that tried to escape its confines. Her already pale face went the color of whey when Daniel introduced himself and Jason, and she politely asked them to wait while she went to inform her employers that they had visitors. Daniel hoped they would not be turned away. It being a weekday, Mr. Holloway might be away from the house if he were a man of business, and his wife could conceivably still be abed at just past eleven in the morning.

The maidservant returned a few minutes later and took their things before directing them toward a well-appointed parlor, tastefully decorated in shades of cream and pale peach. Everything in the room, including a painting of a hunting scene that hung above the mantel, looked new and bright, as if the house had been decorated only recently, and with a generous hand. A man of about thirty-five stood by the unlit hearth, his worried gaze fixed on the visitors as they entered the room. He had sandy hair and brown eyes, his pale cheeks were bracketed by neatly trimmed whiskers, and he wore a carefully waxed handlebar moustache that almost entirely covered his upper lip. He was well dressed, with a gold watch tucked into the pocket of his silk waistcoat and a ruby ring on the pinky of his right hand.

A woman in her mid-to-late twenties was perched on a silk settee, her back ramrod straight, her face tense yet eager. She was attractive, with wide blue eyes and dark hair so like her brother's. Despite her youth, there were lines of grief etched into her face, and her watchfulness reminded Daniel of a frightened doe.

"Is this about Grace?" she blurted out, clasping her hands in her lap as if she had to make a physical effort to keep them restrained. "Have you found her, Inspector?" She looked so hopeful that Daniel felt awful to disappoint her, especially when his news was about to plunge her into a world of despair.

"Mrs. Holloway, I'm afraid we're here about your brother, Sebastian."

"Oh?" Mr. Holloway said, exchanging looks with his wife. "What about Sebastian?"

"I'm very sorry to inform you that your brother is dead," Daniel said, wishing the Holloways would invite them to sit.

"Dead?" Mrs. Holloway echoed. "Was he ill? He wrote to me only a few days ago." Her shoulders slumped as understanding dawned. "No, of course not. You wouldn't be here if he'd died of an illness, would you? Has something awful befallen dear Sebastian?" she asked, her voice quivering with emotion.

"I'm afraid he was murdered, Mrs. Holloway. I'm conducting an investigation into his death, and Lord Redmond, who performed a postmortem on your brother, is assisting me in my inquiries."

The Holloways turned to stare at Jason, whose involvement usually required an explanation, then seemed to recall his rank and instantly altered their demeanor, their questions left unasked.

"Please, sit down, your lordship. Eh, you too, Inspector. Would you care for some refreshment?" Iris Holloway asked, her nervousness intensifying. "I am sorry, I didn't mean to be rude. It was just such a shock when Gwen announced you. We thought..." Her voice trailed off, her gaze turning to her husband in mute appeal.

"How did Sebastian die?" Mr. Holloway asked. He abandoned his spot by the fireplace and came to sit next to his wife, taking her hand gently in his. She leaned against him, not enough to be slouching but just enough to feel his support.

"He was hit on the head, but the cause of death was suffocation," Jason said, phrasing it as mildly as he could.

"So, he was attacked, then strangled?" Mr. Holloway asked.

"He wasn't strangled, no," Jason replied. "He was pushed into an empty grave, his body covered with enough soil to hide it from view."

"He was buried alive?" Iris Holloway cried, bright spots of color appearing in her cheeks in her agitation.

"I'm afraid so," Jason said.

"Did he suffer?" Mrs. Holloway asked, her eyes pleading with Jason to say that Sebastian Slade had died quickly.

"The blow on the head would have rendered him senseless, Mrs. Holloway. I don't think he would have been aware of what was happening." That wasn't strictly true, but there was no sense in distressing the poor woman any further. She seemed to be barely holding herself in check. Had they not been there, she probably would have given in to hysteria, screaming and crying until the tempest of emotion passed and she tired herself enough to finally take some rest.

"Where is he? Where are his remains?" Iris Holloway cried, yanking her fingers out of her husband's grasp and twisting her hands in utter despair.

"He's at the Brentwood police station mortuary," Jason replied.

"We have to get him, Bernard," she implored. "Today."

Bernard Holloway put a restraining hand on his wife's arm. "I will see to everything, my dear. Just leave the funeral arrangements to me." His soothing tone seemed to calm his wife somewhat, allowing her mind to turn to practicalities.

"Sebastian wouldn't have wished for anything ostentatious," Iris Holloway said. "He would have preferred a modest affair."

"Then a modest affair we shall have, for only the closest family and friends. I will contact Stanwick and Sons this very afternoon, and they will dispatch someone to collect the body. You are finished with Sebastian's remains, are you not?" Bernard Holloway asked, glancing at Daniel.

"Yes. The body will be made available to the undertaker when they come to collect it," Daniel replied. *And the sooner the better, given the weather*, he thought.

"Do you know who killed him, Inspector?" Bernard Holloway demanded. "I mean, do you have any suspects?" he hastily amended. Had they known who'd killed Sebastian Slade, it would stand to reason that they wouldn't be conducting an investigation.

"We don't know, Mr. Holloway, and no, we don't have any suspects as yet. Which is why we need to ask you a few questions about Mr. Slade. It will help us find out more about the type of man he was and about the people in his life."

"You think someone he knew did this?" Iris Holloway exclaimed. "Everyone liked Sebastian. He was one of the most generous, loving people I've ever known."

"Yes, people have spoken very kindly of him, Mrs. Holloway, but we must explore every possibility. Can you share with us what Mr. Slade wrote to you in his last letter?" Daniel asked.

Iris Holloway let out a deep sigh, as if preparing herself for an interrogation. "He said he was well, and he'd taken his first ever service that Sunday. He was excited and grateful to have been given the opportunity. He said Reverend Hodges was a kind and patient mentor and seemed to have great faith in Sebastian's abilities," she recited.

"Did he say anything out of the ordinary? Was he at all upset?" Daniel persisted. He wished Jason would pose a few helpful questions, but he seemed to be staring at something on the walnut sideboard, probably the family photographs that were displayed in heavy silver frames.

"He did say that although he had been most disappointed by his new posting at first, he now understood that his past tribulations had all been part of a divine plan."

"Do you know what he meant by that?" Jason asked, turning his attention back to the interview.

"I thought he'd made peace with the changes that had taken place in his life."

"And what changes were those?" Daniel inquired.

"Sebastian had never been fond of the country. He loved London, and Oxford, where he had attended the seminary. He could spend hours in a bookshop, reading contentedly, or debate some obscure theological theory with his fellow seminarians long into the night at some dingy tavern, where they could nurse a tankard of ale for hours and not be asked to leave on account of taking up a table but not spending any money. He was an idealist, a dreamer. He genuinely believed he could change the world, one parishioner at a time." Iris Holloway's eyes glowed with the memory of her brother, a sad smile tugging at her lips.

"Whitechapel or Seven Dials were some of the areas he'd most hoped to work in, but he was excited to be offered a place at St. Dunstan's."

"But his posting to St. Dunstan's was short-lived," Daniel prompted.

"Yes. That is true. Reverend Kent proved to be a harsh, cruel man, drunk on his own power and indifferent to the suffering of those who appealed to him for understanding. Sebastian couldn't stand by and watch him grind those who had already been brought low into the dirt. He felt he had to express his concerns, which he must have done rather forcefully, since the decision led to his dismissal. Sebastian hadn't expected that. He was melancholy for days, going over his time at St. Dunstan's and wondering if there was something he might have done differently."

"Did he live here with you?" Jason asked.

"He liked being part of a family, and he and I had always been close, more so since our parents died."

"Was there anyone else he disagreed with forcefully?" Jason asked, intentionally using Mrs. Holloway's turn of phrase.

"Only on intellectual points. There was never any hard feeling," Iris Holloway replied archly.

"Had he been courting anyone at the time of his transfer to Essex?" Daniel asked.

"No. Even though Anglican clergy are permitted to marry, Sebastian felt that a man of God should remain celibate. To deny his carnal urges and devote himself to prayer and a life of service brought him closer to our Lord. I know that sounds rather Popish," Iris Holloway said defensively, "but it was his own personal decision. It was his right."

"No one is questioning that, Mrs. Holloway," Daniel said in a conciliatory tone. "Would you be able to provide me with the names of some of his friends?"

Iris Holloway nodded. "Yes, of course. George Fisher and Hal Ritchie were his closest friends. George is in Cambridge, and Hal lives in Maida Vale."

"Are they both clergymen?"

"George is, but Hal works in the City."

"Would you have their addresses, Mrs. Holloway?" Daniel asked.

"I believe George is a deacon at Great St. Mary's Church, and Hal works for the Royal Bank of London."

"Thank you," Daniel said as he jotted down the information.

"And who is Grace, Mrs. Holloway?" Jason asked.

Mrs. Holloway paled, the haunted expression returning to her eyes. Her husband took her hand and answered in her stead.

"Grace is our daughter. She is nearly four years old." Iris Holloway let out a strangled moan but didn't interrupt her husband. "Grace was taken from us when she was nine months old."

Daniel considered what Bernard Holloway had said. At first, it had sounded as if the little girl had died, but the man had spoken of her in the present tense, and Mrs. Holloway had inquired if they had brought news of Grace.

"Has the child been kidnapped?" Daniel asked, hoping he wasn't causing these people unnecessary pain.

"Gracie was snatched when her nursemaid, Evans, took her out for a walk in the park. A man knocked Evans to the ground, took the child out of the perambulator, and ran off into the trees. There were two witnesses to the incident. They chased after the man, eager to help," Mrs. Holloway said, her voice quivering with emotion. "But to no avail."

"He got away?" Jason asked, his eyes warm with sympathy.

"No. They caught up with him, but he no longer had the child. When questioned, he swore it was all a mistake and he hadn't been anywhere near Evans and the baby," Mr. Holloway clarified. "They had no other option but to let him go. They'd apprehended the wrong man."

"The police found no trace of Gracie," Mrs. Holloway said, her voice catching on the child's name.

"I'm very sorry," Daniel said. "I can't imagine what you've been through." He'd thought losing Felix had been the worst kind of pain a man could endure, but having your child taken and not knowing if it was dead or alive, content or tormented by its captors, was beyond imagining.

"Did you ever receive a demand for ransom?" Daniel asked, hoping he wasn't overstepping by asking questions about the child.

"No. We did think we might be asked for money, but that never happened. Whoever took Gracie wasn't interested in lining their pockets."

Daniel wrote down his name and the address of the Brentwood police station on a page he'd torn out of his notepad and handed it to Mr. Holloway. "If you hear anything or think of anything that might aid the investigation into Mr. Slade's death, please don't hesitate to write to me."

Mr. Holloway nodded and stuffed the folded paper into his pocket, then pulled out his watch and checked the time, even though there was a handsome carriage clock perched on the mantel. It was their cue to leave, so Daniel and Jason said their goodbyes, collected their hats and gloves from Gwen, and left the Holloway residence.

"What a tragedy," Jason said once they settled into a hansom and the conveyance lurched forward, merging into traffic. "I'm pleased to see they had another child after their loss."

"Did they?" Daniel asked, giving Jason a sidelong glance.

"There was a photograph of Mr. and Mrs. Holloway with a child. You wouldn't have seen it clearly from where you were situated. The child in the picture is about two, so it's not a photograph of Grace. There was another photograph as well," Jason said sadly.

"Of Grace?"

Jason nodded. "It had to be, since it was not the same child as the one in the other photograph."

"It's odd," Daniel remarked, shaking his head in bewilderment as he stared into the middle distance.

"How so?"

"Why take a child if you're not going to demand a ransom? There are hundreds, no, thousands of unwanted children in London. You can have your pick if it's a child you're after. All you have to do is find a baby farm or visit an orphanage, and they'll hand over as many children as you want, even if you are the scum of the earth and will work the child to the bone or abuse them in ways no decent human being would ever conceive of. Why snatch a child, and in front of witnesses, no less?"

"Perhaps they wanted *that* child," Jason pointed out. "But I can't imagine why."

Daniel exhaled loudly. "The only reason I can think of is revenge. Perhaps Mr. Holloway had done wrong by someone, and they wanted to get back at him in the one way that was sure to bring him to his knees. So they snatched his child."

"And did what with her?" Jason asked quietly.

"Killed her. If it was for revenge, what would they want with the child once its purpose had been served? They'd have to pay for her upkeep if they were to let her live. And I'm sure the police checked with all the orphanages and any other charitable organizations, not that there are many. No one cares about all those children. They're a drain on the coffers of the Realm," Daniel said with disgust. "Why feed them and clothe them when you can let them freeze or starve to death, their emaciated corpses blocking doorways and littering the streets? When I was a bobby, I saw men step over them on their way to their clubs and places of business, as if they were nothing more than piles of refuse, not human beings

45

who'd been abandoned, not only by God and their parents, but by a country that has no use for them."

"It doesn't bear thinking about," Jason said. "Surely someone cares."

"Not enough," Daniel replied. "Those who don't die of hunger and exposure are often killed outright. Once money changes hands and the child is left at a baby farm, the proprietress simply smothers the infant or feeds it laudanum to keep it from fussing and crying for food. They all die sooner or later."

"Women should have access to safe and effective birth control," Jason stated matter-of-factly.

"Birth control?" Daniel sputtered. "Are you serious?" He gaped at Jason as if he'd just announced he was the King of Siam.

"There are ways to prevent conception, Daniel. Many different cultures have practiced various forms of birth control for centuries. The Native American Indians, for instance, use certain plants as an oral contraceptive and rely on blue cohosh to terminate unwanted pregnancies."

"That goes against the teachings of the Church, Jason, against God himself," Daniel exclaimed.

"And killing children doesn't?"

"The people who kill them are sinners. They will go to hell," Daniel said, his conviction wavering in the face of Jason's argument.

"Maybe so, but that will not bring back the children they've murdered, nor ease the suffering of the ones who're still alive."

"And do you condone the killing of innocents through abortion?" Daniel asked. He hoped Jason wouldn't be offended by his disapproval, but he felt compelled to ask.

"I do not, but I take no issue with preventing unwanted pregnancy," Jason replied calmly.

"Would you permit your own wife access to a contraceptive?" Daniel asked, utterly scandalized by Jason's radical views.

"Not only would I permit it, I would encourage it, if it were available. She should have free will when it comes to having more children and not try to avoid lying with me for fear of getting pregnant. There are women who give birth every year when they can ill afford to, physically or financially. They are so poor and worn out, they eventually succumb, leaving their children to fend for themselves, therefore perpetuating this cycle of poverty."

"But you and Katherine can afford to have as many children as God gives you, and Katherine is in robust health."

"That's not really the point, though, is it?" Jason asked. "It's not about what we can afford, but about what we want for ourselves."

"Good Lord, how did this conversation even come about?" Daniel asked, deeply embarrassed to be discussing such an intimate topic. "Let's get back to Sebastian Slade. What are your thoughts?"

"I have none," Jason replied, uncharacteristically glum. "It seems the man had no enemies, no vices, and no irritating habits. Either Sebastian Slade was a truly unique individual, or we're talking to the wrong people. Perhaps his friends will be more forthcoming," he mused.

"I do hope so. We can call at the bank after we speak to Reverend Kent," Daniel said as the hansom pulled up before St. Dunstan-in-the-East Church.

# Chapter 8

St. Dunstan-in-the-East was situated between Tower Bridge and the Tower of London, which accounted for the slight cooling in the air and the strong smell of wet mud and rotting fish wafting off the Thames. The church itself was lovely, with a tall spire rising from an ornate tower, and arched stained-glass windows that caught the sunlight and glowed like rainbow-colored portals into a magical world. Jason wasn't much of a churchgoer, but there was something vastly appealing and calmly reassuring about the ancient church. He felt a pang of sympathy for poor Mr. Slade, who'd had to give up a position in such a beautiful setting and take up a post in Upper Finchley, which, although pleasant enough for a small village, could never compare to the old-world charm of St. Dunstan's.

The two men walked through the graveyard and entered the building, their steps echoing on the flagstone floor as they made their way down the nave toward the altar. A young man, presumably the new curate, turned to greet them.

"Good afternoon. I'm Inspector Haze of the Brentwood Constabulary, and this is Lord Redmond, my associate," Daniel informed the man. "Might we have a word with Reverend Kent?"

"Yes, sir. I'll just get him for you. He's in the vestry," the young man said. "This is when he normally takes his luncheon, so you might have to wait a few minutes."

"Of course," Daniel replied, although he was in no mood to wait for the man to finish his repast.

Reverend Kent kept them waiting for close to a quarter of an hour, clearly not inclined to rush. He was much as Jason had imagined him: tall, thin to the point of being gaunt, and unwelcoming in both speech and manner. He made no secret of being galled by the interruption.

"What can I do for you, gentlemen? My time is valuable, so kindly make this quick," he demanded as he strode toward them, his black shirt with a narrow white collar and black coat and trousers reminiscent of a bird of prey that was about to swoop down on some unsuspecting creature and tear it to shreds. Given the man's holier-than-thou demeanor, Jason was surprised to note that he had chosen a more modern form of clerical dress, limiting himself to dark colors and a collar, his attire only marginally different than that of any other gentleman.

"Reverend Kent, I'm Inspector Haze, and this is my associate, Lord Redmond." Daniel was noticeably annoyed by the man's frosty reception and air of superiority. "We'd like to ask you a few questions about Sebastian Slade," he said, striving for an even, polite tone.

"Why?" the vicar demanded angrily.

"Because he's been murdered," Daniel replied.

"Can't say his death is any great loss to humanity," Reverend Kent retorted.

"That's unkind and unchristian, Reverend," Jason said, irritated by the man's unfounded hostility. He'd arrived at the church with an open mind, but it was difficult not to dislike this abrasive cleric.

"And what's your role in this, *my lord*?" Reverend Kent demanded, putting unnecessary emphasis on the title as a means of belittling Jason's involvement.

"I performed the postmortem on the victim," Jason replied, his gaze fixed on the reverend and daring him to question Jason's right to be there.

"Most peculiar," Reverend Kent said under his breath, shaking his head, as if wondering what the world was coming to and if the end might indeed be near. "Fine, what do you wish to know?"

"What sort of man was Sebastian Slade?" Daniel asked.

"An irritating one," Reverend Kent snapped.

"In what way?" Daniel continued, undaunted.

"In every way. He was one of those idealists who think everyone should be comforted and forgiven for their sins, a view that is as misguided as it is impractical. Our task is to keep our parishioners in line and bring them, kicking and screaming if the situation calls for it, into the fold. The poor are responsible for their situation through generations of innate laziness and a refusal to better themselves through worship and penance. I will not congratulate them on their unworthiness or assure them that God loves them anyway, despite their inability to work hard and please their masters." The reverend's dark eyes blazed with the fire of his conviction, and he went on, nearly sputtering in his haste to deliver his message.

"And if I show sympathy toward one fallen woman, a hundred others will expect the same and perceive my compassion in a way that will fit in with their own twisted sense of right and wrong. If a woman lies with a man out of wedlock and falls pregnant, she is a whore and a sinner, and deserves the shame and poverty that's usually a direct result of such a liaison. I will not condone such wanton behavior, nor will I permit some disgraced slut to poison the moral wellbeing of my flock. They will be expelled and not permitted to return unless they've seen the error of their ways and found their way to a respectable resolution."

"And what of the man, Reverend? Does the man who's responsible for said disgrace get expelled as well?" Jason demanded.

"Of course not," Reverend Kent retorted, his bushy eyebrows rising in astonishment. "It is entirely the woman's responsibility to safeguard her virtue. A man has his needs and will slake them on any female weak and lustful enough to permit such a violation."

"Do you slake your needs on some lustful female?" Jason asked, goading the man despite his better judgment.

"I resent your impertinence, sir," Reverend Kent bristled. He would have thrown Jason out had Jason not been of the upper class and therefore virtually untouchable by the likes of the reverend. "I'm married these forty years, and my wife is as respectable as she is devout."

*And probably suicidal*, Jason thought. "So, you disposed of Mr. Slade because he didn't share your views?"

"I disposed, as you put it, of Mr. Slade because he was insolent, ignorant, and willful. Qualities that are wholly inappropriate in a man of his position. Now, if you will excuse me, I've said everything I wish to say on the subject."

He turned on his heel and walked away, head held high, shoulders squared, as if he were going into battle, quite possibly with Lucifer.

"What a prig," Jason said once they stepped out into the brutal heat of the August afternoon. "No wonder they didn't see eye to eye. Imagine having to deal with that zealot every day of your life."

Daniel shrugged dismissively. "When you go into the Church, you are bound to meet more than one cleric who shares Reverend Kent's mindset. He's hardly alone in his worldview. As a curate, Sebastian Slade had no right to challenge the opinions of his superior—not that I wouldn't be hard-pressed not to do the same, were I to find myself in his very uncomfortable shoes. However, I don't think Reverend Kent is in any way connected to the murder. He had no reason to kill Sebastian Slade. Once rid of him, I doubt he gave Slade another thought."

"I agree," Jason said. "Reverend Kent doesn't have a motive for murder unless Sebastian Slade retaliated against him in some way. Shall we find Mr. Ritchie?"

"Do you mind if we get something to eat first?" Daniel asked. "I'm famished, and I could do with a cool drink. How do you deal with this heat, Jason? You don't seem affected in the least."

"New York summers are brutal," Jason replied, "and the time I spent in the Southern States taught me the meaning of the phrase 'from the frying pan and into the fire.' There were days during my imprisonment in Georgia that I actually thought my skin was sizzling. The heat alone was enough to drive you mad, and then there were the mosquitos," he said, grimacing at the unwelcome memory. "I much prefer the gentle English summers."

"If this is your idea of gentle, then I'm glad you're enjoying it," Daniel replied as he pointed out a respectable-looking chophouse. "Shall we?"

"By all means," Jason replied, and followed Daniel as he crossed the street toward the chophouse, his mind still on the pugnacious vicar. He often wondered if it was some innate sense of superiority or one's upbringing that resulted in such an unyielding, high-handed view of the world and the people in it. He wasn't a member of the clergy, but he had been in the army and had come across many a man who had abused his position of power and had been the cause of countless unnecessary deaths.

"I think Sebastian Slade should have considered himself lucky to get away from someone as inflexible as Reverend Kent," Jason said as they settled at a table in the corner.

"That rather depends on what his goals for the future were," Daniel replied. "If he could have found it in himself to be content with the life of a simple country vicar, then yes, he was lucky, more so if he inherited Reverend Hodges's parish. But if he had his eye on a steeper trajectory, then Reverend Kent might as well have cut him off at the knees."

They set their theorizing aside as an elderly waiter approached their table and listed the offerings, which were depressingly few.

# Chapter 9

The high-ceilinged, marble-floored branch of the Bank of London was unnaturally quiet and put Jason in mind of the ornate duomos he and Katie had visited while in Italy. With its tall windows and soaring columns, the bank could easily be mistaken for a place of worship, and for some, it probably was. The few patrons who were being helped spoke in hushed tones, as if they were revealing deep, dark secrets to the men behind the polished counter, who murmured their replies. The clerks were hard at work, black-suited figures dotting the cavernous space.

Jason and Daniel found Hal Ritchie seated behind a small desk in a windowless alcove, head bent over a ledger. He was a stocky young man with carefully pomaded auburn hair and bright blue eyes. Hal Ritchie looked up from his work and smiled politely.

"Can I be of assistance?" he asked.

"Mr. Ritchie, I'm Inspector Haze of the Brentwood Constabulary, and this is my associate, Lord Redmond. I would like to speak to you regarding the death of your friend Sebastian Slade."

Hal Ritchie blanched, his eyes bulging with shock. "Sebastian is dead? What happened?" he cried, and instantly lowered his voice when several disapproving faces turned in his direction. "No, don't tell me," he said. "Not yet. If you have no objections, Inspector, I will meet you in the coffeehouse on the corner in about ten minutes. We'll be able to speak privately there. And a cup of coffee certainly wouldn't hurt," the man added. "I feel rather shaken by the news, truth be told."

"We will see you there, Mr. Ritchie," Daniel said, and turned to leave.

"Are you sure he won't bolt?" Jason asked as they left the bank and strolled toward Barton's Coffeehouse. Even if they hadn't been able to see it from their vantage point on the steps of the bank, they could have simply followed the aroma of coffee that wafted down the street and beckoned, to Jason in particular.

"His shock at the news seemed genuine," Daniel replied, seemingly unconcerned.

"Either that or he's a very good actor."

"If he tries to elude us, we'll simply return to his place of work, not a risk he seems willing to take. He'll come."

Hal Ritchie did come. He slid into a seat across from Jason, ordered a pot of coffee and a plate of toasted crumpets with butter and jam, then leaned against the back of the seat, his shoulders slumping as if he were exhausted beyond words. He stared at Daniel morosely, waiting for him to begin. Daniel quickly filled him in on what had happened in Upper Finchley, watching him intently the whole time.

Hal Ritchie's expressive blue eyes filled with tears. "No," he moaned. "I can't bear it. Knowing that he's dead is bad enough, but to think how he suffered is absolute torture. Sebastian was my best friend. We'd known each other since we were in short pants."

The waiter brought the coffee and crumpets, and Hal Ritchie instantly poured himself a cup and took a long swallow, making a face that could only imply he'd burned his tongue on the scalding liquid.

"How did you meet?" Daniel asked.

"Our families lived next to each other in Portland Place, and our nursemaids took us to Regent's Park for our daily outings. They were only too happy to watch us from a bench as they enjoyed a friendly chat while we played. Sebastian and I always had such a good time together. We remained close friends throughout the years."

"Mr. Ritchie. Hal," Daniel implored, "help us find Sebastian's killer. We've interviewed a number of people, but as of now, we have no leads and no suspects, mostly because no one will tell us the truth of his character. Surely Sebastian had flaws, and secrets."

Hal Ritchie took a more careful sip of coffee, nodded in appreciation, then set the cup down and began to butter his crumpet. "I won't speak ill of Sebastian," he said after a moment's hesitation. "I couldn't even if I wanted to, but I will tell you this," he said, lowering his voice in a confidential manner. "Sebastian always thought that he'd be able to resist temptations of the flesh. He wished to remain pure. That was one thing he admired about Catholicism. He thought priests should be celibate, untainted by earthly desires, but then he met Elena."

"And who's Elena?" Daniel asked, leaning forward so he could hear the answer.

"Elena Cartwright. He met her at a musical evening Iris— that's his sister—had dragged him to when her husband was away on business and she needed an escort. Sebastian loved music," Hal said wistfully. His sadness didn't preclude him from taking a large bite of the crumpet. "Elena was there with a friend," he said once he swallowed. "Had she been some sweet young miss, Sebastian might not have found her appealing, but Elena had just come out of mourning for her husband, and Sebastian was drawn to her obvious melancholy and ethereal beauty. His words, not mine," Hal clarified, and took another bite.

"Did they begin a relationship?" Jason asked.

"They saw each other a number of times before Sebastian left for that ghastly little village he'd been sentenced to. I don't know how close they had become, if you take my meaning, but I believe his vow of chastity was giving him some considerable trouble."

"Would Sebastian have considered marriage had he not died?" Daniel asked.

"I really couldn't say, Inspector, but if he had been considering it, I would think he'd have been conflicted, to say the least."

"Do you know where Mrs. Cartwright lives?" Daniel asked.

"Warrington Crescent. Maida Vale. Not sure of the number, but I wager you can find out easily enough. You are a detective, after all," Hal Ritchie pointed out.

"Was there anyone else he might have been close to or might have had a falling out of some sort with?" Daniel asked.

"I honestly don't know. Sebastian had changed after what happened with Gracie," Hal said. He'd finished the first half of the crumpet and moved on to the second half. "You do know about Gracie, don't you?"

"Yes. How had he changed?" Jason asked.

"He became more reticent, I suppose. He just couldn't believe there was such evil in the world. And having seen what the loss of Gracie had done to her parents, he felt sick with helplessness, knowing he was unable to aid them in any way. After the disappearance, he spent more time with George Fisher."

"Why do you think that was?" Jason asked.

"He met George in his first year at the seminary in Oxford. They had more in common, I suppose, which made me a bit jealous at times. They shared a bond I could never hope to compete with since I wasn't part of the seminarian clique. George was able to shore up Sebastian's faith after Gracie was gone, to convince him that God hadn't forsaken either the baby or her parents. I suppose he was able to find the right words, where all I could do was agree that it was an unspeakable tragedy and there was nothing to be done. I should have offered to pray with him, to join him in good works, but I was busy with my own life and my own tragedies, even if they might have seemed insignificant to Sebastian."

"What tragedies are you referring to, Mr. Ritchie?" Daniel asked softly.

Hal Ritchie looked aggrieved for a moment, his expression that of a hurt child. "My father died suddenly a few months after Gracie was taken. I was devastated; we had been close," he said miserably. "But his death also meant that I had to look after my mother and sister, who depend on me for their very existence. My father had a fondness for the gaming tables, you see, so there wasn't much left after the debts and death duties had been paid. My sister married last year, which was a relief, I don't mind telling you, but I will have to support my mother for the rest of her days, not an easy thing to do on my salary, gentlemen, not if I hope to start a family of my own in the near future."

"Are you married, Mr. Ritchie?" Jason asked.

"I am to be married in October," Hal replied, brightening somewhat. "She's a lovely girl. I still can't believe she chose me. She had her pick, you know."

"My felicitations," Daniel said absentmindedly. "Did Sebastian have any other close friends, besides you and George Fisher?"

"Not that I know of. Sebastian was a private sort of person. He only let a few people in. He was always close with his sister, though. Thought the world of her."

"Had you heard from Sebastian since he arrived in Upper Finchley?" Daniel asked.

"I had one letter. In fact, I received it only two days ago."

"What did it say?" Daniel asked. Jason could sense the tension building in him, the desperate need to learn something that might offer a hint, no matter how small, into what had been on Sebastian's mind in the days before his death.

"Not much, really. He said he was settling in. The vicar and his wife were kind, caring people. Oh, he did mention that something had unsettled him."

"Did he say what it was?" Daniel asked, his eagerness palpable.

"No."

"Can you hazard a guess?" Daniel tried again.

"I couldn't even begin to try," Hal Ritchie replied. "I will say, however, that he wouldn't have mentioned it if it hadn't shaken him to the core. Sebastian was rarely unsettled. He tended

57

to accept whatever life threw at him and make the best of it. I suppose that was the lesson he'd taken from Gracie's disappearance, that sooner or later you have to simply make peace with whatever happens." He drank the rest of his coffee in one gulp and dabbed the serviette to his lips. "I'm sorry, gentlemen, but I must return to work. I hope I have been of some assistance."

"Yes, thank you, Mr. Ritchie. You have been most helpful," Daniel assured him.

Jason tried to hide his smile as Hal Ritchie jammed his hat on his head and departed, leaving Daniel and Jason to settle his bill.

"What could Sebastian Slade have been referring to?" Daniel asked once they'd left the coffeeshop and were walking down the street toward Maida Vale. "What sort of thing would disturb a man in a place he's only just arrived at?"

"Mrs. Monk said that Sebastian Slade had seemed upset after coming back from church on Sunday," Jason said. "That was the first time he'd taken a service, according to Reverend Hodges, so perhaps he'd been unhappy with his performance and realized that he wasn't ready to lead a congregation on his own. He might have expected a more emotional response or maybe had even hoped for praise but received none."

Daniel nodded. "Yes, you might be right. I felt the same way when the body of Alexander McDougal was found in the crypt of St. Catherine's. I didn't believe I was prepared to conduct a murder investigation on my own and felt quite unsure of my abilities."

"Whatever upset Mr. Slade might have nothing whatsoever to do with the manner of his death," Jason said.

Daniel sighed heavily. "I hope it does, because right now, that's our only clue."

# Chapter 10

Warrington Crescent was an oasis of respectability and peace in a city teeming with people from all walks of life who often treated it like a midden heap. It was quiet, clean, and prosperous. The houses were attractive and modern, and in excellent repair. Not a speck of peeling paint or a crack in the plaster was evident as the two men walked down the street, wondering which house belonged to Mrs. Cartwright. A uniformed nursemaid exited the gated park at the center of the crescent, pushing a perambulator as she walked at a stately pace toward the house just across the road.

"Pardon me," Daniel said, "but would you know where Mrs. Cartwright lives?" The nursemaid eyed him suspiciously. "I'm Inspector Haze of the Brentwood Police Constabulary," Daniel added, mentally applauding her reluctance to send two unknown men to the home of a widowed lady. He pulled out his warrant card and showed it to her.

Thus reassured, the woman finally smiled. "That's her house right there," she said, pointing to a home at the far end of the street.

"Thank you," Daniel said, and he and Jason set off.

A young maidservant dressed in a crisp dress and apron opened the door to their knock. "Inspector Haze and Lord Redmond to see Mrs. Cartwright," Daniel said.

The maid looked from Daniel to Jason, then back again. "I'm sorry, sirs, but Mrs. Cartwright is not at home."

Daniel had expected as much, since people were often "not at home" to unwelcome visitors, using their staff as gatekeepers, though they were at home in the physical sense and could theoretically be pressured into seeing whoever had turned up on their doorstep. Daniel tried again.

"We are here on police business, miss. Kindly inform your mistress that we must speak to her on a matter of great urgency."

The woman didn't budge. "Mrs. Cartwright is not here, sir. She's visiting her aunt in Truro."

"When do you expect her back?" Daniel asked.

"Tomorrow afternoon, sir. You're welcome to call then," the maid said, and shut the door in their faces.

"We'll have to come back," Daniel said, disappointed. "I suppose that's it for today, then. I'll be off to Cambridge first thing tomorrow. Care to accompany me?"

"I'm sorry, but Micah and I have an appointment at the Westbridge Academy at noon."

"Oh? Will you be enrolling him for the autumn term?" Daniel asked. Jason had been reluctant to send Micah away to school. He didn't think the boy would be able to adjust to such a structured environment, given not only his traumatic wartime experiences but his Irish heritage, which would make him an oddity at any proper British institution. Micah also wished to remain close to Mary and his nephew Liam, a request Jason couldn't bear to deny.

"If he likes the place, yes," Jason replied. "It's close enough to Birch Hill that I can visit him often, and the headmaster has a reputation for being a fair and progressive man."

"What does that mean, exactly?"

"It means he won't single Micah out for being different. There are a number of boys at the academy who come from the types of families other schools might turn away."

"Why would they be turned away?" Daniel asked. Not having school-aged children or having attended a boarding school himself, Daniel had yet to encounter the prejudice and rigidity of institutions whose only bargaining power lay in their reputation and selectiveness.

"There are two Jewish boys, as well as several children of mixed race. Micah would not be the odd man out."

"I see. And what of his desire to remain close to Mary?" Daniel asked.

"Mary is leaving us," Jason said sadly. "She had promised to stay until Katherine and I returned from our honeymoon, and now she's adamant about returning to the States."

"Pardon me for asking, but what's the urgency? Is there anyone waiting for her?" Daniel asked. As far as he knew, Mary had been entirely on her own, with no one to turn to for help in her hour of need, when the inquiry agent finally managed to track her down in New York. Unmarried, and with a small child to look after, Mary would be entirely dependent on Jason's generosity for the next several years, unless something changed.

"Mary wants Micah to have a proper start in life. As long as she remains at Redmond Hall, Micah will resist going away to school, refusing the education he needs to acquire a respectable profession."

"And what does she plan to do?" Daniel asked.

"Mary has been busy in our absence. She had written to a cousin in Cork, asking after her mother's sister. The cousin wrote back to tell her that Fiona McCollough had immigrated to the States approximately ten years ago. With my permission, Mary wrote to Mr. Hartley, the inquiry agent I had used to track her down, and asked him to locate her aunt. Mrs. McCollough lives in Boston."

"Is that where Mary is going, then?"

"Yes. Her aunt is expecting her, so Mary won't be entirely alone once she returns to America. Micah has grudgingly agreed to let her go, and Mary, in turn, has extracted a promise that Micah will complete his education before making any decisions about his future."

"Clever girl," Daniel said, nodding in approval. "Does Micah wish to return to the States?"

"A part of him does, but Micah is no fool. He grew up surrounded by ignorance and poverty. He has a chance to better himself and ensure that his family will never live as his ancestors did, barely scratching out a living in Ireland and then doing much the same thing in Maryland, surrounded by the same prejudices and limitations his parents thought they'd fled. As much as he dreads being parted from Mary and Liam, he realizes that he has a once-in-a-lifetime opportunity to make something of himself."

"I wish you success at the school, then."

"Thank you. I do hope Micah likes the place. The school has extensive grounds and a variety of sports that might appeal to him."

"And what of Mr. Sullivan?"

"Mr. Sullivan initially agreed to a year's employment, which is nearly up," Jason said. "He's an excellent tutor, but I think he feels isolated and extremely lonely. He misses his life in London."

"Has his liaison with Harry Chadwick come to an end?" Daniel asked. No one ever alluded to Shawn Sullivan's homosexuality, but Jason and Daniel had discovered during a recent investigation that he had been romantically involved with a member of a prominent local family.

"I believe so. It is my understanding that Harry is departing for Egypt at the end of the month."

"Is he, indeed?" Daniel asked. "But he's still in mourning for his wife."

Jason shrugged. "Observing the mourning etiquette can be burdensome when one isn't actually grieving for the deceased."

"Yes, you have a point there," Daniel said.

"Micah and I should be back by teatime. I do hope you will stop by. I'd like to discover what you've learned."

"If anything," Daniel said sourly.

# Chapter 11

The pitter-patter of rain beat against the windows, the night sky as dark as the yawning grave Jason had been dreaming of. He slid out of bed, pulled on his dressing gown, and made his way downstairs, suddenly desperate for the comforting glow of the oil lamp Mrs. Dodson kept on hand in the kitchen, and a glass of something cold. Jason's bare feet slapped against the flagstone floor once he descended to the kitchen, and a smile tugged at his lips when he saw the welcoming light of the lamp.

Mrs. Dodson sat at the table, her frothy fair hair neatly braided and her flowery dressing gown belted tight at the waist.

"Can't sleep?" she asked. "There's still tea in the pot."

"Is there any cold milk?" Jason asked.

"I'll get you some."

Setting a cup of milk before Jason, she resumed her seat and looked at him, her head cocked to the side, her gaze as curious as that of a magpie that had seen something shiny in the grass. "I think congratulations are in order," Mrs. Dodson said, smiling at last.

"How did you know?" Jason asked, instantly realizing the silliness of his question. The servants knew everything, and Mrs. Dodson more than most.

"A honeymoon baby," Mrs. Dodson said. "Always a blessing."

"Yes."

"You don't seem happy," she observed.

"I am. Very. It's just that things are going to change," Jason said. He hadn't realized he'd been thinking it until the words left his mouth, but the conversation with Daniel must have brought his reservations to the forefront.

"Things will change either way," Mrs. Dodson said softly. "They always do. Is it Micah you're worried about?"

"Micah, and Mary, and Katherine," Jason admitted. "They're the only family I have. I don't want to lose them."

Mrs. Dodson sighed. "Mary and Micah are not yours to keep," she said wisely. "They will always care for you, but it's time you let them go. They don't belong here, and I think you know that. As far as Katherine, her wellbeing and that of the baby are in God's hands. Trust in Him to see them through safely."

"I've seen so much death, Mrs. D," Jason said softly. "I couldn't bear it if anything happened to them."

"With you as her husband, Katherine has a better chance than most women of delivering safely. She will be—what is that word you use?—okay," she said, recalling the unfamiliar term. "Love her, comfort her, and see to her health. That's all you can do."

"Of course, I will. Why can't you sleep?" Jason asked. Mrs. Dodson suffered from bouts of insomnia, but they weren't as frequent since Jason had prescribed an infusion of valerian root to help her sleep through the night.

She smiled guiltily. "Same as you. I've grown fond of the Donovan children. And Liam…" She let the sentence trail off. "I'll miss that little rascal," she said, her eyes tearing up. "Even Mr. Sullivan has grown on me." She sighed. "After your father left, the house became so quiet. It felt so empty for so many years. And now it's full of people. I see their youthful faces and hear their laughter, and I feel needed and energized. Once they're gone… Once you're gone…"

"I'm not going anywhere, Mrs. D," Jason said, surprised by her prediction.

"Yes, you are," she said, sighing loudly. "You just don't know it yet. Well, goodnight, my lord. I'm for my bed."

"Goodnight, Mrs. D." Jason watched as she walked out of the kitchen.

Having finished his milk, Jason turned out the lamp and went upstairs, but did not return to the bedroom. He wouldn't be able to go back to sleep anyway and had no wish to disturb Katie with his tossing and turning. Instead, he walked into the dark drawing room and settled in his favorite chair, which offered the best view of the rolling lawns and parkland during the daylight hours. He leaned his head against the back of the chair and stared out into the charcoal darkness, with only his turbulent thoughts for company. Was Mrs. Dodson right? Did he wish to leave? Did she see something he didn't? Or maybe he did see it but wasn't ready to address it just yet.

He did miss home; that was true. But it wasn't the buildings or the streets of New York that kept a hold over his heart; it was the hospital where he'd worked, and the life of purpose he'd led before his capture and imprisonment, and even after, when he'd tended to the men of Andersonville Prison, doing his best to treat them without the benefit of medicine or surgical tools. He'd tried to keep them alive for as long as possible, or at the very least help to make their deaths more comfortable, if only by offering spiritual comfort or a sympathetic ear. He'd always meant to return to the hospital once he'd recovered from the physical effects of his captivity, but that had been before he'd known of the deaths of his parents, or the estate he'd inherited in Essex.

City Hospital had been his home, his refuge, his life's calling. He missed surgery, and he missed making a difference in the lives of people who came to him for help. His fingers itched to hold a scalpel, to cut out the cancer or amputate an infected limb. He missed the mental challenge and the physical exhaustion, as well as the camaraderie of other surgeons with whom he could discuss the latest techniques and scientific breakthroughs.

He never wanted to relive the horrors of the Civil War, but he had done important work, had saved countless lives. What was he doing now? Investigating the death of a saintly curate, whose life, although important to those who had known him, had no bearing on Jason's own. Was he looking for something to fill the hours, to make him feel as if he wasn't wasting his precious time? Was he eager to perform postmortems for the sake of maintaining his surgical skills? Perhaps. His position precluded him from practicing medicine in any meaningful way, and the hours of idleness weighed heavily on him.

Even now, he felt uncomfortable with his title, embarrassed at the change that came over most people once they realized he was of noble rank and gazed upon him in sycophantic admiration, as if he'd suddenly become a better person, right before their eyes. He wanted to be respected for his knowledge, his skill, even his sense of honor, but not for a rank he'd done nothing to achieve.

Katie made him incredibly happy, but he didn't feel complete, not as long as he had no true purpose. Did he want his children to grow up in England, boxed in by the demands of their station? And did he believe it wise to allow them to grow up to be idle, privileged human beings who cared nothing for those around them and perpetuated the status quo? His father had escaped, longing to be a part of something modern, someplace where change was not only possible but happened every day. And Jason had completed the circle, winding up right back in the place his father had despised.

Jason exhaled loudly as he considered these weighty questions. He had Katie to think of. He could hardly uproot his pregnant wife and drag her back to the States, not when everything she knew and loved was right here. No, he would bide his time, Jason decided as the first glimmer of morning light pierced the eastern sky and shone a light into his restless soul. Once Katie was safely delivered, he'd ask himself these questions again, but for now, his needs were not a priority. They probably wouldn't be for some time.

# Chapter 12

## Thursday, August 8

Rising early, Daniel tiptoed out of the bedroom and closed the door softly behind him. Sarah and Charlotte were still asleep, the baby snug in her cradle, which Sarah insisted on keeping in their room, fearful of being parted from Charlotte for even a few hours. Daniel was secretly glad and often woke during the night and lay very still, listening to Charlotte breathe. Only once he was certain that she was sleeping soundly did he allow himself to go back to sleep, a wonderful sense of wellbeing settling over him.

Daniel washed, shaved, and dressed in the adjoining bedroom, which would eventually be Charlotte's room but now acted as a dressing room of sorts. He brushed his hair, cleaned his spectacles and put them on, then adjusted his tie, which was a bit crooked. He then made his way downstairs. Although Tilda and the cook were already up, the house was still silent, the rooms lost in the half-shadow of predawn. Cook was just lighting the stove when Daniel entered the kitchen, surprising her into nearly dropping the taper she was holding to the bits of newspaper she'd inserted between the wood to get the fire started.

"Good morning, sir," Mrs. Glen said as she blew steadily on the flame for a few moments to get it going, then closed the iron door, satisfied with her efforts. "You're up early this morning."

"Good morning, Mrs. Glen. I must be off early today. Police business," he added. "Can I trouble you for some tea and buttered bread?"

"Course, sir. Tilda will bring it to ye in the dining room."

"Thank you."

Daniel settled in the dining room, his gaze fixed on the bay window as the first rays of the sun pierced the murky gray sky, bands of bright pink spreading outward from the shimmering orb and painting the room in a rosy light. He loved watching the sunrise and never tired of the ethereal beauty of the moment when light vanquished dark. By the time a bleary-eyed Tilda brought his breakfast, the room was bathed in a golden glow, the trees outside the window weeping silently as the rainwater from last's night downpour slid down the lush leaves to shower Sarah's flowers and soak into the loamy earth.

"I'll need a ride to the railway station," Daniel said to Tilda, who nodded and went to wake the stable boy.

Daniel took his first sip of tea, sighing with pleasure as the hot liquid slid down his throat. That was another pleasure he always looked forward to, that first cup. Daniel buttered two slices of bread, spread them with homemade marmalade, and tucked into his breakfast. He had a long day ahead of him. He would travel to Brentwood by dogcart, then take a train to London, where he would make his way crosstown to the depot at Liverpool Street and then transfer to an east-bound train that would take him to Cambridge. He wasn't sure how long the journey would take, but he was allotting two hours, at the very least. Once in Cambridge, he would head directly to Great St. Mary's Church and ask to speak to George Fisher. With luck, the man would be there and would impart something of value. Once the interview was concluded, Daniel would make the journey in reverse. All in all, it would take the better part of a day.

Daniel finished his meal, remembered to take his umbrella should the heavens open up again, and stepped outside, filling his lungs with the wonderfully fresh air of early morning. Tom was already outside, his hat pulled down low as he sat hunched on the bench of the dogcart. He yawned hugely and instantly covered his mouth, casting a sidelong glance at Daniel, who climbed in and stared straight ahead.

"Well, let's go. I don't want to miss the train," he said to the boy, who seemed to still be half asleep.

Daniel arrived in Cambridge around eleven, and after asking for directions at the railway station, he headed for St. Mary the Greater, as he was told it was referred to, not to be confused with St. Mary the Lesser or Little St. Mary's. He'd never been to

Cambridge before and enjoyed a brief burst of excitement, feeling like a tourist rather than a police inspector about his business. He wished he could spend the day, wandering around aimlessly and taking in the sights and sounds of the university town. Students in black robes hurried past him, stacks of books under their arms, gazes distracted, brows furrowed with whatever problems were occupying their minds. He saw several dons, looking exactly like the students only a bit more mature, their steps not as springy. He even spotted a young man on a velocipede, a curious contraption with two wheels and awkwardly placed pedals that seemed to propel him forward without tipping to the side, a wonder to Daniel, who expected the rider to hit the pavement at any moment and possibly cause himself serious injury.

Passing a quaint coffeehouse, Daniel decided that he would treat himself to a pot of hot chocolate and a slice of sponge once he finished with George Fisher, or maybe he'd find a respectable-looking tavern and enjoy a steak and ale pie and a pint instead. Yes, he decided as he continued along, that was a much better idea, given that it had been nearly six hours since breakfast and his stomach was making embarrassing rumbling sounds. He'd need something hearty to tide him over till dinnertime. Cook was making mutton chops with mint jelly, one of his favorite meals.

Daniel dragged his mind away from his stomach as the church came into view. St. Mary the Greater was magnificent, the light ochre exterior dominated by a four-pointed tower adorned with a whimsical clock just above the arched doorway. The inside was no less impressive, with Georgian galleries suspended over the ground-floor pews for additional seating and massive stained-glass windows that, on this bright afternoon, bathed the interior in multi-colored light.

Daniel saw a young man in clerical garb and approached him, wondering if he might be lucky enough to have found George Fisher so quickly. He wasn't. The young man asked Daniel to wait and set off in search of Mr. Fisher, an endeavor that took more than a quarter of an hour, since Mr. Fisher had stepped out for a cup of tea and a bun and had yet to return. Daniel could only assume that Mr. Fisher was not supposed to have left his post, since the middle-aged vicar, who was now glaring at Daniel in a most disapproving manner, had not been aware of his absence.

When George Fisher finally appeared, he looked nervous and upset, his gaze darting frequently toward the vicar until the older man turned on his heel and retreated toward the vestry, leaving Daniel and the young deacon blessedly alone. George Fisher finally seemed to relax and invited Daniel to take a seat in one of the pews. He was a slight man with dark blond hair that was already receding at the front and artfully combed to distract the eye from this affliction. He had neatly trimmed sideburns and soulful brown eyes fringed with long but nearly colorless lashes. His stole was diagonally placed over the alb, from left shoulder to right hip, and Daniel suspected that he must have left his post directly after the morning service, not having taken the time to remove his vestments.

"I'm sorry to have kept you waiting, Inspector Haze," George Fisher said. "I overslept this morning, a result of staying up late to finish a rather absorbing book, I'm afraid." He smiled apologetically. "I tend to feel faint if I don't eat at regular intervals, so I was forced to abandon my duties and seek sustenance immediately after the morning service, since I hadn't had time for breakfast this morning," he explained. "How can I help you?" George Fisher asked, the realization that a police inspector had come looking for him seemingly sinking in at last. "Is something wrong?"

"Mr. Fisher, your friend, Sebastian Slade, was found dead Tuesday morning. Murdered. I'm here to ask you some questions."

"What?" Fisher gasped, his hand flying to his breast. "Seb is dead? But that can't be. Who'd want to hurt him? It must have been an accident, surely. Yes, a terrible accident," he concluded lamely.

"I'm afraid it wasn't an accident, Mr. Fisher. It was very deliberate, and rather brutal."

"Oh no," George Fisher moaned. "I can't believe it. Does Iris know?"

"Yes, Mrs. Holloway has been informed."

George Fisher nodded miserably, his head drooping like a wilted flower, his hands clasped in his lap. Daniel thought he might be crying. The alb didn't appear to have any pockets, so Daniel took out his own handkerchief and handed it to the deacon.

"Thank you," George Fisher muttered, and blew his nose after dabbing at his eyes. "I'm sorry. Now I've gone and soiled your handkerchief."

"Keep it," Daniel said.

George Fisher nodded his thanks. He straightened his shoulders, closed his eyes, and took a deep breath before releasing it slowly and turning to Daniel. "I'm quite recovered now, Inspector. Anything I can do to help; you only need to ask." He turned sideways to face Daniel, his back rigid and his gaze determined.

"When was the last time you saw Sebastian Slade?" Daniel asked, hoping the man wouldn't dissolve into tears again before the end of the interview.

"Just over a month ago," George Fisher said. "I came to London to visit my mother. Sebastian and I met for supper."

"Was Sebastian in good spirits?"

"Not really. He was having difficulties at work. As it happens, he lost his position only a few days after we met, a consequence he hadn't anticipated. Luckily, he was offered a post in the village of Upper Finchley. Is that where he was killed?" George Fisher asked.

"Yes, I'm afraid it was. Have you heard from Sebastian since he arrived in the village?" Daniel inquired.

"I received a letter just yesterday. He must have posted it on Monday."

"Was there anything unusual in his letter?"

George thought about that for a moment. "He did say that now he thought he understood why he had been sent to Upper Finchley and that his inability to get on with Reverend Kent and his subsequent exile to Essex were all part of God's great plan."

"What plan was that?" Daniel asked, already knowing what George would say.

"I have no idea. I really don't. I assume he would have told me in the fullness of time, but given what's happened…"

"Did Sebastian seem pleased with this divine plan he was referring to?" Daniel asked, now grasping at straws.

"I really couldn't say, Inspector."

"And what led him to believe that his banishment was part of a plan?"

"I think he saw someone, someone who obviously meant a great deal to him, but for the life of me, I can't imagine who it might have been."

"Could it have been Elena Cartwright?" Daniel asked.

George shook his head. "Oh, no. Sebastian and Elena didn't have the kind of relationship where she would come to visit him, especially unannounced."

"What kind of relationship did they have?"

"It was a friendship that would have certainly blossomed into love, given time. I believe Elena would have been an ideal companion for Sebastian."

"Why is that?"

"They shared similar views on life, faith, and family. Had they had time, I think they would have found solace and joy in each other's company. Sebastian was quite taken with her."

"Have you met Mrs. Cartwright?" Daniel asked.

"Yes, I have met her on two occasions. I found her to be charming, intelligent, and compassionate."

"Did Mrs. Cartwright have any other admirers?"

"Yes, as a matter of fact, there was an army captain who pressed his suit most ardently."

"Do you know his name?"

"Captain Reginald Herbert. Sebastian mentioned him when we met."

"In what context?"

George Fisher smiled sadly. "He was afraid Elena might be swayed by his romantic overtures."

"Oh?" Daniel said noncommittally.

"Captain Herbert is rather well off, from what I gather, so he has the means to woo the lady in a rather extravagant manner. Seb couldn't hope to compete. He was always a bit skint."

"What did Sebastian do with his money?" Daniel asked. "It is my understanding that his lodgings were paid for by the Church, and I believe he received a stipend."

"No one goes into the Church for the money, Inspector. It's a comfortable, but not a lucrative proposition, and he had yet to attain the living. Yes, Seb's lodgings were paid for, and he received a modest stipend, but a man has other expenses, doesn't he?"

"Such as?" Daniel pressed.

George Fisher shrugged. "To be honest, we never discussed it outright, but I do think—and this is mere speculation, mind you—that Seb had a fondness for cards. I only suspect that because Hal Ritchie mentioned once that his father had nearly ruined the family with his gambling, and Sebastian grew quite defensive. He said that as long as a man was able to govern his passions, there was nothing wrong with allowing himself a bit of a diversion from time to time."

"Would Sebastian have been able to govern his passions?" Daniel asked.

"I would have thought so, but many a man has courted ruin at the gaming tables, Inspector. I, myself, would never indulge. It's a slippery slope, so to speak, and I have no expectations of coming into funds through marriage or inheritance."

"Had Sebastian married Mrs. Cartwright, would the marriage have been financially beneficial for him?" Daniel asked.

"Oh, I expect so. Mr. Cartwright left his wife well provided for, or so Seb told me," George Fisher added.

"Had Sebastian Slade and Captain Herbert ever met?"

"Yes, they met several times, but I wouldn't describe their relationship as a cordial one. The captain could barely hide his dislike for Sebastian, and the feeling was mutual. Sebastian thought the captain belligerent, godless, and generally uncouth, and was deeply concerned that Elena would permit the man to court her, given his brash manner."

"And why would Mrs. Cartwright allow this man to pursue her, in your opinion?" Daniel asked. Of course, George Fisher couldn't speak for Elena Cartwright, and everything he said was complete hearsay, but it was always interesting to get an impartial opinion, if George Fisher was capable of being impartial in this case.

"A woman should be married, Inspector. It is her divine purpose to be a wife and a mother. A widowed lady, such as Mrs. Cartwright, must choose from the suitors that are available to her and not dismiss a chance of matrimonial happiness based on someone else's point of view. I think Sebastian would have made a good husband to her, but Sebastian had reservations about entering into such a union, while Captain Herbert had made his intentions clear. A bird in the hand is worth two in the bush, and all that."

"So, you think Mrs. Cartwright was open to a proposal from the captain?"

"I don't know, Inspector, but I think she would consider it carefully if it came."

"Was there anyone else you can think of who might have had a reason to dislike Sebastian?"

"No, I really can't. Sebastian didn't have many close friends, but he knew how to talk to people and always left a favorable impression on those he'd met. He would have made an excellent vicar, had he lived. His death is a tragic loss."

"Thank you, Mr. Fisher. I will ask you to forward the letter you received from Mr. Slade to me at the Brentwood police station. I would like to see it for myself."

"No need, Inspector. I have it here. I put it in my pocket after I had read it and forgot to take it out. My coat's in the vestry. I'll just be a moment."

Having received the letter, Daniel said his goodbyes and left the church, heading to a tavern George Fisher had recommended in parting. He placed his order and took out the letter, eager to read the message for himself. It was as Fisher had said, a general account of Sebastian Slade's days leading up to the murder. Except for his prophecy about his posting to Upper Finchley being part of God's greater plan, there was nothing at all to indicate that anything was amiss or that Sebastian Slade considered himself in any danger. Perhaps he had simply been making the best of a bad situation and had tried to convince himself that the new posting was a step forward rather than a setback. The letter did not specifically mention him seeing someone he'd known, but it did say he intended to make a trip to London to visit Elena Cartwright in the near future.

Daniel folded the letter and pushed it into his pocket once his food arrived. Despite the lack of concrete evidence, he was pleased with the morning's work, since he had learned several vital facts about the deceased. Sebastian Slade had been jealous of Captain Herbert, whom he had described as belligerent and uncouth. Perhaps it had been jealousy speaking, but it was also entirely possible that the romantic rivalry between the two men had crossed a line from emotional distress to physical confrontation, a theory worth exploring. Sebastian Slade also might have had a gambling problem, which could have spiraled into debt. He may have borrowed money unwisely or been unable to repay someone who'd grown tired of waiting and had taken matters into his own hands.

As Daniel tucked into his steak and ale pie, he reflected that for a man who supposedly admired the celibate lifestyle of Catholic priests and thought that abstinence would bring him closer to God, Slade wasn't averse to gambling, a vice much more corrosive than carnal knowledge of one's lawfully wedded wife. Daniel swallowed, took a pull of his ale, and allowed himself a small smile. Sebastian Slade had not been nearly as saintly as he'd first appeared. At last, Daniel had something to work with.

# Chapter 13

Daniel boarded a London-bound train immediately after lunch, his desire to take a walk around Cambridge surpassed by his eagerness to speak to Mrs. Cartwright, who would hopefully be at home when he called on her this afternoon. This was a woman who had known Sebastian Slade as well as anyone and might help him to identify possible suspects in the case. Perhaps she was a suspect herself, Daniel mused as he gazed out the window at the lush countryside beyond. He hailed a hansom as soon as he exited the station and gave the address in Warrington Crescent, hoping there wouldn't be too much traffic and he'd get there quickly.

To his immense relief, the maidservant he'd met yesterday informed him that Mrs. Cartwright was indeed at home and would receive him. She took his umbrella, hat, and gloves, and escorted him to the drawing room, which was as elegant as its mistress. Elena Cartwright was in her mid-twenties, a strikingly beautiful woman with silvery fair hair, cornflower-blue eyes, and a heart-shaped face that was pale and strained by grief. She wore an exquisite gown of lavender silk adorned with a silver-hued lace fichu that shimmered as bright as her hair, which was parted in the middle and wound into an elaborate chignon. Her only jewelry was a delicate necklace of jet beads and matching earrings, her attire consistent with half-mourning.

"I'm so sorry I wasn't here yesterday, Inspector," she said once they were seated and Elena had called for tea. "I didn't know about Sebastian, you see. I only just learned of his death from Iris Holloway when I returned home this afternoon. I'm…" Her voice trailed off. There was no need to complete the sentence. Daniel could see that she was shattered by Sebastian Slade's death. "If I can help in any way," she said, her eyes imploring him to allow her to be useful.

"Mrs. Cartwright, please tell me about Sebastian Slade."

Elena Cartwright folded her hands in her lap. She looked like a schoolgirl about to recite a poem. "I would never normally discuss my innermost feelings with anyone, least of all a policeman, but I believe this is a time for plain speaking. I do hope the things I tell you will be held in confidence."

"Of course," Daniel replied, cringing inwardly. He couldn't guarantee that he would keep the woman's secrets if they had bearing on the investigation, but he would do his best to protect her privacy.

"I met Sebastian six months ago at a musical evening hosted by a mutual acquaintance. I had only just come out of full mourning for my husband, and that was my first foray into society following his death. After two years of near solitude, I had longed for company, but once I arrived, I felt guilty and out of place. Sebastian noticed my discomfort and approached me. He was a dear man, Inspector," Elena Cartwright said softly. It was obvious she was holding back tears. "He listened to me and assured me that slowly getting on with life was part of the mourning process, and it was natural to feel as if I were betraying the dead by allowing myself to seek the company of others and longing to experience the small pleasures I had so missed. He invited me to go for a walk the following day, and I readily agreed. Our walk in Regent's Park became a part of my weekly routine."

"Mrs. Cartwright, how would you describe your relationship with Mr. Slade?"

Elena sighed. "I was—still am—in love with him, Inspector. Sebastian was the first man to ever make me feel... I suppose the right word is 'worthy.' To him, I wasn't just an ornament, or a necessary step in the process of begetting an heir. To him, I was a person—a thinking, feeling person who has opinions, and interests, and dreams."

"And did he feel the same about you?" Daniel asked gently, not wishing to upset her any more than she already was.

"Yes and no. Sebastian was in love with me, I do know that, but he wasn't ready to commit to marriage, nor would I have accepted him had he made me an offer."

"Why not?" Daniel asked, surprised by the admission.

"Some men are not cut out for marriage, Inspector Haze. Sebastian didn't go into the Church to please his parents or guarantee himself a living. He was passionate and devoted and eager to make a difference. One of his fondest dreams was to become a missionary and go to places where men like him were truly needed."

"But an Anglican priest is permitted to marry," Daniel pointed out. "He could have been both a husband and a clergyman. And if you were in love…" Daniel allowed the sentence to dangle, hoping Elena would elaborate, because her sentiments didn't make much sense to him.

"Call me selfish, Inspector, but I don't wish to compete for my husband's affections. God doesn't disappoint, but a wife grows tiresome and demanding, especially a wife who craves attention and companionship, and I would. I desire a true partnership of mind and body, not a mere status, and Sebastian would not have been capable of giving me that."

Elena went quiet when a middle-aged maidservant brought in the tea tray and set it on a low table. Elena poured and invited Daniel to try some of the teacakes that looked and smelled very appetizing. Daniel helped himself to a cake and took a sip of tea as he waited for the maid to depart so he could continue his conversation with Elena Cartwright.

"And what of Captain Herbert?" Daniel asked. He hated to admit that he knew something of her private life, but this was a murder inquiry; he had no choice.

She winced. "So, you know about the captain."

"I do."

"Reggie is an old friend. I met him years ago, before I married. He was a friend of my brother. He had feelings for me then, but I only had eyes for Michael Cartwright," she said sadly. "We renewed our acquaintance a few months ago."

"And does he still have feelings for you?" Daniel asked.

"He does."

"Mrs. Cartwright, I'm not sure if you realize, but as the two men both had romantic intentions toward you, that made them rivals and gave Captain Herbert a motive for murder."

Elena Cartwright looked shocked by the suggestion, her mouth opening slightly as she stared at Daniel. "Inspector Haze, Reggie would never hurt Sebastian."

"I was led to believe that Captain Herbert has something of a temper." That wasn't precisely what George Fisher had said, but it served Daniel's purpose to exaggerate and see what Elena Cartwright would say in response.

She set down her cup carefully, her expression pained. "Yes, he does. He's a soldier, Inspector Haze. I think most military men tend to eschew diplomacy in favor of dealing with threatening situations in a more decisive manner."

"Did Captain Herbert feel threatened by Sebastian Slade?"

"Not threatened, no. But he did feel insecure. I assured him that he had nothing to worry about. You see, Reggie and I are to be married in December, so he had no motive whatsoever to kill Sebastian. Sebastian was no threat to him, and Reggie has known that for several weeks now. In fact, I had gone to visit my aunt to tell her the happy news."

"But you freely admitted to me that you're in love with Sebastian Slade. Surely your feelings for the man would pose a threat to your future spouse."

"Reggie never knew how I felt about Sebastian. You are the only person I've ever shared that with."

"He may have guessed," Daniel suggested.

"He didn't. He's not that perceptive," she replied with a small smile. "Or more accurately, he's not that honest with himself. Reggie wants to believe that I love him, so he does."

"So, you have chosen to marry a man you don't love versus a man who made you feel worthy, as you yourself put it."

"Yes," she replied simply. "Reggie loves me the way a man loves a woman, Inspector, whereas Sebastian loves me—loved me—in a more abstract way. He wished to put me on a pedestal, to admire me and spiritually guide me, but I don't believe what he felt for me was romantic love." Her face colored. "You see, Michael wasn't able to give me children, and it is my fondest wish to be a mother."

Daniel took a sip of lukewarm tea to hide his knowing smile. Elena Cartwright had chosen a passionate, virile man to be her husband rather than a mincing cleric. The thought put Daniel in mind of Charles Darwin. This surely was a fine example of survival of the fittest, and Sebastian Slade had been found lacking where it mattered most.

"And please, don't assume I don't love Reggie," Elena went on, spurned by Daniel's silence. "I simply love him in a different way than I loved Sebastian. A more intimate way," she added, her cheeks turning a charming shade of rose. Elena Cartwright was a sensual woman who wasn't willing to risk tying herself to a man who would not relish his husbandly duties and would leave her lonely and childless.

"You don't need to justify your decision to me, Mrs. Cartwright. You know best what will make you happy. Now, if you don't mind my asking, what did your husband die of?"

"He hanged himself," Elena said softly. "In this very house."

"Had he been melancholy?" Daniel asked, wishing he didn't have to intrude on the woman's obvious grief but compelled to learn more.

"Our childlessness was his fault, and he wished to free me so I could marry again. That's what his note said."

Daniel stared at Elena Cartwright, bewildered by her statement. "He killed himself so that you could remarry?"

"Yes."

"And what made him think he was responsible?"

Elena Cartwright looked up, her gaze no longer sad but filled with anger and resentment. "My husband had contracted syphilis during one of his many forays into the brothels of London. As soon as he discovered he was afflicted, he withdrew from my bed so as not to infect me or any offspring we might have. He did away with himself a year later."

"I'm very sorry," Daniel said. He wasn't quite sure what he was sorry about, the man's death or the fact that he had felt the need to lie with whores when he had such a beautiful, charming wife.

"His death was an act of love, an apology for the life he'd ruined. But now that I am free, I must choose wisely."

"Yes, I can see why you would." Daniel set down his cup and stood. "I would like to speak to Captain Herbert. Where would I find him?"

"He's quartered at the Regent's Park barracks. Very near here," she added, a small smile now tugging at her lips.

Daniel couldn't help wondering if the captain paid the lovely Mrs. Cartwright nocturnal visits, but then reminded himself that it was none of his business and the couple was, after all, to be married.

"There is something I feel I should tell you, Inspector," Elena Cartwright said as Daniel turned to leave. "Sebastian shared this with me in confidence shortly before he left for his new post. I would never betray his trust if I didn't think it might have bearing on the case."

"Please, go on," Daniel said, sitting back down.

"Sebastian did not see eye to eye with Reverend Kent, who's the vicar at St. Dunstan's Church. He thought the man cruel and autocratic."

"Yes, I am aware of that."

"What you probably don't know is that Reverend Kent had publicly humiliated and expelled a young woman who had become pregnant out of wedlock and had asked Sebastian for help. Her name is Jenny Ross."

"I know that too," Daniel said, gravely disappointed that Elena Cartwright had nothing new to tell him.

"Sebastian had an altercation with Reverend Kent following the incident. I believe he called the reverend all sorts of awful names, which led to him being sacked from St. Dunstan's and sent to Essex as punishment for his inappropriate behavior."

"Are you suggesting that Reverend Kent might have killed Sebastian Slade because of the verbal abuse he had suffered as a result of his treatment of Miss Ross?"

"No," Elena said, shaking her head. "That wasn't what I was suggesting at all. You see, Inspector, Sebastian felt awful for what happened to Jenny. I suppose he felt responsible, being a member of the clergy at St. Dunstan's, so he made it his business to seek her out and help her in a private capacity."

"That's very kind of him, but what does that have to do with his death?" Daniel asked. He wished the woman would get to the point. She seemed to be drawing out her statement, as if reluctant to speak of the incident, which didn't seem all that scandalous to Daniel. Reverend Kent certainly wasn't the first vicar to bring down the sword of judgment on the head of a fallen woman, nor would he be held accountable for his actions by the Church. Doctrine held that a woman who had given herself to a man without the benefit of wedlock and become pregnant was no better than a whore and a creature of Satan and deserved no understanding or pity, having brought about her own downfall.

"Sebastian had a soft heart. He wished he could help every woman who'd come to shame, but God had put this poor creature in his path, and he couldn't turn his back on her. The child's father had abandoned her, and her own father, a violent man, by all accounts, had threatened to beat the child out of her and then kill the man responsible."

"What did Sebastian do?" Daniel asked.

"He helped Jenny get away from her father and set her up in rooms of her own, pledging to support her and her baby until the child was of age or until she married. I think maybe Mr. Ross felt

Sebastian had no right to interfere and thought to teach him a lesson," Elena said.

"Which went too far," Daniel finished for her.

"Exactly. Or perhaps the child's father thought there was a reason Sebastian had taken such a personal interest in Jenny's plight."

"Do you happen to know the man's name?" Daniel asked.

"Sorry, no. I don't think Sebastian knew it either. And now that he is gone, Jenny will have no means to pay for her lodgings and will have to return home, which will not go well for her, given her father's temper," Elena said sadly.

"Do you know where Jenny Ross can be found?"

"I promised not to reveal her whereabouts."

"Mrs. Cartwright, I will not return Jenny to her father. I only wish to speak to her," Daniel pointed out.

"Of course. I will write down the address for you. Inspector Haze, I wonder if I might beg a favor of you."

"Certainly."

"I won't be a moment," Elena said, and left the room. She returned a few minutes later and held out a ten-pound bank note and a scrap of paper with an address. "Please, give this to Jenny. Sebastian would want to know that she is safe, and this will see her through a few months at the very least, longer if she's frugal. But don't tell her it's from me. If you tell her Sebastian left it for her, she'll be less likely to question it."

"That's very kind of you, Mrs. Cartwright," Daniel said, and pocketed the note.

"It's nothing I can't easily afford, and it will make all the difference to someone in her position. I will speak to Iris Holloway after the funeral and see if some kind of provision can be made for Jenny Ross out of the monies Sebastian left behind. Iris will wish to honor her brother's promise."

Daniel nodded and stood. He was touched and surprised by Elena Cartwright's generosity toward a young woman she'd never met, but then, she seemed a remarkable woman, and he genuinely wished her happiness in her new marriage.

"Thank you for your help, Mrs. Cartwright. And again, I'm sorry for your loss."

Elena Cartwright inclined her head in acceptance of his sympathy and walked him to the door of the drawing room. "Goodbye, Inspector Haze. I hope you get justice for Sebastian. He didn't deserve what happened to him."

*Few murder victims do*, Daniel thought, but said nothing.

# Chapter 14

Taking advantage of the barracks' proximity to Warrington Crescent, Daniel walked to Albany Street, where the barracks were located, and, after showing his warrant card to the young soldier on sentry duty, asked after Captain Herbert. The man pointed toward a doorway some distance from the entrance to the barracks and directed Daniel to inquire there. Daniel followed his instructions and walked toward the office, taking in the squat, colorless buildings grouped around a parade ground and flanked by a long, low building that had to be the stables. Had he not known better, he might have thought this was a workhouse or a mill of some sort. Daniel could easily understand why Captain Herbert would wish to seek refuge at Elena Cartwright's lovely townhouse, where the decor was tasteful, comfortable, and pleasing to the eye.

"I'll have someone fetch the captain for you," the officer who greeted him said. "He's probably in the mess. Won't be a minute." His tone was civil, but Daniel could see the suspicion and resentment in his narrowed gaze. He was sure they didn't get too many policemen sniffing around and didn't welcome the intrusion. The army was a law unto itself.

It took considerably longer than a minute to locate Captain Herbert, but Daniel didn't mind. As long as he spoke to Captain Herbert today, he would be free to return to Upper Finchley tomorrow and continue his inquiries there. While he waited, he wondered how Jason had got on at the school and if Micah would agree to being parted from him now that he felt more secure in his surroundings. He hoped so. Jason and Katherine should have the time to settle into marriage without the constant demands of children that weren't even their own. Perhaps he was being unkind, Daniel thought as he paced before the young man's desk, his hands clasped behind his back. Both Micah and Mary had suffered more in their short lives than most adults did in a lifetime. Jason genuinely cared for the Donovan children and would be heartbroken to find himself parted from them.

"Inspector Haze." A man of about thirty, tall, broad-shouldered, and dashing in his uniform, had entered the office. The captain did not come near, but remained by the door, as if waiting for Daniel to state his business before he committed to the interview.

"Is there somewhere private we could talk?" Daniel asked.

"What's this about?"

"It's about the murder of Sebastian Slade," Daniel said, wondering if the man was intentionally feigning ignorance. If he had had any communication with Elena Cartwright since her return, he'd know of Slade's death.

"I see." Captain Herbert turned toward the officer, who was watching the exchange with great interest.

"You can use my office," the man said. "I'm going to go find a cup of tea."

"Thank you," the captain said. He waited until the young man shut the door behind him, then turned to Daniel again. He did not invite him to sit. "How can I be of assistance, Inspector?" the captain asked, a ghost of a smile tugging at his lips.

Daniel pictured Elena Cartwright on the arm of Captain Herbert and thought they would make a fine couple. The captain's thick dark hair was slick with pomade, and his lean cheeks were cleanly shaven. He wore a neatly trimmed moustache extended into points that seemed to serve the all-important purpose of drawing attention to the deep dimples in his cheeks. He was a handsome man in the prime of his life, and Daniel could understand only too well why a woman like Elena Cartwright might choose the dashing officer over the indecisive curate.

"Captain Herbert, the body of Sebastian Slade was found Tuesday morning in the village of Upper Finchley," Daniel began.

"That's dreadful news, old chap, but I don't see what it's got to do with me."

"Given your relationship with a woman Mr. Slade held in high regard, you are—"

"A suspect," the captain finished for him, clearly amused.

"Yes."

"There are at least a dozen men who can account for my whereabouts on Tuesday morning," Captain Herbert said.

"I said Mr. Slade was found Tuesday morning. I didn't say that's when he was killed."

"When was he killed?"

"The night before, which would have been Monday."

Captain Herbert nodded. "In that case, the only person who can confirm my whereabouts is my uncle, with whom I dined at his club on Monday night. Oh, and all the other members of White's who saw us together," he added smugly. Captain Herbert cocked his head to the side, studying Daniel as if he were an interesting specimen he'd never seen before. "Out of curiosity, why do you think I'd want to kill him?"

"He was in love with the woman you intend to marry," Daniel replied.

Captain Herbert laughed. "Sebastian Slade was never a real threat, Inspector. Elena enjoyed his company at a time when she felt lonely and vulnerable, but a sexually repressed priest who didn't have a pot to piss in is not the husband she wants."

"Perhaps, given her late husband's less-than-repressed tastes, that's exactly what she wants," Daniel countered, despite the fact that Elena had said the opposite not an hour ago. "And what do you know of Sebastian Slade's financial situation?"

"Only that the man had a fondness for cards and wasn't averse to joining games with high stakes, where he frequently suffered considerable losses. He would have a great deal more to gain by marrying Elena than she would by marrying him. Michael Cartwright left Elena a sizeable estate."

"And who's to say you're not after that estate yourself?" Daniel asked.

"I don't need Elena's money. I'm comfortably off in my own right, and I'm my uncle's heir. I will not touch her money once we wed. It is hers to do with as she pleases."

"Not legally," Daniel pointed out.

"Look here, Inspector, I have loved Elena since I first met her eight years ago. I would have married her then, but she chose Cartwright over me, and I can't say I blame her. At the time, I had little to offer in the way of worldly goods and future prospects. Things have changed since then, for us both. But do you know what hasn't changed? My feelings for her. I will never cause her a moment's doubt when it comes to my devotion to her. All I want is to make her happy."

"A pretty speech, Captain," Daniel said, "but that still doesn't mean you wouldn't have considered eliminating the competition."

Captain Herbert shrugged. "If that's what you believe, then the burden of proof is on you. Good evening, Inspector Haze."

The captain turned on his heel and strode out, leaving Daniel to look at his retreating back.

# Chapter 15

Daniel returned to Brentwood at half past six. The logical thing would have been to go home. He'd been gone since early morning and Sarah would be worried about him, but he took a hansom to Redmond Hall instead. He needed to speak to Jason, analyze what he'd learned, and test his theories; otherwise, he'd never be able to get to sleep tonight. Emptying out his purse to pay the cabbie, he hoped the constabulary would reimburse him for the expenses he'd incurred this day, which were considerable, since no cabbie wanted to drive out to Birch Hill without some added incentive.

Jason smiled warmly when Dodson escorted him to the drawing room.

"Daniel, good to see you. Drink?"

"Please," Daniel said as he settled in his favorite chair. "I hope Katherine won't mind the intrusion too much. I'll make sure to leave before dinner."

"Stay. Join us," Jason invited.

"Thank you, but I need to go home."

"All right, then. Have you made any progress on the investigation?"

"Possibly," Daniel said. He quickly filled Jason in on everything he had learned during the day. "If Sebastian Slade whisked Jenny Ross away from her father without his knowledge, that would certainly give Ross a plausible motive for murder, but I'm not completely discounting Captain Herbert. Despite his vehement denial, he might have felt threatened by Slade's hold over Elena Cartwright and decided to do away with him, arrogantly assuming that no one would be able to tie him to the crime. It would have been simple enough for him to travel to Upper Finchley, kill Slade, and return that same night."

Daniel took a sip of his drink and continued. "However, in the letter to George Fisher, dated Sunday, August sixth, Sebastian Slade makes it clear that something had unsettled him that very day. It stands to reason that it wasn't an encounter with anyone from Upper Finchley, since he'd only just made everyone's acquaintance. Therefore, it must have something to do with his life in London. Likewise, both George Fisher and Captain Herbert alluded to Sebastian Slade's weakness for the card tables. Perhaps Slade had failed to pay his debts and suffered the consequences."

Jason considered this theory. "I agree that the motive for the murder probably originated in London, but whoever killed Sebastian Slade did so on the spur of the moment, which effectively rules out Mr. Ross, Captain Herbert, or some disgruntled moneylender."

"Why do you think so?" Daniel asked, feeling unexpectedly deflated by Jason's response. After all, that was what he'd come for, an honest opinion and an exchange of theories. But Jason had just eliminated all his suspects in one fell swoop.

"The killer used whatever they had to hand, namely a shovel left by the gravedigger and a freshly dug grave. If either Captain Herbert, Mr. Ross, or some nameless bookie had come to Upper Finchley with the intention of killing Slade, do you not think they would have come armed?

"Likewise, no one you questioned in Upper Finchley mentioned encountering any strangers, so the person must have arrived after dark and gone directly to the graveyard, which leads me to believe that the meeting had been prearranged. Sebastian Slade must have trusted his killer, since he didn't come to the meeting armed."

"Few curates would," Daniel pointed out.

"Few men would meet their would-be killer in a graveyard at night if they believed their life to be in danger."

"So, what you are saying is that Sebastian Slade didn't perceive the danger until it was too late."

"Exactly so. Slade met his murderer by design, an argument broke out, and the person grabbed the shovel and bashed Slade on the head in a fit of anger. Perhaps, believing him to be dead, they pushed him into the grave and shoveled the dirt to cover the body, fearing the consequences of their actions and hoping to avoid discovery. This undermines the case against Mr. Ross and Captain Herbert. I simply can't see why Sebastian Slade would agree to meet either man at night in the middle of a graveyard given that they clearly bore him ill will."

"What about the bookie?" Daniel asked, needing to fit at least one suspect for the crime. "Not wishing anyone in Upper Finchley to see him colluding with such a personage and thinking he could talk his way out of paying the debt immediately, he might have agreed to the meeting."

"Yes, he might have, but by killing Slade, the bookie would forgo any chance of collecting the debt, which would be counterproductive to his purpose."

"Unless tempers flared and the bookie killed Slade without considering the consequences," Daniel theorized. "And I'm still not entirely convinced it couldn't have been Captain Herbert. If we are calling this a crime of passion, then Herbert had the most cause to feel passionate, since his heart was engaged."

Jason shook his head stubbornly. "Elena Cartwright confided to you that she loved Sebastian Slade, but I doubt she made it as clear to her intended. But assuming Captain Herbert was astute enough to figure this out for himself and decided to travel to Essex to meet his rival in a graveyard in the middle of the night, do you honestly believe he would leave things to chance and hope someone might have left a shovel for him to use and an open grave to hide the body in? Being a soldier, he has a cache of weapons at his disposal, and he's well trained in using them. He's also a man who understands the benefit of having a strategy. No, Daniel, he would not have come unprepared."

"Perhaps he never meant to kill Slade, only warn him off," Daniel replied.

"He'd hardly have to sneak into the village and meet the man in a graveyard at night to do that. Sebastian Slade was sent to Essex, which was the best possible outcome for Captain Herbert. His rival was out of the way, and the woman he'd loved for years had finally agreed to marry him. Why would he want to jeopardize that by committing murder?"

"Maybe something Slade said set him off, and he reached for the shovel and brought it down on his head without thinking. He may have been armed, as you suggest, but grabbed the first thing he saw instead of going for his weapon. Besides, discharging a pistol would have alerted the villagers to the altercation."

"True, but what could Slade have said that would provoke such a volatile reaction?" Jason mused. "What Elena Cartwright felt for Sebastian Slade was not romantic love. She said as much herself. She didn't think he would be a proper husband to her, nor did she think she could compete with his devotion to God. This is a woman who knows her own mind and has made a decision with a view to securing her future and starting a family. Were I in Captain Herbert's shoes, I don't think I would consider Sebastian Slade much of a rival, not in any way that matters, anyway. Besides, you said he has an alibi," Jason pointed out.

"Yes, he said he was dining with his uncle at his club, which is easy enough to verify. But let us consider Mr. Ross, Jason. Perhaps he'd tracked down Sebastian Slade in the hope of discovering the whereabouts of his daughter," Daniel suggested. "He may have even gone to St. Martin's that Sunday, but Slade convinced him to meet in a more private setting later. Tempers flared, and Sebastian was killed."

"At this stage, we only have Elena Cartwright's version of those events, or more accurately, Sebastian Slade's. It may be just as he told her, but what if Jenny Ross is not an innocent victim but a clever chit who found a path to independence through hoodwinking a naïve curate?"

"Until we know otherwise, we have to count the child's father and Jenny's own father among the list of suspects, which is pitifully short," Daniel said, sighing in dismay.

"All right. But consider this. Let us say that Mr. Ross found a way to get to Upper Finchley. Perhaps he'd taken a train to Brentwood and then hitched a ride to the village. He'd shown himself to Slade sometime on Sunday, frightening Slade, an occurrence he alludes to vaguely in his letters. For one, someone would have seen Mr. Ross in the village. For another, why would he wait until Monday night to meet with Slade if he was there as early as Sunday morning? Where would he have been from Sunday morning until Monday night?"

"He might have returned to London," Daniel replied. "Having arranged to meet Slade on Monday night, he went home and then made a return journey to the village on Monday."

"And no one saw him?" Jason asked, his skepticism obvious. "Upper Finchley is about the size of Birch Hill. Are you telling me that someone wouldn't see a stranger who'd appeared in the village not once, but twice in the space of two days?"

Daniel's shoulders slumped in defeat. "You have a point there. It seems I must return to London tomorrow."

Jason smiled guiltily. "I'm sorry I tore your theories to shreds, Daniel."

"Don't be. Everything you said makes perfect sense, which is why this case is so confounding. We still don't have a solid motive, nor any obvious suspects."

"Would you like me to accompany you tomorrow?" Jason asked.

"I would," Daniel said, smiling tiredly. "You see things from your own unique point of view, which I find extremely helpful."

"I will collect you around nine, then," Jason said. "Joe will drive us to the railway station. We will verify Captain Herbert's alibi, find Jenny Ross and get her version of the truth, then question Mr. Ross."

"That's a sound plan. How did your visit to the school go?" Daniel asked, ready to talk about something other than murder.

"Micah liked the school. It wasn't nearly as awful as he thought it would be. He grudgingly agreed to give it a try."

"Are you pleased or disappointed? I can't tell," Daniel joked, taking in Jason's pained expression.

"A little of both, I suppose. I'm glad Micah is receptive to forgoing the security and comfort of Redmond Hall. I think it will do him a world of good to be on his own for a while. But I will miss him."

"He'll come home for the holidays."

"I know, but it won't be the same. It was just me and Micah for so long."

"But you're also striking out on your own."

Jason smiled happily. "I am. I suppose I'm a little apprehensive about the coming changes."

"That's understandable. Nothing alters your point of view like starting your own family, and Micah is no longer a child. He must see to his own future. All you can do is give him the means to succeed."

Jason nodded. "Yes, you're right."

"And Mary? When will she be leaving for Boston?"

"As soon as I can book her passage," Jason replied sadly. "She wishes to leave before Micah starts school, to make it easier for him."

"That's kind of her," Daniel said. "I hope she finds happiness in Boston. Well, I'd best be going. Katherine will be expecting you to change for dinner. Till tomorrow, then."

"Till tomorrow," Jason said.

# Chapter 16

## Friday, August 9

Having arrived in London, Daniel and Jason proceeded directly to the address Elena Cartwright had provided, hoping to speak to Jenny Ross first. The Swan Tavern on Cannon Street was as nondescript as the textile warehouses that lined the street and supplied most of its customers. The interior was dim and could have done with a thorough cleaning, and the odors of fermentation and grease hung in the air. The Swan was virtually empty, except for a young boy, probably the publican's son, who was wiping down the tables and managing to leave them as dirty as they had been before the application of his filthy rag. A woman of about forty came forward to greet them, her mouth lifting in a smile of welcome.

"Gentlemen, please come in," she said, making an expansive gesture toward the empty tables. "Sit anywhere ye like. Can I start ye with a jar of ale, or perhaps ye'd like some cider? We'll 'ave fresh steak an' ale pies in about an 'our, but if ye're 'ungry, I can offer ye some bread and cheese to tide ye over."

"Thank you, but we are not here to eat, madam," Daniel said politely, noticeably disappointing the woman. "We'd like a word with Jenny Ross. This is the address we have for her."

"And what d'ye want with Jenny?" The smile of welcome was gone, replaced by something resembling a snarl.

"I'm Inspector Haze of the Brentwood Constabulary, and this is my associate, Jason Redmond," Daniel said. They'd agreed not to use Jason's title for fear of intimidating Jenny.

"She's done nothin' wrong," the woman said, her hands resting on her ample hips. "She's a good girl."

"I've no doubt she is," Daniel said in his most placating tone. "I simply wish to ask her a few questions regarding a case I'm working on. I mean her no harm," he reiterated.

The woman still looked unconvinced, but then finally waved them toward what had to be the kitchen. "She's in there."

The kitchen was an airless space, with soot-covered beams and ancient plaster walls covered in cracks so thick, they resembled varicose veins. A bucket of potato peelings stood in the corner, and a hunk of rancid-smelling bacon sat on a sideboard, fat flies perched on its slimy surface. A bowl of dubious-looking meat, presumably filling for the pies, stood in readiness on the pine table. A girl of about seventeen was hard at work, her hands covered in flour as she rolled out the dough for the steak and ale pies. She looked up when they entered, lines of fatigue and disappointment etched into her young face. She was fair-haired and blue-eyed, but so thin that the huge belly that protruded from beneath her apron made her look grotesquely deformed. She had to be mere weeks from giving birth.

"Jenny?" Daniel asked softly. She took a step back, clearly frightened. Daniel held up his warrant card. "My name is Inspector Haze. This is Mr. Redmond." Daniel didn't bother to explain Jason's presence.

"I've done nothing wrong," she choked out.

"I'm not accusing you of anything. I only want to speak to you for a few minutes, if that's all right."

"About what?" Jenny asked. She appeared poised for flight, even though there was nowhere for her to go, since she'd have to get past Daniel and Jason to get to the door.

"Jenny, Mr. Slade was murdered on Monday night in the village of Upper Finchley. I believe you knew him."

She nodded. Her lips were trembling, and her hand instinctively went to her belly. She was clearly upset by the news.

"Mr. Slade left this for you," Daniel said, and held out the money Elena Cartwright had asked him to pass on.

Jenny snatched the money and shoved it in the pocket of her skirt, the lines of despair around her mouth relaxing somewhat. "Thank you, sir. This will go a long way to providing for us."

"Why don't you sit down," Daniel suggested, gesturing toward a three-legged stool in the corner.

"I have pies to prepare," Jenny replied. "The warehouses break for dinner at noon."

"All right, then. Why don't you work while we talk," Daniel agreed.

Jenny resumed her stance at the table and reached for the rolling pin.

"I was told that Mr. Slade had helped you in your hour of need and promised to provide for you and your baby. Can you tell us how that came about?"

Jenny nodded again, her shoulders slumping with misery. "I'll have to start from the beginning, then," she said.

"Start wherever you think is the right place," Jason said kindly.

Jenny finished rolling out the dough and reached for a cutter to divide it into even circles that she would later fill with meat. "A new customer came into my father's shoe shop last autumn," she began. "John Simpson. He was a learned man, a gentleman," she added wistfully. "My father wasn't there that morning, so I took his measurements and showed him drawings of the different shoe styles he could choose from. He took his time, debating the merit of each style, but eventually settled on an ankle lace-up shoe in dark brown." Jenny sighed, as if remembering that day was particularly painful.

"Please, go on," Daniel prompted. He was surprised by Jenny's speech. She sounded almost ladylike.

"He returned the next day. I thought he wished to cancel his order, but he had changed his mind about the color and decided to go with classic black instead. My father assured him the shoes would be to his satisfaction. When my father stepped into the back room for a moment, Mr. Simpson asked me to meet him at the coffeehouse down the street for a cup of chocolate and a bun. I agreed."

"What happened then?" Daniel asked, glad to add the name of John Simpson to his list of suspects.

"John and I continued to meet in secret for several months. I told him that my father goes to Bermondsey every other Tuesday to visit the tanneries, since he can't afford to buy a quantity of stock all at once, and John came when he knew father would be out." Jenny blushed violently, making it clear what she and John had done to pass the time. "John said he loved me. He said he'd speak to my father and ask for permission to marry me once I turned seventeen." A silent tear slid down her flushed cheek.

"You became pregnant?" Daniel asked, and ignored Jason's raised eyebrow. The answer was blatantly obvious.

Jenny nodded miserably. "I told John in March, once I was sure. I thought he'd speak to my father then, but he became angry and said it was all my fault and I was a wicked girl for allowing such a thing to happen. He stormed out and didn't return. I hoped and prayed that once he'd had time to think, he'd come back and everything would be all right between us, but several months passed and I hadn't heard from him." She was crying openly now, the tears rolling down her cheeks. She wiped her nose with the corner of her apron.

"Did you ever see him again?" Jason asked. It was obvious he felt sad for this lonely girl who'd been so ill-used by a man she'd loved and trusted.

Jenny angrily wiped her eyes. "By the end of June, I couldn't wait any longer. I was showing, and no amount of holding objects in front of me or standing behind counters or chairs was going to disguise the fact that I was with child. My father was beginning to look at me in that questioning way, already knowing the truth of the matter but still hoping he was mistaken. So, I swallowed my reservations and went to the lodging house where John told me he lived. The landlady said she had only one tenant, but not by that name. When I asked her to describe her lodger, she said he was a man in his fifties with muttonchop whiskers, a head as bald as an egg, and a strong Yorkshire accent. It wasn't John."

Jenny slid the tray of finished pies into the old-fashioned brick oven and turned to face Daniel and Jason. "It was after I returned from the lodging house that my father told me I had to leave. He had a respectable business and would lose customers if they learned of his daughter's disgrace. I begged him not to cast me adrift, but he said I'd made my bed and now I had to lie in it, alone or with the man who'd brought me so low. I was desperate," Jenny cried. "I didn't know what to do or where to go."

"Was that when you went to St. Dunstan's?" Daniel asked.

"Once, I had seen a program from St. Dunstan's in John's pocket, so I decided to try there. I packed a small valise and set off, thinking that if that was his regular place of worship, he might be there for the Sunday service and I could speak to him, and if not, I would go round the taverns and ask for work."

"He wasn't there?" Jason asked, his tone warm with sympathy.

"No, he was," Jenny said, her eyes suddenly blazing with anger. "Right there at the pulpit, dressed in his vestments, or whatever they're called."

"Are you referring to Reverend Kent?" Daniel asked, staring at her in incredulity. Surely the man was too old to tempt a girl like Jenny, but there was no accounting for taste.

"No, Inspector, I'm referring to Sebastian Slade."

Jason let out a low whistle and gave Daniel a sidelong glance. Here it was, the sound of the angel tumbling from Heaven and landing on the ground with a deafening thud.

"Did you confront him?" Daniel asked.

"Not immediately. I was too shocked. I sat in one of the back pews and waited for the service to finish. Once it did, I went straight up to John and asked him to help me. I had nothing left to lose, so I thought I'd shame him into facing me and taking responsibility for the child he'd so carelessly sired. It was then that the vicar saw fit to intercede. He called me a harlot and told me to leave and not come back unless I had mended my ways and was once again worthy of the Lord's forgiveness."

A sob of despair escaped from Jenny's thin chest. "I never felt so wretched in my life. I ran outside and would have kept going, but I felt so ill, I leaned on one of the gravestones to keep from falling. That's where John—Sebastian—found me. Maybe he truly regretted the way he'd treated me, or maybe he couldn't bear to lie to my face in the sight of God, but he said he would look after me and the baby. I thought that meant he'd set me up proper, but he brought me here and said I could work in the kitchen in exchange for room and board. That was the extent of his generosity. Still, I have a roof over my head and enough to eat, so I'm grateful."

"Have you seen your father since?" Jason asked.

"No. We've had no contact since the day he threw me out. And we never will. He chose his pride and respectability over his only child and grandchild, knowing when he told me to go that he might be sending us to our deaths. I'm through with men," Jenny said, her anger palpable. "We'll be all right, my girl and me," she said, laying a hand over her belly. "We'll manage. And before you ask me, Inspector, I don't know anything about the murder, nor will I grieve the man."

"Where were you Monday night, Jenny?" Daniel asked, but there was no sternness in his voice, only pity.

"I was right here, Inspector, ladling out stew and slicing endless loaves of bread. I cleared up and went up to bed close to midnight. There are plenty who saw me."

"Was your father ever unkind to you?" Jason asked. "Did he beat you?"

"Lord, no," Jenny sputtered, clearly surprised by the question. Her earlier anger toward her father seemed to have dissipated, and she looked like a sad little girl. "It was I who was unkind to him. He'd always done his best by me. He thought book learning was important, even for a woman, so he educated me and encouraged me to better myself. He wanted me to make a good marriage and have a comfortable life. Instead, I squandered my virtue on the first man who showed an interest in me and ruined it all. What a fool I've been," Jenny whispered as fresh tears began to fall.

"Jenny, if you're ever in need of employment, come to Redmond Hall in the village of Birch Hill." Jason extracted a bunch of coins from his pocket and handed them to Jenny. "This will cover the cost of the train and hansom. Think of it as a contingency plan," he said.

"What's that?" Jenny asked, her eyes wide with surprise.

"It's just something to fall back on, that's all."

"Thank you, sir. You're very kind," Jenny said, pocketing the money. "Redmond Hall," she repeated under her breath.

"We'll need directions to your father's shop," Daniel said awkwardly. He admired Jason for his boundless generosity but couldn't help being marginally annoyed by his tenderhearted need to collect strays. Jenny Ross wasn't his responsibility. She had made decisions that had cost her dearly, but so did a great number of people. That was life, and people had to learn to fend for themselves.

Jenny shrugged. "You won't find what you're looking for. My father had nothing to do with Sebastian's murder."

*I'll be the judge of that*, Daniel thought bitterly. This investigation was making him feel terribly inadequate, and he wished some solid evidence would finally present itself so that he could redeem himself in his own eyes.

"Thank you, Jenny. Be well," Jason said. They left the kitchen, passed through the taproom of the Swan, and headed out into the overcast morning.

# Chapter 17

The shoe shop consisted of a tiny front room, where customers were received, and a workroom at the back. There was a strong smell of leather and polish and an even stronger stench of despair. A man of about fifty came forward to greet them, his pale blue eyes downcast with sadness, his once-dark hair streaked with gray. He was thin, like his daughter, and his shoulders were stooped with either years of bending over a workbench or abject misery.

"Mr. Ross?" Daniel asked.

"Yes. How can I help you, gentlemen?" Mr. Ross asked breathlessly.

Daniel introduced himself and Jason and plunged in. "One of your customers, a man known to you as John Simpson, was murdered on Monday night."

"I'm pleased to hear it," Mr. Ross said, a hint of a smile tugging at his mouth. "He got his just deserts, then."

"Where were you on Monday evening?" Daniel demanded.

Mr. Ross barked out a laugh that turned into a cough that lasted for a few seconds. "You think I did it?"

"You certainly had a motive for wanting him dead," Daniel replied.

"Inspector, as you yourself just said, I knew the man as John Simpson. A fictitious name given along with a fictitious address. Had I wished to kill him, I wouldn't even know how to go about finding him. Although I would be lying if I said I didn't dream of killing that scoundrel every night."

"Your daughter could have told you his real name. It wouldn't be hard to discover that he'd been sent to a parish in Essex," Daniel said. Jenny might have lied about having no contact with her father. Perhaps she'd tried to appeal to him despite his harsh treatment of her.

"I have not spoken to nor seen my daughter since I asked her to leave this house in June. At that time, she believed her lover's name to be John Simpson. Have you seen Jenny?" Mr. Ross asked. "Have you spoken to her?" There was such desperation in his voice, Daniel actually felt sorry for the man.

"Jenny is well," he replied.

"Please, Inspector, tell me where she is. I want to go to her, to beg her to come home. I was a foolish, proud man, concerned with my reputation and business, but nothing means anything without my Jenny."

"If your daughter means so much to you, why did you not support her when she needed you most?" Jason demanded, clearly still angry on Jenny's behalf.

Mr. Ross's shoulders sloped even lower. "She lied to me. She met that man in secret and gave herself to him as no decent girl would. I warned her time and time again that there would be men who'd try to sweettalk her, make false promises. She should have known better, should have trusted the father who loves her. What sort of man makes advances to a girl nearly ten years his junior and seduces her in her father's shop? A reprobate, a trickster," Mr. Ross answered his own question. "A man who's only after one thing." He sighed deeply. "I had always treated Jenny with respect, had talked to her, and educated her. I wanted her to have the comfort and security a woman can only achieve through a good marriage. And now she's ruined forever, saddled with a child that should never have been, all of life's doors forever closed to her. I was angry and disappointed, I freely admit that, but I was wrong. I was foolish. I miss my girl," he said wheezily. "How I miss my girl."

"Mr. Ross, where were you on Monday night?" Daniel asked again.

Mr. Ross sighed dramatically. "I was next door at Mrs. Coley's. She's been widowed these three years, and once Jenny was gone, I found myself looking for companionship. We sup together most nights. It holds the loneliness at bay for a short time," Mr. Ross replied.

"We'll be speaking to Mrs. Coley," Daniel said sternly.

Mr. Ross shrugged. "Do. I have nothing to hide, Inspector. I wish I would have killed that swine for the way he treated my Jenny. Perhaps if I'd had more courage, I would have found a way to track him down," he said, squaring his shoulders defiantly.

"Good day, Mr. Ross," Daniel said, and turned toward the door.

"Wait, please," Mr. Ross cried. "Please, tell me where I can find Jenny. I only want to speak to her, to make amends."

"I'm afraid I can't do that, Mr. Ross," Daniel said.

"But we will pass on your sentiments to Jenny," Jason cut in, glaring at Daniel like an avenging angel.

"Will you really?" Mr. Ross asked, looking at Jason as if he were indeed his guardian angel.

"You have my word," Jason said. "Good day, Mr. Ross."

"Was that wise, Jason?" Daniel asked once they stepped outside. "The man is technically still a suspect, and he had a powerful motive for wanting Slade dead. In fact, he freely admitted that he wished he'd killed him. It's not difficult to entice a lonely widow to lie on one's behalf."

Jason made a dismissive gesture with his hand. "Ross didn't kill Sebastian Slade. I'd be surprised if he had the strength to lift a shovel, much less bring it down on a man's head swiftly enough to take him by surprise. The man's lungs are severely compromised, probably from breathing in all those compounds used for tanning leather in an airless room for the past several decades. I don't think he has too many years left to him, and I, for one, see no reason to stand in the way of a reunion. Besides, he seems genuinely contrite."

"What if Mr. Ross's contrition is all an act?" Daniel asked. "If he's as ill as you suggest, he might simply want his daughter back so she can look after him."

"He might," Jason agreed, "but that's what children do for their parents. I don't believe he's a violent man, nor do I think

Jenny will be in any danger. Many a father chastises their child and sometimes even casts them out, but more often than not, love prevails over wounded pride, as I hope it will do in this case. Even my grandfather came around in the end and wished for a reconciliation with my father," Jason said sadly. "I wish they would have found a way to forgive each other before it was too late."

"Is that why you decided to come to England? To bridge the gap?" Daniel asked.

"In part. I think my father would have approved of my decision," Jason said. "And you know what they say, Daniel— blood is thicker than water, and no matter how hurt Jenny Ross might feel, her father is still her only family."

"All right. You've convinced me," Daniel admitted grudgingly. "Let's stop in and speak to Mrs. Coley, then we'll return to the Swan and relay Mr. Ross's regrets to his daughter. I hope this situation at least will have a happy ending."

Mrs. Coley was a plump, kindly looking woman of middle years who seemed to relish the opportunity to talk and gladly invited Daniel and Jason into her front parlor, where she offered them refreshments, which they declined.

"Oh, yes," she said when asked. "Eugene dined with me on Monday evening and every other evening before and since. I took pity on the man when 'is Jenny went off, but I must admit it's been nice 'aving a bit of company. I'm not looking to get married again, mind ye," she went on. "My William left me comfortably off, thank the Lord, so I don't need to tie myself to another man, especially one who's not long for this world."

"Did Eugene Ross tell you he's ill?" Jason asked.

"He didn't 'ave to, did 'e? Any fool can see 'im wheezing and coughing. And truth be told, I did feel a little guilty 'bout 'is Jenny."

"Why did you feel guilty, Mrs. Coley?" Daniel asked.

"I'd seen 'er, ye know," she admitted, lowering her voice as if imparting a secret. "Seen 'er with that cove as got 'er with child. I should 'ave said somethin' to Eugene, should 'ave intervened. But I thought, she ain't my girl. What business do I 'ave telling tales? Jenny's a smart girl, I said to myself. She'll not fall for 'is tricks. But she did, the poor lamb. Perhaps if her dear mother were still alive, things would 'ave turned out differently. But I should 'ave said somethin'," Mrs. Coley went on, now in full flow. "'Specially when I seen 'im looking at Mabel as 'e 'ad."

"And who's Mabel?" Daniel asked.

"Mabel is Mrs. Potts' daughter. They're just across the street," she said, pointing toward the house on the opposite side of the road. "Mabel were just coming back from the market, so it must 'ave been Friday. Always goes to the market on Fridays. Anyroad, she 'ad 'er basket slung over 'er arm, and it looked 'eavy. Well, Mr. Simpson, or whatever 'is real name was, 'ad just come out of Eugene's shop and was walking down the street. 'E saw Mabel and went right over to 'er. 'Let me 'elp ye,' 'e said, all solicitous like. 'That looks 'eavy.'"

"Is it so unusual for a man to offer help to a woman?" Daniel asked.

Mrs. Coley scoffed. "It is in these 'ere parts, and let me tell ye, Inspector, 'ad 'e seen me struggling, 'e'd 'ave walked right past. Mabel is sixteen, and fresh as a daisy. Fair curls, blue eyes, and a lovely figure to boot. 'E were trying it on, but Mabel, she's smarter than Jenny, it seems. Told 'im, 'No thank ye, good sir, I'm nearly 'ome.' I could see 'e were disappointed. 'E looked after Mabel for a long while after she walked away."

"Thank you, Mrs. Coley. That was most helpful," Daniel said as the men stood to leave.

"Always glad to 'elp the police," Mrs. Coley said, beaming. "There's some as won't, but not me."

"Do you realize what this means?" Daniel asked once they were back out in the street. He was brimming with frustration and yanked at his stiff collar, feeling as if it were strangling him.

"That we're back where we started. I have no doubt White's will confirm Captain Herbert's presence at the club on

Monday evening, which will mean that neither Eugene Ross nor Captain Herbert was anywhere near Upper Finchley on the night Sebastian Slade was killed. But we have learned something new," Jason pointed out.

"And what's that?"

"Sebastian Slade was not as conflicted about indulging in carnal relations as he had led those close to him to believe. There's Jenny Ross, and he'd shown an interest in Mabel Potts."

"And what does that tell us, exactly? That he was just a man who liked a pretty face?" Daniel asked archly.

"It tells us that he seemed to have a preference for young, fair-haired, blue-eyed girls," Jason pointed out.

"That's hardly a crime," Daniel replied. "And, incidentally, Elena Cartwright is fair and blue-eyed as well."

"It's certainly not a crime to be drawn to a particular type of woman, but it's a pattern of behavior we shouldn't ignore."

"We need a real lead, Jason," Daniel said, shaking his head. "All this speculation is getting us nowhere."

"We need to return to Upper Finchley. The motive for the murder might have originated in London, but I think the answer lies in Essex, my friend."

Daniel nodded. "I agree, but there's one more person I'd like to speak to after we confirm Captain Herbert's alibi."

"Really? Who?" Jason asked.

"Bernard Holloway."

# Chapter 18

Bernard Holloway was an easy man to find. He was at his office in the City, his desk, clearly visible through a glass door, strewn with papers and reports, his brow furrowed as he read something and then reached for a pen and dipped it in ink before scribbling a note across the page.

"Do you have an appointment?" a young clerk demanded when Daniel asked to speak to his employer.

"I'm afraid not, but this will only take a moment."

"I'm afraid Mr. Holloway is rather busy," the clerk insisted.

"This is police business, and it will not wait," Daniel replied calmly, knowing the man was only doing his job.

"I see. I will ask Mr. Holloway if he'll speak to you," the clerk replied, and went into the office to consult his employer.

"Go on in," the clerk said once he returned.

Bernard Holloway had abandoned whatever he was working on and sat back in his chair, looking welcoming and relaxed as Daniel and Jason entered the office.

"Gentlemen, please, have a seat. How may I be of service?" he asked. His gaze was expectant, perhaps because he believed they'd come to deliver news of the investigation.

"Mr. Holloway, since your wife is not here, perhaps we can speak frankly," Daniel said, cutting across the pleasantries. "What can you tell us about Sebastian Slade?"

"How do you mean, Inspector?" Bernard Holloway asked, but Daniel thought the man knew precisely what he'd meant.

"What do you know of your brother-in-law's sexual conquests?"

Bernard Holloway gave Daniel a hard look as he leaned forward and clasped his hands on the desk, his shoulders stiffening with tension that hadn't been there a moment ago and his mouth twitched beneath the carefully groomed moustache. The man's gaze slid away, fixating on something outside the window. This was clearly not a conversation he wished to have, probably out of loyalty to his wife, or maybe because he valued his professional reputation and wished to keep his name from becoming associated with the murder.

"Mr. Holloway, anything you tell us will be treated as confidential," Daniel said, hoping the promise would loosen the man's tongue.

"Iris idolized Sebastian," Bernard Holloway said at last as he reluctantly tore his gaze from the window. "She thought the sun shone out of his arse. I suppose I could see why she'd think that, since the side of him he showed to her was one of kindness and humility."

"Tell us about the other side," Jason invited.

Holloway sighed. "Sebastian had a penchant for young girls. That was one of the reasons he'd never married. The thought of watching a beautiful young woman turn into a matronly vicar's wife whose body has been ruined by numerous pregnancies and the ravages of time was repugnant to him. He was attracted to underdeveloped girls who were hovering on the verge of womanhood. He liked to witness their awakening—their metamorphosis, he called it."

"But he had no interest in staying for the final act," Daniel said, the image of Jenny's pinched face and huge belly swimming into his mind.

"No. Once his lovers began to exhibit signs of sexual awareness, he lost interest in them," Bernard said.

"Do you know of any young women he debauched?" Jason asked, barely controlled anger in his voice.

"I know of two. One was Jenny Ross, the daughter of a cobbler he'd visited. The other was Dorothy Fry, our scullery maid. There might have been others."

"And you turned a blind eye while he seduced a young woman under your roof?" Jason asked belligerently.

Bernard Holloway started, as if he'd been slapped. "I had no idea what he was up to. Sebastian was still at the seminary when Iris and I married and only moved in with us when Gracie was six months old. I would have preferred for him to rent his own rooms, but Iris insisted. We had plenty of room, and she thought it would be nice to have her brother with us for a time. This was never going to be a permanent arrangement, you understand," Bernard Holloway said forcefully, clearly regretting the decision to allow his brother-in-law to settle under his roof.

"I only found out about Dorothy after she'd complained to Cook, who beat her for spreading vicious lies and sacked her on the spot. Iris never knew the reason for the dismissal. She assumed the girl was lazy or insolent and had her replaced, but Sebastian mentioned the incident to me. He was quite put out that Dorothy had been dismissed. It seems he wasn't yet finished with her."

"So, what did you do?" Daniel asked.

Bernard Holloway shrugged. "What was there to do?"

"Did you not think to chastise him, or seek Dorothy Fry out and recompense her for the injustice she'd suffered while in your employ?" Jason demanded.

"Would you have? What right did I have to chastise him? Many a man I know makes free with the staff or avails himself of whores while his wife believes he's dining at his club. Am I supposed to challenge them all or recompense the whores for the injustice of their situation? What men do is between them and their conscience, and from what Sebastian told me, Dorothy had been a willing participant, so it was no one's fault but her own. It is a woman's responsibility to safeguard her virtue. I did ask Sebastian to keep his peccadilloes out of our home," Bernard Holloway added sourly.

"And how did you find out about Jenny?" Daniel asked.

"Sebastian told me about her. No, *boasted* would be a more accurate word. He was quite pleased with her until she got with child. Then he wanted nothing more to do with her. I assume he was in the market for a replacement, but then the trouble with

Reverend Kent started, and he was packed off to Essex. Now, if you will excuse me, I have work to do."

"Thank you, Mr. Holloway. This conversation has been most illuminating," Daniel snapped. He stood and turned on his heel, more than ready to leave. Jason followed him outside.

"The insufferable prig," Daniel fumed. "It's a woman's responsibility to safeguard her virtue. Many a man I know makes free with the staff," Daniel mimicked, his outrage boiling over.

"Calm down, Daniel," Jason said, but his expression was grim. "Infuriating as the man is, sadly, he's right. There will always be those who will deceive, violate, and abuse. A woman must be ten times as vigilant as any man when it comes to protecting her future."

"It seems Sebastian Slade was just as vigilant about protecting his," Daniel replied. "He turned the confrontation with Jenny into a crusade for tolerance, making sure Reverend Kent never suspected that when Jenny asked Slade for help, she was doing so because he was her child's father. He may have lost his position at St. Dunstan's, but he managed to safeguard his reputation. Had he not been murdered, he would most likely have taken over Reverend Hodge's living once the old vicar passed. Upper Finchely might not be London, but he'd be a law unto himself in a place where he'd have complete trust from the female population."

"Well, perhaps some member of the female population had decided it was time to mete out her own justice," Jason said. "Can't say I blame her. Come. Let's go home. Tomorrow is another day."

"Another day that we'll start with no motive and no leads," Daniel pointed out bitterly.

"The motive and leads exist, and we will find them," Jason said.

# Chapter 19

By the time Jason returned to Redmond Hall, he felt tired and irritable and wanted only to spend a peaceful hour with Katherine, but that was not to be. She ran out to meet him as soon as he walked up the steps.

"Katie, what is it?" Jason asked, frightened by the anxiety in her eyes.

"Mary's gone."

"How long has she been missing?" Jason asked as he handed his things to Dodson. He followed Katherine into the drawing room, where she poured him a brandy and took a small glass of sherry for herself.

She sat heavily on the settee and took a sip. "After you left this morning, I heard Liam crying. I didn't think anything of it at first, but then he continued to cry and call out for his mother. Worried, I knocked on the door, but there was no answer, so I went in. Mary's bed hadn't been slept in, and Liam was standing up in his cot, reaching out for me to take him."

Jason glanced at the carriage clock on the mantel. It was past three in the afternoon. "Have you spoken to Micah?" he asked.

Katherine nodded. "He is very upset."

"Did Mary not say anything to him before leaving?"

"It would appear she didn't. I can't imagine where she's gone," Katherine said, and sipped more sherry. "What if she's hurt? Or dead?" she whispered.

"Who was the last person to see Mary last night?"

"I was. I wished her a good night when I saw her entering her bedroom around nine. She seemed fine. She had some warm milk for Liam."

"So, sometime between nine in the evening and this morning, Mary left this house. Is it possible that she went to meet someone?"

"I can't think of anyone she might have met with. Mary doesn't have any friends in the village."

"Have you spoken to Kitty?" Jason asked.

Katherine nodded. "She knows nothing."

"And Mr. Sullivan? He and Mary have become quite close over the past few months."

"He's as much in the dark as I am."

"I think I'd like to speak to him myself," Jason said. He tossed back the remainder of his brandy and stood.

"I'm so glad you're home, Jason," Katherine said.

Jason took the glass out of her hands, set it aside, and pulled her up, taking her in his arms. "Everything will be all right, Katie. Please don't worry. Who's with Liam?"

"Kitty is looking after him. Mrs. Dodson was able to spare her for a few hours."

"Let me speak to Shawn. I might be able to glean something."

Jason found Shawn Sullivan in the library, a book in his lap. He looked drawn and sad, his colorful waistcoat and puff tie bringing undue attention to his pallor. He sprang to his feet when Jason entered, behaving as if he were doing something untoward instead of quietly reading.

"Please, sit down, Mr. Sullivan," Jason said, and took the armchair opposite him. "Shawn," Jason said, using the man's Christian name because he saw no reason to stand on ceremony. "You and Mary are great friends. Has she said anything to you?"

Shawn looked uncomfortable, his eyes sliding away from Jason's probing gaze. "No."

"Has someone been courting her?"

Shawn shook his head. "Henley tried it on a few times, but she wanted no part of him."

"Did he do anything to make her feel unsafe?" Jason asked, thinking he was going to wring his valet's neck if he had.

"No, not at all. Mary just wasn't interested in him in that way."

"Might it have been someone from the village?"

Mary had previously indicated that she had no interest in finding a beau for fear of having to settle in England permanently if she met someone who truly touched her heart, but perhaps the situation had changed, and she'd been seeing someone on the quiet. Such a relationship might cause her to change her mind about leaving.

"She wasn't interested in courtship, sir."

"So, what was she interested in?" Jason asked, thinking that despite all their conversations, he didn't know Mary at all.

"Freedom," Shawn said, taking Jason by surprise.

"Freedom from us?"

"No, freedom to make her own way in the world."

"But no one tried to deny her that. Are you saying she ran away?"

"I'm not saying anything, sir. Mary didn't confide in me. She only said that she felt like a bird in a gilded cage."

"I see," Jason replied, not seeing at all. "Thank you, Shawn. Please let me know if you think of anything else."

"I will, sir."

Having left the library, Jason made his way downstairs, where he sought the guidance of someone wiser than he, at least in household matters. Mrs. Dodson had been like a surrogate mother to him, and to Micah and Mary, as well. It was as if she'd taken the motherless Americans under her wing, offering comfort, support, and sometimes baked goods to soothe ruffled feathers, quiet fears, or just lend an ear.

Mrs. Dodson was red in the face from the heat of the kitchen, her frothy fair hair limp and damp at the temples. She was peeling potatoes but set the knife down when Jason slid into his customary seat at the pine table.

"Would you like a cool drink?" she asked. "I can sure use one."

"Please," Jason said, and shrugged off his coat, tossing it on the bench.

Mrs. Dodson set a glass of lemonade before him and sat down, sighing with relief at taking the weight off her tired feet.

"A cold supper would be just fine, Mrs. D," Jason said. "It's way too hot down here to be cooking and baking."

She waved his comment away. "Don't you worry about me. I will serve my lord and lady a proper meal, no matter the weather."

"Mrs. Dodson, has Mary said anything to you?" Jason asked.

"She said a great many things to me, but I'm not sure I should repeat them," Mrs. Dodson said.

"I don't understand. Have I done something to offend her?"

"Not intentionally," Mrs. Dodson replied cryptically. Seeing Jason's confusion, she smiled sympathetically at him. "Captain, you are a kind and generous man, and you've been a safe harbor for Mary and Liam, but it's time you let her go."

"But I wasn't holding her back," Jason replied, growing even more uneasy. "And why would she leave Liam behind?"

Mrs. Dodson took a long pull of lemonade and sighed, shaking her head at Jason's shortsightedness. "Just because someone's poor don't mean they don't have their pride."

"Have I offended Mary's pride somehow?"

"What did you offer her?" Mrs. Dodson asked, smiling at him kindly.

"I offered her passage home, the use of my Washington Square house and staff should she decide to settle in New York, and the means to live independently for the rest of her life."

"And what did she offer you in return?" Mrs. Dodson asked.

Jason felt anger welling in his chest. "Are you suggesting that I asked for payment in kind?"

"Not at all, which is precisely what I'm telling you. The girl's got her pride."

"Mrs. Dodson, speak plainly," Jason said. "I'm too tired and upset to decipher riddles."

Mrs. Dodson nodded. "All right. You asked for it. Mary is not your kin. She's not your responsibility. It made her feel beholden to accept charity from you. You brought her to England, so passage home was her fair due, but what would an Irish girl from a farm in Maryland do in a grand house in Washington Square? Socialize with your society friends? And how would the staff treat her when she's no better than they are? Hm?" Mrs. Dodson demanded. "And what has she done to earn a lifelong allowance?"

"I only wanted her to feel safe and cared for," Jason protested.

"Well, you made her feel indebted. She needs to find her own way, and she can hardly do that with a small child and no husband to support her."

"So, she left us Liam to raise?" Jason asked. "As you pointed out, we're not her kin."

"She'll send for him, I'm sure. She left you the most precious thing she has because she trusts you with her life. Take care of that boy and then send him back to her with Micah, once he's done with his studies."

"But how did she think she'd get to Liverpool?" Jason asked, still baffled by this unexpected turn of events.

"Oh, I suspect she had help."

"From whom?"

Mrs. Dodson grinned. "From Moll Brody, who was the closest thing she had to a friend in this village aside from Kitty. I expect you'll find that Matty Locke took her to the railway station this morning and she caught the first train out of Brentwood."

"Why didn't you tell Lady Redmond?" Jason asked, irritated with Mrs. Dodson for allowing Katherine to worry so.

"Because telling her wouldn't bring Mary back, and you're the one she was running from."

Jason felt a great weight settle on his chest. He'd wanted to help, but it seemed he'd not only caused offense but had been the means of separating mother and son.

"Don't blame yourself," Mrs. Dodson said, as if reading his thoughts. "You did what any feeling person would do. You reunited brother and sister, and you gave Mary a safe place to recover from the ordeal she'd been through during the war. But now you must let her go. Liam is a good boy. He won't be too much trouble, and he'll be a companion for your own little one," she said with a kindly smile.

"Thank you, Mrs. Dodson. What would I do without you?"

"You'd be just fine, my lord," she said, smiling at him. "You don't need me to tell you that."

"Perhaps I do."

"You're a good man, and don't let anything change you."

Jason nodded his thanks and left the kitchen, trudging up the stairs warily to explain the situation to his wife.

# Chapter 20

Jason found Micah in the garden, sitting on a wrought-iron bench in the shade of a leafy tree and staring into space. Micah's gaze shifted when Jason came into view, and he smiled sadly, his eyes filling with tears.

"I'm sorry," he mumbled.

"You've nothing to be sorry for," Jason replied as he sat next to him.

"I do. Mary is my sister, and she repaid your kindness with ingratitude."

"I'm not sure it's that simple," Jason replied. He looked closely at Micah and then asked the question that had been plaguing him since Katherine informed him of Mary's departure. "Micah, do you really have an aunt in Boston?"

Micah shook his head. "Mary made her up. She felt uncomfortable with all the things you were offering but couldn't bear to refuse to your face and hurt your feelings. She thought you'd stop if you thought she had family to go to."

"So, where did she go?"

Micah shrugged. "I don't know. She didn't even say goodbye. She just left." He hung his head, but Jason could still see the tear that slid down his pale cheek. "I suppose she thought she was doing me a favor."

"How so?"

"She wants me to go to school, to better myself, to become a proper gentleman."

Jason nodded in understanding. "You wanted to go with her, didn't you? That's why she ran off without saying goodbye."

"I hated the thought of being parted from Mary and Liam. I thought maybe I could go to school in Boston. That was when I believed there really was an aunt."

"Why do you think she left Liam behind?" Jason asked, but he already knew.

"Because she knows you'll do right by him. She trusts you. And as long as Liam is here, she knows I'll stay and not follow her back." Micah raised his tearstained face to Jason. "Maybe we can still catch her, in Liverpool, I mean. Convince her to come back."

Jason laid a hand on Micah's shoulder. "I don't think so, Micah. Mary is a grown woman, and she's made her choice. I will not be the one to bring her back."

"What about Liam?" Micah asked.

"We'll look after him. You've nothing to worry about on that score."

"Should I still go to school?" Micah asked wistfully.

"Of course. As soon as I'm done with this case, we'll go into Brentwood and order your kit. There's quite a long list of things you'll need. Are you looking forward to going?" Jason asked.

"Yes and no. I'm scared," Micah admitted, his voice barely audible.

"I know you are. Every boy is scared when starting a new school, but you will be just fine. You'll make friends in no time."

"What if no one wants to be my friend?" Micah asked miserably.

"If you don't settle in by Christmas and want to leave, I'll take you back, no questions asked," Jason said.

"Really? You promise?"

"You have my word."

Micah smiled up at Jason and leaned into him, resting his coppery head on Jason's shoulder. "I love you, Captain," he said. That was the first time he'd said it out loud, and it brought tears to Jason's eyes.

"I love you too. Now, stop moping and come inside. It's teatime, and I hear there's cake."

"I like cake," Micah muttered.

"I know," Jason replied with a smile. Some things, as least, never changed.

# Chapter 21

## Saturday, August 10

Saturday morning found Jason and Daniel heading to Upper Finchley. Jason expertly drove the chestnuts, while Daniel looked morosely over the passing countryside. Come Monday, he'd have to report to Chief Inspector Coleridge, and he had promised to update Bishop Garner on the progress of the investigation. As of this morning, he had nothing of value to share with either man. Sebastian Slade had been immoral and duplicitous, but if every man who fit that description were killed, the country would be strewn with corpses. Daniel did not see a clear motive for the murder, nor did he have any viable suspects.

This morning, the plan was to interview the two people who would know most about what went on in the village, namely the publican and the postmistress, but Daniel worried that they'd simply be frittering away precious time without much to show for it. Had either one known something pertaining to the case, surely they would have come forward already.

"People rarely realize what they know," Jason said, correctly interpreting Daniel's gloomy silence. "What might seem commonplace to them can in actuality be an important clue."

"You are right, of course," Daniel replied. "I suppose I'm putting undue pressure on myself, since failure to solve this case can affect my future with the police service."

"Daniel, no detective solves every case. Surely you know that."

"I do. I suppose it's terribly vain to think I can be that one exception."

"Vanity is not a character trait I associate with you, but doggedness is. Odds are the more people you speak to, the better chance you have of stumbling upon someone who either saw or heard something."

"I suppose," Daniel replied, smiling despite his determination to remain negative.

"Would you prefer to interview the publican or the postmistress?" Jason asked, grinning.

"I'll take the publican. The ladies are way more impressed with you than they are with me."

"Sorry, old chap, I just can't seem to tone down my American charm," Jason joked.

"That'd be funny if it weren't true," Daniel replied in jest. He suddenly felt lighter. Jason was right. Not every case got solved, and even the commissioner himself had suffered a few setbacks in his day, some of them quite well documented in old issues of the *Illustrated Police News*.

Once they arrived in the village, Jason left the curricle by The Black Boar and continued on foot toward the post office, while Daniel went inside to speak to the publican.

The publican, a Mr. Brockton, was in his forties. He was short and stocky, with a florid complexion and a luxuriant moustache that hung like a fur curtain above his mouth. He raised a hand in greeting, no doubt having recognized Daniel from when he'd seen him at the graveyard on Tuesday. A young woman, who resembled him too much not to be his daughter, hovered nearby, her gaze following Daniel as if she were afraid to miss something important.

"Good day to ye, Inspector. Would ye care for a jar of ale or a cup o' cider? We make it ourselves, and it's the finest in the county," Mr. Brockton boasted.

"Thank you, no," Daniel replied. "I was hoping I could ask you a few questions."

Mr. Brockton pursed his lips and folded his arms across his chest. "I'd like to help ye, but I don't know nothin', Inspector."

Daniel didn't think that was quite true. Perhaps Mr. Brockton didn't care to get involved, or placed an unusually high value on discretion for fear of losing custom if he revealed something unsavory about one of his patrons. Daniel decided to try a different approach.

"A publican is much like a vicar, in my opinion. He knows everything that goes on in the village but keeps his own counsel and protects the privacy of those who entrust him with their innermost thoughts," Daniel said.

Mr. Brockton nodded in agreement. "Ye got that right, guv."

"Even a vicar must betray a confidence at times when he knows it's the moral thing to do. Mr. Brockton, someone brained the curate with a shovel and buried him alive. That person must be brought to justice."

"And ye think I know who done for 'im?" Mr. Brockton asked, incredulous.

"I'm not suggesting that you know who killed Mr. Slade. But I do think you might have seen or heard something that could put me onto the murderer."

Mr. Brockton looked thoughtful. "Nope. Ain't seen or heard nothin'. Everyone liked the new curate. Thought he was a fine man."

Daniel tried to harness his irritation. The man wasn't willing to budge. "I'll remain in the village for an hour or two, so if you happen to think of something, please find me," he said.

"I won't."

"Thanks all the same," Daniel said, and left the pub.

He hadn't gone more than a few feet when he heard someone behind him. Daniel spun around, unnerved by the stealthy footsteps and nervous breathing. He was surprised to find the publican's daughter, who held a finger to her lips and beckoned him to follow her. She led him behind a shed that her father likely used for storage and looked out to make sure no one had seen her.

"Da won't like me talking to ye," she said.

"What is it you wish to tell me?" Daniel asked. Seeing her up close, he realized she was younger than he'd first thought. Thirteen or fourteen, at most.

The girl was nervous. "I left my *Book of Common Prayer* inside the church on Sunday." The stealthy look on her face implied that she'd probably done it on purpose. Perhaps she had arranged to meet someone, and this was the excuse she had needed to return.

"Please, go on."

"When I went inside, Mr. Slade was sitting on the step leading up to the altar, 'is face white as chalk," she whispered.

"Was he frightened, do you think?" Daniel asked.

"More shocked, I'd say," the girl said. "'E looked like 'e'd seen a ghost."

"Was there anyone else inside the church?"

"No, but I 'ad seen someone 'urrying away just before I reached the lychgate."

"Did you recognize this person?"

The girl nodded. "It were Mr. Gale."

"Is there anything else you wish to tell me?"

"No, sir."

"Well, thank you, Miss Brockton. I appreciate you sharing this information with me," Daniel said.

"Is it important?" the girl asked eagerly.

"I am sure it is."

She smiled happily. "Will my name get in the paper if it were Mr. Gale as killed the curate? It's Elsie. Elsie Brockton."

"Most definitely, Elsie," Daniel replied. "Good day to you."

The girl seemed eager for attention and was probably dramatizing the incident for his benefit, but he didn't have any other leads. He would seek out Mr. Gale and see what he had to say for himself.

# Chapter 22

The Upper Finchley post office was located at the back of the village shop, which sold everything from produce to tools, and at the moment smelled strongly of raw meat. Jason smiled politely at the man behind the counter and proceeded toward the back, where a comely woman in her thirties was sorting through some letters and parcels that had just been delivered by the mail coach that served villages that weren't on a railway line. A young man in uniform stood by, waiting patiently to be handed the mail to deliver. It would probably take him several hours to cover the area on foot, delivering letters and parcels to farms that were miles away from the village center.

"Good morning, sir. How can I help you today?" the postmistress asked Jason once the young man had set off.

"Good morning, Mrs. Curtis." Jason had made sure to learn the postmistress's name before approaching her. "My name is Jason Redmond, and I work with the police."

"Yes. Of course. I saw you the other day. You examined the body," Mrs. Curtis exclaimed, attracting the attention of the man behind the shop counter. She raised an eyebrow at him as if reminding him to mind his own business.

"My husband," she explained. "Curious as a magpie, that one." She turned her attention back to Jason. "Do you know who killed him?" she asked, lowering her voice. "Was he still alive when they buried him?"

"I'm afraid he was," Jason replied. He had to give her something if he hoped to get something in return, and she was clearly as curious as her spouse.

"Strange, that," Mrs. Curtis observed. "He seemed such a mild man. Who'd want to do that to him?"

"That's what we're trying to find out."

Mrs. Curtis consulted a small watch pinned to her bodice. "I'm gasping for a cup of tea. Will you join me, Mr. Redmond? I can't allow you back here, it's against regulations, but we can sit right over there, companionable-like," she said, indicating a small table and two chairs that were either used for the postal workers to eat during their dinner break or for the wrapping of parcels and copying out of addresses by people who'd failed to do so at home.

"It would be my pleasure," Jason said.

"Good. The kettle's just boiled, so I won't be a moment."

Mrs. Curtis stepped into the back room to make the tea while Jason waited patiently for her to return. She brought out a small tray with a teapot, milk jug and sugar bowl, two delicate cups and saucers decorated with a floral pattern, and a plate of shortbread.

They sat down at the table, and she poured. Jason accepted the cup of tea, refused the milk and shortbread, and took a sip. Mrs. Curtis took her time fixing her tea just the way she liked it, then reached for a biscuit.

"I always have to have something around this time," she explained, "or I grow faint and my hands start shaking. Tea with lots of sugar usually does the trick."

"Perhaps you have low blood sugar, Mrs. Curtis," Jason said. "You should consult a doctor."

She looked at him in surprise. "Low blood sugar?"

"Yes. That's why drinking sweet tea makes you feel better."

"And how would a doctor be able to tell?"

"He can test your urine," Jason replied.

Mrs. Curtis looked scandalized. "Are you a medical man, then?"

"I practiced medicine in New York before coming to England."

She wagged a finger at him. "So that's why you have that accent. I thought I'd better not ask. Didn't want to cause offense, but you do sound odd to my English ears. We are not much used to foreigners here."

"Yes, I know," Jason replied patiently.

"I didn't offend you, did I?" Mrs. Curtis asked.

"Not at all. Now, Mrs. Curtis, if I could ask you those questions."

"Yes, of course. I do tend to go on, don't I? Terrible thing that, the murder. Who would have thought something like that could happen in a place like this? Why, I was born and bred here, and my parents and grandparents before me, and never has such a thing happened."

"You mean there's never been a murder in Upper Finchley?" Jason asked, genuinely surprised.

"I'm sure there have been murders," Mrs. Curtis amended, "except they weren't treated as such. Why, there was the time John Randall caught his wife with the blacksmith. Everyone knew he beat her to death, but the magistrate said it was a husband's right to punish his wife and if she died of her injuries, well, it was 'Death by Misadventure.' It was a misadventure, all right," she said, raising her eyes heavenward. "A misadventure that he came upon them during their adventure." She laughed at her own witticism.

"And there was the time some village boys went swimming in the river. Twenty years ago now, that was. They were horsing around and holding each other down underwater. Well, it's all fun and games until someone drowns, isn't it, Mr. Redmond? One of the boys died. Was it murder? The magistrate didn't think so. There's such a thing as intent, isn't there, and I don't think anyone intended to hurt anyone. It was just a prank gone wrong, but still, it was a life lost through someone else's actions. But what happened to Mr. Slade… Why, it's downright barbarous what someone did. Fiendish!" she exclaimed.

"Yes, it certainly was, which leads me to believe that something Mr. Slade had done elicited a strong emotional response. Mrs. Curtis, we know that something occurred on Sunday to distress Mr. Slade. Can you tell me everything you recall from Sunday morning until the time you heard of Mr. Slade's death?" That was a tall order, but given how chatty the woman was, Jason hoped she'd prattle on until she let something important slip.

"Well, I don't rightly know, Mr. Redmond. Oh, one second, please," she said as someone approached the counter.

"Two stamps," the customer said. Mrs. Curtis served the woman and returned to the table, ignoring the customer's curious stare and her husband's pointed one.

"Let me think. The vicar felt unwell, so Mr. Slade took the service. It was his first time, so he was a little nervous, and he told us so right at the start. He seemed happy, though, excited. This is what he'd trained for, wasn't it?" She stopped speaking for a moment. "Now that you mention it, I do recall that he paused right after he told us that, as if he'd seen something unexpected. He blanched. Yes, that's the right word. Blanched, and seemed to completely lose his train of thought. I just thought he was more nervous than he was letting on."

"Did you see what drew his attention?" Jason asked, his tea forgotten.

"No."

"Was there anyone present that you didn't recognize?"

Mrs. Curtis shook her head. "No."

"So, the congregation was made up entirely of locals?"

"Indeed, Mr. Redmond. It was all people I know and help here at the post office and my Larry serves at the shop. Just friends and neighbors."

"Mrs. Curtis, are there any newcomers to the village?" Jason asked.

"You mean besides Mr. Slade? Well, not newcomers, exactly, but there are some as came back. There's Rob Hanson, who'd worked as a navvy for nigh on five years," she said.

"What's a navvy?"

"It's someone who works on laying down the railroad tracks," Mrs. Curtis explained patiently. "He came back and married Polly Forbes. She'd been mooning over him since they were children."

"She waited for him all that time?" Jason asked.

Mrs. Curtis scoffed. "Not like anyone else would have her. Got a face like a gorgon, that one. I'm sorry. That's unkind," she instantly backtracked. "She's a nice girl, Polly. And she's a good wife to Rob."

"Anyone else return recently?" Jason asked.

"Well, there's Miss Lundy. Moved in with her widowed sister, but she's sixty if she's a day," Mrs. Curtis supplied. "She's earned a bit of rest, the poor dear. Went into service at fourteen and hadn't been back in all that time. You'd think Chelmsford was on the moon," she said disapprovingly.

"Is that all?" Jason asked, disappointed.

"The Goodwins moved to the village a few years ago. Rose had grown up here, but her husband is originally from Dover, or Southampton, or one of them port towns. I'm really not sure. They moved in with Rose's father. He passed last year, poor man. Suffered an apoplexy and was bedridden for months. His right side was all frozen-like. Couldn't speak properly or chew. Rose took care of him, fed him like a babe. I think he could have gone on like that for years, but he had a mind to die. Didn't fancy being an invalid and making his daughter's life a misery, so he quietly slipped away one day. Went to sleep and never woke up."

"And Mr. Goodwin? What does he do?"

"Works the farm. It was a rundown old place before the old man died, but Neil Goodwin has turned it around. Fixed up the house, bought fancy machinery, even hired a farmhand."

"And the farmhand, is he local?"

"Oh, yes. Solly Higgins. He's not too bright, the poor lad, but he's strong and hardworking. He's happy with the Goodwins, and they look after him."

"Is there anyone else you can think of?" Jason asked.

Mrs. Curtis shrugged. "This is a small village, Mr. Redmond. Four people settling here in the space of five years is quite a lot."

Jason nodded. She was right. Places like Upper Finchley didn't change much over the years. They might get a post office, try new methods of farming after years of resisting newfangled machinery and pontificating over a pint how the old ways of doing things were best, but the nature of the community didn't change. There wasn't much new blood, and the flow of new ideas was quickly staunched by the elders, who wished to keep things much as they had been for generations. Jason had seen similar towns and villages in the United States, when he'd fought in the Civil War— backward, resistant to change, suspicious of "city folk," as they referred to anyone who came from any place bigger than their own.

"That's why it's such a shame about Mr. Slade," Mrs. Curtis continued, a faraway gaze in her eyes. "He was a fine prospect, and all the unmarried girls were eager to catch his eye. He'd be needing a wife soon, no doubt about that, and if he stayed on, then all the better because his wife wouldn't need to be separated from her family."

"Was there any one woman he seemed to notice?" Jason asked. He was sure someone like Mrs. Curtis would not be oblivious to the signs of a budding romance.

"He was equally pleasant and charming to all the young ladies." Mrs. Curtis's face suddenly darkened, as if a cloud had passed over the sun. "I had hopes for my own Clarissa. She's beautiful, and bright as a newly minted penny. Are you married yourself, Mr. Redmond?" she asked.

"I am. Just two months," he added as an unbidden smile sprang to his lips.

"Ah, you love her," Mrs. Curtis said. "I don't think my Larry ever smiled like that when asked about his matrimonial state."

"Mrs. Curtis, did anything else happen during or after the service, or the following day, that seemed unusual to you?" Jason asked, trying to redirect her thoughts from his personal life.

"After the service, we returned home and had Sunday dinner. Afterward, I spent some time in the garden. Sunday is my only day off, so I try to enjoy it as much as I can. Larry remained indoors. He likes to have a kip on Sunday afternoon, and Clarissa had cleared up after dinner and then joined me in the garden, where we had tea."

"And Monday?" Jason tried again.

"Mr. Slade came in on Monday morning to post some letters," Mrs. Curtis said.

"How many letters did he have? Who were the letters addressed to?"

"I can't tell you that, Mr. Redmond. A person's correspondence is private."

"You are right. I shouldn't have asked. Can you tell me how he seemed?"

"He was a bit jittery, now you mention it. I asked him if he was all right, and he said he hadn't slept well. He handed over the letters and left. Said he was going for a walk."

"Where would he have walked to?" Jason inquired.

Mrs. Curtis shrugged. "No shortage of open space here. He could have gone anywhere."

"Good morning, Mrs. Curtis. I'd like to send a package," a young man who'd entered the shop said as he approached the counter.

"Another novel you're trying to sell, Billy?" Mrs. Curtis asked, smiling at the young man sympathetically.

"This will be the one they like, Mrs. C," the young man said, grinning shyly. "This one is really good."

"Well, good luck to you, son," Mrs. Curtis said as she accepted the brown-paper-wrapped manuscript and laid it on the scale.

Jason stood. "Thank you for the tea and the chat, Mrs. Curtis," he said.

"It was my pleasure, Mr. Redmond."

The young man's eyes widened, and he took a step toward Jason. "Are you the Lord Redmond who assists the Brentwood police in their inquiries? I've read about you. You were mentioned in the paper when that girl was murdered in a Gypsy caravan a few months ago."

"Yes, I'm afraid I am," Jason admitted, eager to leave.

"*Lord* Redmond?" Mrs. Curtis asked, nearly choking on his title. "You didn't say."

"I apologize if I misled you," Jason said. "It didn't seem relevant."

Mrs. Curtis blushed like a young bride. "It was a pleasure talking to you, my lord," she said. Jason feared she just might sink into a curtsy. "I hope I was helpful."

"You absolutely were, Mrs. Curtis," Jason said, and escaped the hot confines of the shop, glad to get away from the stench of raw meat and Mrs. Curtis's admiring gaze.

# Chapter 23

Jason met Daniel outside the shop, and they fell into step as they headed down the street. "Were you able to learn anything?" he asked.

"The publican's daughter saw a man leaving the church on Sunday. He might have been the last person to see Mr. Slade after the service, except for Miss Brockton, who returned to retrieve her prayer book. She thought the curate looked troubled. You?"

"Not much. Sebastian Slade seemed distracted by something at the beginning of the service, but Mrs. Curtis didn't notice anything out of the ordinary. He posted several letters on Monday morning. She's not at liberty to say how many or to whom. She did say that several people have returned to the village over the past few years, but given that Slade had only arrived two weeks ago, all the villagers were new to him, unless he'd met them on a previous occasion."

"Do you think he may have?" Daniel asked.

"I think it's unlikely. Miss Lundy is an elderly woman who's spent the past few decades in service in Chelmsford. Mr. Hanson worked on the railways for five years before returning to Upper Finchley. And the Goodwins hail from some port city, according to Mrs. Curtis. Given that Sebastian Slade had studied in Oxford and then returned to London, I can't see how their paths would have crossed, but we should certainly speak to them, if only to rule them out."

"First, I think we should re-interview Mrs. Monk, then speak to Mr. Gale, the man seen leaving the church," Daniel suggested. "Then we can interview the rest."

"Yes, that sounds logical."

Mrs. Monk greeted them like old friends. "Come in, come in, gentlemen. Would you care for some refreshment?"

"That's very kind, but we're in something of a hurry," Daniel said, not wishing to waste any time. "Mrs. Monk, please think back to Monday. When was the last time you saw Mr. Slade?"

Mrs. Monk's brow furrowed as she tried to recall. "I usually do laundry on Mondays, so I had spent much of my time in the kitchen and then outside, hanging the washing. As I told you before, Mr. Slade went out after breakfast to post some letters."

"What time did he return?" Daniel asked.

"He came back in time for luncheon. I had cold meat and salad for him, on account of the laundry," she explained.

"Did he go out at all after luncheon?"

"No. He sat in the parlor, reading until suppertime. I was surprised because it was a fine day, heat notwithstanding, and it wasn't like him not to budge from his spot all afternoon. He didn't even go out into the garden."

"And did anyone come to see him during this time?" Jason asked.

"No, no one came."

"Can you direct us to Mr. Gale's house?" Daniel asked.

"Of course." Mrs. Monk explained where to find the Gales.

"Thank you, Mrs. Monk," Daniel said. "You've been most helpful."

"Was she?" Jason asked pointedly once they were back outside.

"Not really," Daniel replied irritably. "But I can hardly tell her that. How is it possible that in a village the size of a pinhead, no one saw or heard anything? Come, let's speak to Mr. Gale."

They headed toward the end of a row of cottages that lined the only street in the village. The Gales lived in the second to last. It was a neat little house with a green-painted door and several rosebushes dotted with blood-red blooms, but it showed signs of neglect. The step looked unswept, the rosebushes were choked by weeds, and the windows looked grimy in the harsh light of the midday sun.

When they knocked on the door, a man of about forty answered. His brown gaze seemed glazed, his hair looked unkempt, and his powerful shoulders stooped as if he carried a heavy burden. He was well dressed, but his shirt could have used a wash and his somber waistcoat had a stain down the front.

"Good day, Mr. Gale. I am Inspector Haze, and this is my associate Jason Redmond. I wonder if we might have a word."

Mr. Gale stepped aside to let them in and invited them to sit down in the parlor. It was tastefully decorated but, like Mr. Gale himself, looked a bit grubby. Mr. Gale sank onto a stained settee and looked at them expectantly.

"Mr. Gale, you were seen leaving the church some considerable time after the Sunday service ended," Daniel began.

The man looked puzzled. "Are you suggesting I did something wrong?" he asked, his voice low and devoid of emotion.

"Not at all. We simply wanted to inquire if you might have noticed anything suspicious," Daniel rushed to reassure him. "Was there a reason you stayed back?"

"I wanted a word with Mr. Slade."

"What about?" Daniel prompted. The man was clearly reluctant to speak of it, or perhaps just reluctant to speak in general. He seemed dazed. "Mr. Gale?" Daniel prompted when the man failed to answer.

"My wife, Sylvie, passed in May," Mr. Gale finally said, his shoulders stooping even further. "She was a wonderful woman, Sylvie—kindhearted, warm, and loving. Our daughter, Victoria, has had difficulty accepting her mother's death. She's been lashing out at me, threatening to leave if I so much as try to speak to her, and refusing to help around the house. I work at the smithy all day. I have no time or skill when it comes to domestic chores." He sighed deeply. "I thought I'd speak to Mr. Slade and ask for guidance on how to manage Victoria's outbursts."

"Why did you choose to speak to Mr. Slade rather than the vicar, who's probably known Victoria since the day she was born?" Daniel asked.

Mr. Gale smiled sadly. "You've met the vicar, Inspector. He was Victoria's age at the turn of the century or thereabouts. I thought a younger man might have greater insight."

"And did he?" Jason asked.

Mr. Gale sighed deeply again. "He said that Victoria is grieving for her mother and that grief takes many different forms. She's angry at having her mother snatched from her and probably frightened that she will lose me as well. Mr. Slade advised me not to be harsh with her but allow her to accept her mother's passing in her own time. He offered to have a word to see if he could find a way to unite us in our grief."

"That sounds like sound advice," Jason said. "Very modern, in fact."

"Yes, I suppose it was," Mr. Gale agreed. "But he seemed distracted. Ruffled. I could tell he was eager for me to leave."

"Do you know what had unnerved him?" Daniel asked.

"No. How could I?" Mr. Gale replied.

"Mr. Gale, how old is Victoria?" Jason asked, his gaze fixed on Mr. Gale's face, which seemed to crumple.

"She's fourteen. An age when a girl needs her mother."

As if on cue, a fair-haired, blue-eyed girl walked into the parlor and froze, surprised by the presence of two unfamiliar men. "I'm sorry," she muttered. "I didn't know you had company."

"We were just leaving," Daniel said, smiling at her.

"Are you here about the murder?" Victoria asked, looking from Daniel to Jason with surprising forwardness in one so young.

"Yes, we are. Is there anything you wish to tell us?" Daniel asked, still smiling at her as if she were a charming child.

"No."

"Did you like Mr. Slade?" Jason asked, his manner friendly.

"Oh, yes," Victoria gushed. "He was—what is the right word—charismatic," she said slowly, as if savoring the word on her tongue. It was probably the first time she'd had an occasion to use it.

"He was handsome too," Jason said. "For a curate."

"He looked like Lord Byron," Victoria said dreamily. "Have you read his poems?"

"Yes," Jason replied.

"No," Daniel admitted.

Victoria began to recite:

> She walks in beauty, like the night
> Of cloudless climes and starry skies;
> And all that's best of dark and bright
> Meet in her aspect and her eyes;
> Thus mellowed to that tender light
> Which heaven to gaudy day denies.
>
> One shade the more, one ray the less,
> Had half impaired the nameless grace
> Which waves in every raven tress,
> Or softly lightens o'er her face;
> Where thoughts serenely sweet express,
> How pure, how dear their dwelling-place.
>
> And on that cheek, and o'er that brow,
> So soft, so calm, yet eloquent,
> The smiles that win, the tints that glow,
> But tell of days in goodness spent,

*A mind at peace with all below,*

*A heart whose love is innocent!*


Victoria's recitation had stunned her father into silence. She looked rapt, her lips slightly parted, her eyes shining with the romantic fervor of youth.

"That's quite enough, Victoria," Mr. Gale barked once he'd regained his composure, his cheeks stained with an embarrassed flush.

"That is a beautiful poem," Jason said, ignoring Mr. Gale. "One of my favorites, in fact. Who introduced you to Lord Byron's poetry?"

Victoria's gaze slid toward her feet, her hands clasping before her. "Eh, no one," she said. "I came across it in one of my schoolbooks."

"Do you know any of his other poems?" Jason continued.

"I like this one too," Victoria said, lifting her gaze to meet Jason's.

*It is the hour when from the boughs*

*The nightingale's high note is heard;*

*It is the hour — when lover's vows*

*Seem sweet in every whisper'd word;*

*And gentle winds and waters near,*

*Make music to the lonely ear.*

*Each flower the dews have lightly wet,*

*And in the sky the stars are met,*

*And on the wave is deeper blue,*

*And on the leaf a browner hue,*

*And in the Heaven that clear obscure*

*So softly dark, and darkly pure,*

*That follows the decline of day*
*As twilight melts beneath the moon away.*


Jason nodded in appreciation. "It is beautiful, isn't it? Are you a devotee of Lord Byron's poetry, Mr. Gale?"

"Never heard it till this moment," Mr. Gale replied gruffly.

"I happen to have a book of poetry by Lord Byron," Jason said, smiling at the girl. "May I gift it to you? I know the poems by heart."

Victoria's eyes lit up. "Oh, that would be so kind, Mr. eh…"

"Redmond."

"I will treasure it," Victoria gushed.

"There's really no need," Mr. Gale protested.

"It's no trouble at all. I will bring it by tomorrow. Perhaps, if it's all right with you, Mr. Gale, Victoria can read a few poems aloud to me. It's quite a different experience when read by someone other than oneself. I think you might enjoy them as well."

"I'm not a man given to flights of fancy," Mr. Gale said, "but I have no objection to Victoria reading to you, in the garden, perhaps, as long as I can see you both from the window," he added. "For lack of a proper chaperone."

"Of course. You are right to feel protective. Till tomorrow, then," Jason said, rising to leave.

"Thank you, Mr. Gale, Miss Gale," Daniel said, and followed Jason out into the street.

"What in blazes was that?" Daniel demanded as soon as they were out of earshot of the cottage. "You are going to read Byron's poetry with a fourteen-year-old girl? We have a murder to solve."

Jason laughed. "Which is exactly what I'm doing. Victoria is young, vulnerable, and susceptible, and bears a striking resemblance to Jenny Ross, or had you not noticed?"

"I did, as it happens," Daniel grumbled.

"She clearly harbors romantic feelings for Sebastian Slade, and I mean to find out if he ever did anything to encourage those feelings or take advantage of her innocence, which is why I need to speak to her alone."

Daniel permitted himself a chuckle. "You really are a card, you know that."

"Am I?" Jason asked innocently. "If Slade made advances to Victoria or despoiled her, Mr. Gale would have a clear motive for wishing to bash his head in. Any father would. And if you had been paying attention to Victoria's charming recitation, you'd have noticed that both poems make mention of the night, a most romantic time for secret lovers to meet, wouldn't you say?"

"I would," Daniel admitted, feeling a bit foolish to have missed something so obvious. "Do you think she'll speak to you?"

"I will do my best to put her at ease and glean as much as I can," Jason promised. "Have faith in my American charm."

Daniel laughed. "You plan to charm her in full view of her father?"

"I do, indeed."

"Slade gave Jenny a false name and address to protect himself. Do you think he would try to seduce Victoria openly in a village with less than a hundred residents?" Daniel asked as they continued along the street.

"Perhaps he'd grown careless. Or had availed himself of a prophylactic to prevent another pregnancy. Victoria is young enough that he could play on her innocence and convince her to keep their relationship a secret, much as Jenny had done until she had no choice but to seek him out."

"I must admit that now that I have a daughter, I can easily understand how a man could be driven to murder," Daniel said.

"Mr. Gale certainly wouldn't be the first man to resort to violence to protect his child."

"Do you think he was telling the truth about his conversation with Slade?" Daniel asked.

"Yes. I don't think Mr. Gale has what it takes to come up with such insightful and pragmatic advice on his own. I do believe the conversation took place, just not necessarily last Sunday. Perhaps Gale remained after the service to have a different kind of discussion with the curate."

"If Slade had refused to acknowledge his guilt or ridiculed Mr. Gale's concerns, he might have gone to meet Slade in his daughter's place, if only to prove that he knew of their affair."

"And availed himself of the shovel and a grave he knew to be there when things became heated," Jason remarked.

"Yes," Daniel agreed. "That theory does fit the facts. Shall we return to Birch Hill? We can interview the others tomorrow, since we now have to return to the village for your rendezvous with Victoria Gale."

"Yes, but first I must stop in Brentwood," Jason said.

"Why?"

"Because I need to find a book of Byron's poems," Jason explained.

"I thought you had one."

"I lied. In fact, I'll take you home and then ask Katie if she'd like to come with me. She can never say no to a new book, and she seems to feel better in the afternoons so will enjoy the drive. I miss her," Jason admitted with a shy smile.

Daniel grinned. "I miss Sarah and Charlotte as well. I could spend hours watching the baby sleep. She's such a miracle."

"Babies usually are, except when they aren't," Jason answered cryptically.

# Chapter 24

"Do you really think Sebastian Slade seduced Victoria Gale?" Katherine asked as they lay in bed that night.

"I think it's a possibility. He seduced Jenny Ross and left her without a backward glance when he found out she was with child. A pregnancy didn't fit into his plans."

"I'm sure it didn't," Katherine said with disgust. "What a vile man."

"There are more men like him than you realize," Jason replied.

"But he was a man of God. That should mean something," Katherine exclaimed.

"Priests can be as lecherous and corrupt as anyone, all the more so because they have the guise of respectability to hide behind," Jason said. "They inspire trust, especially in those who are innocent enough to trust them without reservation."

"Knowing what you do, do you still want to find his killer and bring him to justice?" Katherine asked, unwittingly voicing Jason's own reservations.

Jason thought about that for a moment. "Yes, I do," he said at last. "Sebastian Slade wasn't an honorable man, but that doesn't mean someone had the right to snuff him out and hide his body from view. Had the corpse not been discovered by Arthur Weeks, no one would have ever known what became of him. His poor sister would be heartbroken."

"Especially since she doesn't know the fate of her daughter," Katherine said softly. "What a tragedy. To lose a child and not even be able to mourn her. It's a wonder the Holloways have found the strength to go on."

"Human beings are more resilient than we realize," Jason said sadly.

"Jason, would you be disappointed if we had a girl?" Katherine suddenly asked, watching him intently.

"Katie, how can you even ask that?" Jason exclaimed, wounded by the suggestion. "Of course I wouldn't."

Katherine looked momentarily contrite but didn't drop the subject. "I didn't mean in that respect. I know you'd love a daughter just as much as a son. It's just that being a father to a girl is more complicated, isn't it? A girl is so much more vulnerable than a boy."

"One certainly has to remain vigilant," Jason agreed, somewhat mollified. "Girls are always more vulnerable, but boys can be abused too."

"You don't mean…" Katherine's voice trailed off as she stared at him in disbelief.

"I do. I've seen it happen. There was a young man in my regiment. He was very handsome, and young. Not yet seventeen. He was wounded during a battle and brought to me to patch up. His injury wasn't serious, a flesh wound, but I noticed he could barely sit still when I tried to stitch the gash. It took some persuading, but he finally confided to me that one of the older men had forced himself on him in the woods and threatened to cut his throat if he told anyone. He allowed me to examine him," Jason said, sighing at the memory. "The other soldier had not been gentle."

"Did you report him?" Katherine asked, clearly horrified by the story.

"No, but I did have a quiet word. With a scalpel held to his balls," Jason added with a grin.

"I wouldn't want to get on the wrong side of you, Captain Redmond," Katherine said with an affectionate smile.

"You could never do that," Jason said, pulling her closer.

# Chapter 25

## Sunday, August 11

Having accompanied his wife to Sunday services at St. Catherine's, Jason left her at the vicarage to enjoy luncheon with her father and share the happy news, and returned to Redmond Hall to collect Micah, who'd refused to attend the Catholic Mass in Brentwood. Micah had been begging to drive the curricle, and Jason thought he could use a distraction from Mary's abrupt departure. Micah had been melancholy and silent the past few days, moping around the house and pretending not to be at home when his friend Tom Marin had come to see him.

Jason found Micah in the garden with Liam, who was happily crawling on the ground and trying to stuff fistfuls of grass into his mouth. Jason scooped up the child and glared at Micah.

"He's going to get sick."

"A little grass never hurt no one," Micah said defensively. "I guess Mary doesn't care if he gets sick, or she wouldn't have left him behind."

"If you're not too busy feeling sorry for yourself, maybe you'd like to come with me to Upper Finchley."

"Why would I want to do that?" Micah asked sullenly.

"Because you can drive the curricle there and back," Jason replied smoothly.

"Really? You mean it?"

"I do. But first, we need to find someone to look after this little rascal."

"Kitty will do it," Micah replied. "She's just back from church."

"All right. Let's ask Kitty," Jason said, and followed Micah inside the house. Now that Mary was gone, they'd have to hire a nanny to look after the child. It wasn't fair to expect the female staff to step in, regardless of how fond they were of the little boy.

Kitty was happy to take Liam, who went to her eagerly, wrapping his pudgy little arms around her neck.

"Are you sure you don't mind, Kitty?" Jason asked, not wishing to abuse his position of power.

"Not at all, sir," Kitty gushed. "I love Liam. 'E is so sweet. I'll be 'appy to look after 'im until ye return."

*And then what?* Jason thought irritably. He'd have to broach the subject with Katherine this evening.

"Can we go now?" Micah whined. "I want to drive the curricle."

"All right. Let's go," Jason said, hoping Joe had the carriage waiting for them. He did, and Micah climbed in and grabbed the reins, his impatience palpable.

"Go on, then," Jason said once he was settled. "They're all yours."

Micah smiled happily as the chestnuts trotted down the lane, the sun gleaming off their smooth coats. "This is fun!" he cried. He gave Jason a sidelong glance. "Can I take Tom for a drive one of these days?"

"Let's see how you do today, shall we?" Jason replied, not sure if he was ready to surrender his curricle to a twelve-year-old.

"Please," Micah pleaded. "Just for a half hour. I'll take good care of the horses. I promise."

"We'll see," Jason replied noncommittally. "We can start by you walking the horses while I speak to Miss Gale."

"All right. Is she pretty?" Micah asked.

"She is," Jason replied with a smile. Micah was starting to show an interest in the opposite sex, which was perfectly normal at his age, and also kind of endearing. "But she lives too far away for you to make friends with her."

"I know," Micah replied matter-of-factly. "I was just asking. Kitty never wants to talk to me anymore. She says she's too busy."

"I thought you were in love with Fanny," Jason teased. Micah was awfully fond of their pretty maidservant.

"I was, but she treats me like a child," Micah replied petulantly.

"To her, you are a child," Jason said.

"She's only twenty-two," Micah protested.

"Exactly, ten years your senior."

"I don't suppose I'll get to meet any girls at that posh school you're sending me to," he said without rancor.

"Maybe you will. Perhaps one of your friends will invite you to visit, and you will meet his charming sister," Jason said.

Micah brightened. "You think so?"

"Could happen."

"I mean, do you think someone will invite me to stay?" Micah asked.

"Why wouldn't they? That's what friends do, and I have no doubt you will make lots of new friends."

"I'm a little nervous," Micah admitted.

"It's natural to be nervous. You're embarking on a new chapter of your life, but this is nothing compared to going to war."

"Yeah, you're right. I'm not scared."

They pulled up in front of the Gale house, and Jason descended from the carriage. "I shouldn't be long. No more than a quarter of an hour."

"See you," Micah said, and snapped the reins. His face broke into a beatific smile as the horses began to walk at a stately pace. He was in heaven, for the moment, at least.

Jason knocked on the door and was pleased when Victoria opened it. She had been waiting for him. "Good afternoon," she said eagerly.

"Good afternoon, Victoria."

"Please, come through to the garden. Father is just in the kitchen."

"I'd like to say hello to your father first," Jason replied. It would be rude not to.

Mr. Gale was standing at the sink, his shirtsleeves rolled up, a greasy rag in his hand. He ran the rag over the dirty dishes, then poured hot water from a pitcher over them, shook them off one by one, and set them on a draining board. The cleaned dishes looked greasy in the sunlight that filtered through the dusty windowpanes.

"Good afternoon, Mr. Gale," Jason said, feeling sorry for the man.

"Good afternoon, your lordship," the man replied sourly. So, word had spread that Jason was no commoner. At this stage, he didn't think it would make any difference to the investigation.

"Victoria and I will just sit in the garden for a few moments," Jason said politely.

"Not like I can stop ye," the man mumbled under his breath.

Jason followed Victoria into the garden, grateful for the leafy tree that shielded the bench from the blazing sun.

Once seated, Jason took out a beautifully bound copy of Byron's poems and handed the book to Victoria.

"Oh, it's beautiful," she gushed. "It looks brand new."

"It is," Jason confessed. "I couldn't find mine, so I drove into Brentwood and purchased this book."

"You didn't have to do that," Victoria said, clearly touched that he would go to such trouble on her account.

"I made you a promise."

"People don't always keep their promises, especially men," Victoria said wisely.

"No, they don't, but I do. Will you read me one of the poems?"

"Which one?"

"Whichever one you like. How about one you haven't heard before?"

Victoria leafed through the book, chose a poem at random, and began to read.

"That was lovely," Jason said once she finished. "You have a flair for the dramatic."

"Do I?" Victoria asked, blushing.

"You do. You don't simply read the poems; you experience them," Jason said. "Tell me, did Mr. Slade introduce you to poetry?"

Victoria looked taken aback, but then nodded shyly. "He did. He said reading the poems would help me deal with my grief. I miss my mother," Victoria said, her eyes filling with tears.

"I'm sure you do. You'll always feel the loss of her, but the grief will lessen in time. I lost my mother not so long ago as well."

"But you're a grown man. You don't need a mother."

"Sometimes I feel as though I do. My wife is expecting a baby," Jason confided. "I wish I could share the news with my mother and ask her some questions about parenting. I have much to learn about being a father."

"You seem kind. I'm sure you'll be a wonderful father to your baby."

"Victoria, when did Mr. Slade talk to you of poetry?" Jason asked, wondering how the curate had managed to get Victoria on her own.

"He came up to me when I was visiting my mum's grave. I was crying, and he comforted me."

"That was kind of him," Jason said.

"He was a kind man. Sensitive," Victoria said. Jason thought she must have learned the word from Slade.

"Did he ever ask you to meet him?"

Victoria set the book down on the bench and stared into her lap. "You're trying to trick me into telling you bad things about him."

"I'm not trying to trick you; I'm asking you straight out. Someone killed Mr. Slade, and we need to find out who did it and why."

"And you think it was my father?" Victoria asked, momentarily silencing Jason with her astuteness.

He sighed. He hadn't wanted to tell her about Jenny, but if he was to learn anything about her relationship with Sebastian Slade, he'd have to be honest with her. "Victoria, there's a girl in London, not much older than you, who's about to give birth to Mr. Slade's child. He used her and abandoned her, and now she's frightened and all alone."

Victoria lifted her chin defiantly and glared at Jason. "Sebastian told me about her. He said she was a harlot and she'd been with other men. He said he'd loved her and wanted to marry her, but his conscience wouldn't allow it. He needed someone pure, someone godly. He said if I waited for him, he'd marry me once I turned seventeen."

"And did this waiting involve anything else?" Jason asked.

"How do you mean?"

"Did he kiss you, Victoria?" Her flaming cheeks were answer enough. "Did he tell you it would be all right for you to give yourself to him because you would be married?"

She nodded miserably.

"And did you?" Jason asked gently. "You can tell me. I'm a doctor, and I can help you if the need arises. No one would have to know." Sebastian Slade had only arrived in the village a few weeks ago, so Victoria wouldn't know if she was with child, but he wanted her to know that she wasn't alone should she find herself in a precarious position.

Victoria shook her head. "I told him I was scared."

"Did he pressure you?" Jason asked, his anger simmering just beneath the surface.

"Sebastian said I was right to be frightened. It was a big step, and he would wait as long as he had to for me. He said I was his 'beauty,' just like the girl in the poem."

"Did you ever meet him at night?" Jason asked, wondering if it had been the promise of seeing Victoria that had led him to the graveyard.

"No. We met during the day, by my mother's grave. I felt safe there, like my mother was looking out for me. I think she would have approved of Sebastian, had she been alive."

*I think she would have flayed him alive*, Jason thought, but kept that opinion to himself. "Mr. Slade was considerably older than you are," he pointed out gently.

"Not so much older, only ten years. My father was ten years older than my mother. They married when she was sixteen. That's only two years older than I am now. And they were happy. They loved each other."

"I've no doubt they did. Victoria, may I offer you a piece of advice?" Jason asked, hoping she wouldn't become defensive.

"Go on," Victoria said.

"Never trust a man who asks you to meet in secret. If a man is serious about you, he will have the courage and the respect to speak to your father and ask for permission to court you. That's what an honorable man does."

"Did you do that when you met your wife?" Victoria asked.

"Not right away, but my wife is considerably older than you, and she knows her own mind. She's one of the most independent women I know."

"I know my own mind," Victoria countered. "I would have married Sebastian had he not died, and now I will remain alone forever."

"You will meet someone wonderful one day," Jason promised.

She looked at him, her expression dubious. "You think so?"

"I know so. You're too lovely and smart not to. But while you wait, I think you should try to help your father. You are the lady of the house now, and your mother would have wanted you to act like it. Your father is grieving too. He's lost the woman he's loved for nearly half his life. Be kind to him."

Victoria hung her head in shame and nodded. "I will. I promise."

"I'm glad to hear it. Enjoy the poems. I hope they bring you comfort. I must go. My friend is waiting for me."

"Inspector Haze?"

"No. My ward, Micah. He's twelve years old, but he has been to war, and he then looked after me while we were in prison. He stood at my side at my wedding."

"And he's twelve?" Victoria asked, incredulous.

"It's not how old you are that determines your worth," Jason replied.

"Thank you," Victoria said. "You've been very kind. My mother would have liked you."

"That's the best compliment you could have paid me." Jason reached for her hand and bowed over it, as if she were a lady of rank. "Good day, Miss Gale."

Jason felt Mr. Gale's gaze on him as he walked away, making his way around the house, through a wooden gate, and into the street. Micah was already waiting for him, and he climbed into the curricle and pulled his hat lower to block out the sun.

"Where to, Captain?" Micah asked.

"Home, I suppose. Oh, wait," Jason suddenly said, and jumped out of the curricle, striding toward Mrs. Curtis, who was walking down the street toward them.

"Mrs. Curtis, what a pleasure to see you again," Jason said, tipping his hat.

"Good afternoon, my lord," Mrs. Curtis replied, looking up at him as if he were the royal consort himself.

"I'm sorry to trouble you, but I have two questions to put to you. I hope you can spare me a few moments."

"Of course," Mrs. Curtis replied. "I'll help in any way I can."

"Is anyone in Upper Finchley related to Eugene or Jenny Ross?"

As the postmistress, Mrs. Curtis would know if anyone had written to either father or daughter, and as someone who'd been born and bred in the village, she was sure to know every familial connection, no matter how obscure.

Mrs. Curtis shook her head. "No. No one has relations by the name of Ross as far as I know. What's the second question?"

"Has anyone from the village spent a considerable length of time in London?"

Mrs. Curtis nodded, happy to have a positive reply for him at last. "Yes. Rose Goodwin was in service to a lady in London before she met her husband."

"And would you know the lady's name?" Jason asked.

"Sorry, no. She never mentioned it. I believe her employer died."

"I see. Well, thank you all the same, Mrs. Curtis. You are a gem."

Mrs. Curtis blushed to the roots of her hair, drawing raised eyebrows from her husband, who'd stepped outside to meet her, having spotted her through the window. He hadn't heard the exchange but could see her obvious pleasure and glowered at Jason as if he were about to call him out. Jason wished them both a good day and climbed back into the curricle.

# Chapter 26

On the way home, Jason dropped Micah off near the Marin cabin so he could visit with Tom, then continued on to Daniel's house to report on his meeting with Victoria. Tilda opened the door and escorted him into the drawing room, where Daniel, Sarah, and Sarah's mother, Harriet Elderman, were taking tea.

"Jason, it's so lovely to see you," Sarah exclaimed. She looked calm and well rested, a marked improvement on the last time Jason had seen her. "Will you take a dish of tea?"

"Yes, thank you," Jason said, taking a seat across from Sarah.

"Daniel was just telling us about the case," Harriet said, her eyes sparkling with mischief. She loved theorizing and offering her opinions, whether they were wanted or not.

"Yes, this case is proving to be tricky," Jason said noncommittally. He had no wish to discuss what he'd learned in front of the ladies. "And how's dear Charlotte?" he asked. "May I take a peek at my goddaughter before I leave?"

"Of course. She's sleeping now," Sarah said, her face alight with maternal tenderness. "She's wonderful, Jason. So sweet."

"I hear you have news of your own," Harriet said, giving him a meaningful look.

"It's not public knowledge yet," Jason said, wishing Daniel would have kept Katherine's pregnancy in confidence. It was early days yet, and anything could happen. They had decided to wait a few weeks before telling anyone who wasn't family or staff.

"Of course. I'm sorry. We're just so pleased for you," Harriet said.

"Thank you," Jason replied stiffly.

Sarah handed him a cup of tea and directed a warning look at her mother.

"I do think this case is awfully strange," Harriet said, undeterred. "The logical conclusion would be that someone had followed the curate from London with the intention of settling a score, but it seems that there were no strangers in the village in the days leading up to the murder. So it must have been a local," Harriet mused. "What do you think, Jason?"

"I think that nearly everyone in the village witnessed an event that led to Sebastian Slade's murder last Sunday, but unfortunately, they didn't know what they were seeing."

"How do you mean?" Sarah asked. She looked perplexed.

"We've been told by several people that something distracted Sebastian Slade during the service. He was moody when he returned to his lodgings and went up to his room, where he spent the remainder of the day and wrote several letters to people closest to him. He posted the letters on Monday, and then was murdered later that day. Something important happened within that window of time. We're missing a vital clue that's a key to this mystery," Jason explained.

"Well, we'll leave you two to sort it out," Sarah said as she set down her cup and stood. "Come, Mother, let's allow the men to talk. They clearly have much to discuss."

Harriet looked crestfallen at being ordered to leave but didn't argue with her daughter. She set down her own cup and rose laboriously to her feet. "I have no doubt you two will work it out," Harriet said in parting.

"Shall I ask Tilda to brew a fresh pot?" Sarah asked before leaving the room.

"No need, my dear," Daniel replied, his gaze tender. "We'll be just fine."

The ladies left the room, and Daniel turned to Jason, who was helping himself to another tiny teacake. "Any luck with Victoria Gale?" Daniel asked eagerly.

"Yes and no. Sebastian Slade did indeed try to romance the girl, but their relationship was in the early stages. He hadn't had time to do too much damage."

"That's good news, I suppose," Daniel said. "He certainly didn't waste any time, did he? The rogue."

"No, he didn't," Jason agreed. "Sebastian Slade's behavior toward Victoria certainly gives Mr. Gale a motive, except that I don't think he knew anything about his daughter's budding relationship with the curate."

"He may have," Daniel argued.

"Victoria met Slade by her mother's grave. No one would question a curate offering a bit of comfort to a bereaved child if they saw them together. And I doubt Mr. Gale was even aware they'd met. He's doing his best to cope with his own grief."

Daniel sighed heavily. "If Gale didn't kill him, then who did? If we keep discounting every lead, we'll never solve this case."

"I meant what I said, Daniel. We're missing a vital clue that will put everything in perspective. Something happened at the service, and everyone in that church witnessed it. We need to speak to someone who sat at the back of the church."

"Why? What does it matter where they sat?" Daniel asked, intrigued.

"Because those at the front would have been facing the pulpit. They might have seen Slade lose his composure, but they wouldn't know what had caused the momentary slip since whatever it was had likely been behind them."

"We need to return to the village and question a few more parishioners," Daniel agreed. "Mrs. Hodges would know who normally sits at the back."

"Yes, I think she would. By the by, as it happens, I ran into Mrs. Curtis this afternoon and took the opportunity to ask her something I should have thought of the last time," Jason said.

"What's that, then?"

"I thought that perhaps Jenny Ross had relations in the village, who might have wished to teach Sebastian Slade a lesson, but she doesn't, at least not as far as Mrs. Curtis is aware.

However, Mrs. Curtis did mention that Mrs. Goodwin, who recently returned to Upper Finchley with her husband, had been in service to some dowager in London. Mrs. Goodwin might have had a run-in with Sebastian Slade while in her employ."

"What are the chances that Mrs. Goodwin had met this one man in a city the size of London?" Daniel asked, visibly discouraged.

"Stranger things have happened," Jason replied.

"They certainly have, which raises a number of questions in my mind."

"Go on," Jason invited.

"We're working under the assumption that something happened last Sunday to set the murder of Sebastian Slade in motion, but what if we are wrong? What if he simply felt ill during the service and needed a moment to compose himself, unsure if he'd be able to continue? Elsie Brockton said she'd found him sitting on the step after the service, looking pale and shocked. What if it wasn't shock but a bad case of indigestion?" Daniel asked, his frustration mounting. Nothing about this case had been straightforward or even remotely logical. "Slade managed to finish the service but refused luncheon when he returned to his lodgings and went directly upstairs. He may have simply felt unwell and wished to rest."

"That could very well be, but someone still saw fit to kill him. I doubt they bashed him over the head because he had an upset stomach and momentarily lost his train of thought during the service," Jason pointed out.

"But what if his death had nothing to do with anything that had come before? It could have been a robbery gone wrong, or a scuffle that had broken out spontaneously. It's entirely possible that, feeling better on Monday, Sebastian Slade had gone for an evening walk and was set upon by someone intent on mischief. He might have been lured or dragged to the graveyard, where a confrontation ensued and the killer used whatever was to hand to silence Slade. It might have been nothing more than a random occurrence rather than a prearranged meeting between two people who had a previous connection," Daniel concluded.

"Or he may have offended someone without realizing it. Hit a nerve, so to speak," Jason said, ignoring Daniel's bout of self-pity. He could understand his frustration, but pessimism didn't solve crimes; the dogged pursuit of facts did.

"As far as we know, Sebastian Slade had not had disagreements with anyone since coming to the village, or grievances lodged against him. Everyone seemed to think him kind and pleasant," Daniel pointed out.

"And maybe he was outwardly kind and pleasant, but pleasant people are not exempt from being murdered."

"What could he have said that would have led to his murder?" Daniel asked. "It would have had to be something fairly inflammatory."

"Whatever he said or did cost him his life," Jason said. "Perhaps we should ask Reverend Hodges about the sermon Slade delivered last Sunday. Someone might have taken it too much to heart."

"I think that's a good idea," Daniel said. "Let's start with the vicar and Mrs. Hodges and then interview the recent additions to the village."

"All right. I'll come for you at nine," Jason replied, and rose to leave. He wasn't particularly looking forward to returning to Upper Finchley.

# Chapter 27

Daniel wished he could remain at home for the rest of the day and enjoy some time with Sarah and Charlotte, but he'd promised to update CI Coleridge on his progress, and since he'd be going directly to Upper Finchley in the morning, now was as good a time as any. He asked Tom to bring around the dogcart and drove into Brentwood, hoping CI Coleridge hadn't left for the day. He kept strange hours but could usually be found in his office toward the end of the day, dealing with the inevitable paperwork that went with every arrest and complaint.

"Come in, Haze," CI Coleridge said gruffly when Daniel knocked on his door. The older man had removed his coat and was in his shirtsleeves and waistcoat, a cigar dangling between his lips. Several sheets of paper were before him on the desk, but he stuffed them into the upper drawer before giving Daniel his full attention. "Well? Have you narrowed down a list of suspects?" Coleridge asked.

"Not quite, sir."

"What does that mean?"

"I have been able to identify several suspects, but I don't believe any of them did it."

"Why not?"

"Lack of motive, opportunity, and the method of the crime itself," Daniel replied, cringing inwardly at his choice of words. He sounded ineffectual and unprofessional.

CI Coleridge turned around and grabbed a newspaper off the credenza behind him, then tossed the paper on the desk, the headline facing Daniel. It screamed:

### The Curious Case of the Cleaved Curate

"Clever, no?" Coleridge asked with obvious disgust. "A play on words. That's what the reporters do at our expense. They make clever little jokes. Would you care to read the story? I'll spare you the time and give you a summary, shall I? They refer to us as 'clueless clodhoppers.' Another alliteration for the amusement of the readers. But you know what, Haze? They are not all wrong. You've been investigating for days, and all you have is a rather short list of suspects whom you don't believe did it. Well, someone did. Someone nearly cleaved that man's head in half. Surely there are not that many people out there who felt such strong hatred toward a simple curate."

"It's more complicated than that, sir," Daniel protested.

"Is it? Bishop Garner called on me at home this morning. Did I tell you that? He wants to know what's taking so long. I believe the phrase he used was, 'Finding a killer in a village the size of Judas's arsehole should be as easy as shooting fish in a barrel.'"

"And he'd be right, if we knew for certain that the killer is someone in Upper Finchley," Daniel said. "Yes, the murder was committed in the village, but the motive lies elsewhere. I'm sure of it."

"Make an arrest, Haze. Even if you have to let the culprit go later on, at least it looks like we're doing something."

"I will question some of the inhabitants of the village tomorrow, but I can't promise I'll make an arrest," Daniel replied. "I need a reason to accuse someone of murder."

"I suggest you find one before they call you a 'bungling boob' in the press. We need the goodwill of the people to do our job, Haze, and that means catching killers."

"But does it mean sending innocent people to the gallows?" Daniel demanded, really angry now.

"No, it doesn't. That's why we pay you to get the right man. Now, out with you. I still have work to do tonight."

"Goodnight, sir," Daniel said tersely as he stood to leave.

"If only it was," Coleridge replied archly. "If only it was."

# Chapter 28

## Monday, August 12

Daniel sat in pensive silence as Jason guided the curricle toward Upper Finchley. Jason could understand his despondency. They'd been at it for days, but nothing they had learned pointed toward a clear motive or an obvious killer. Sebastian Slade must have made his share of enemies, but there was a world of difference between hating a man and taking a shovel to his head. As Bernard Holloway had callously pointed out, many a man availed himself of women he had no legal claim to. It was easy enough to do in a society that showed little regard for women and was ready to cast them out should they make one wrong choice, often leaving them broken and destitute.

For most men, women fell into one of several categories: respectable young lady, wife, whore, servant, spinster, relation, or target of seduction. Sebastian Slade had divided the women they'd questioned so far into those obvious categories. Iris Holloway was the devoted sister, Elena Cartwright the potential wife, had Slade proposed marriage before Captain Herbert had and been accepted. Jenny had been branded a whore, and Victoria Gale had been a target of seduction. But none of those women appeared to be the motive for the murder. There had to be something else, something they weren't seeing.

Jason brought the curricle to a stop before The Black Boar and handed the reins to a boy waiting outside the tavern livery. Jason tossed him a coin and instructed the boy to water the horses, then followed Daniel toward the vicarage, just across the village green.

"Good morning, gentlemen," Mrs. Hodges gushed when the servant led them into the drawing room. "Please, do sit down. Shelly, tell the vicar we have visitors," she told the young maid. "He'll be right down," Mrs. Hodges said. "He'll be pleased to see you. He's been so upset about this awful business. I hope you have some news that will cheer him up."

"Unfortunately, we've made little progress, Mrs. Hodges," Daniel said. "Which is why we've come to speak to you again."

"I told you everything I know, Inspector," Mrs. Hodges said. "I've been able to think of little else over the past few days, but nothing new springs to mind."

"I was actually wondering if Mr. Slade might have given the vicar a copy of his sermon for last Sunday's service," Daniel said.

"You'll have to ask him that, but I doubt it. You see, the change of plans was rather last minute. My husband took ill on Saturday evening and was still unwell come Sunday, so Mr. Slade wasn't given time to prepare. He had to improvise, the poor dear," Mrs. Hodges said. "He was very nervous."

"Gentlemen," Reverend Hodges said as he entered the room. He looked even older and grayer than he had on Tuesday, the past few days having taken a toll on him, according to his wife. "Any news?" he asked, gazing upon Daniel with great hope.

"I'm afraid not. We were just asking Mrs. Hodges about last Sunday's service," Daniel explained. "Did Mr. Slade tell you what he was going to speak about?"

The vicar nodded. "Forgiveness. He thought it was a fitting choice for his first service, and although I wasn't there to hear it, everyone seemed to have enjoyed it."

Mrs. Hodges nodded vigorously in agreement. "It wasn't a very long sermon, but that was to be expected given that Mr. Slade was still only a curate and not a full-fledged vicar. He acquitted himself well."

"Mrs. Hodges, can you tell us who normally sits at the back of the church during the services?" Jason asked.

"Why, what an odd question," Mrs. Hodges said, eyeing Jason with suspicion.

"It's only that we'd like to ask if they might have noticed anything unusual during the service. Several people have mentioned that Mr. Slade seemed to have faltered for a moment."

"Did he?" Reverend Hodges asked, turning to his wife.

"It was really for just a moment," Mrs. Hodges replied irritably. "He was nervous is all."

"We'd still like to speak to someone who had a different perspective," Daniel insisted.

"The Hansons and the Goodwins tend to sit toward the back," Mrs. Hodges said. "Both families have young children that can at times be disruptive. As I mentioned last time, the Goodwins left early. Their boy, Johnny, had kicked up a fuss, so they had to take him outside."

"Thank you, Mrs. Hodges," Daniel said.

"It really is extraordinary that you haven't yet caught the killer," Reverend Hodges said, pinning Daniel with a look of intense disapproval. "This is a small village, Inspector. Surely the suspects are not that difficult to identify."

"Really?" Daniel asked, failing to mask his annoyance. "I would love to hear your thoughts, Reverend Hodges. Which of your parishioners do you believe capable of such an act?"

"Well, I really couldn't say," Reverend Hodges backtracked. "I only meant to suggest that surely there are obvious clues."

"Nothing about this case is obvious, Reverend Hodges," Daniel snapped. "Thank you for your assistance. Good day."

The two men stepped back out into the hazy August morning. "The nerve of the man," Daniel fumed. "You'd think this was a parlor game and the killer left me obvious clues, as if this were a scavenger hunt. It's not bad enough that I have to hear it from Chief Inspector Coleridge, who's none too pleased, I have to tell you, but now I have to explain myself to the vicar as well."

"Daniel, I know you're frustrated," Jason began.

"I'm sorry," Daniel said, frowning guiltily. "I have allowed this case to get under my skin. I suppose I've grown accustomed to attaining a good result. I've grown overconfident. Perhaps this is a lesson in humility I needed to learn."

Jason rolled his eyes, eliciting a small smile. "Daniel, there's an American expression I must share with you."

"Really? What is it?" Daniel asked, intrigued.

"Snap out of it!" Jason commanded. "Not every case will get solved in a matter of days, and not every case will get solved. Period. As I'm sure Chief Inspector Coleridge knows, and Reverend Hodges doesn't. Now, set aside your doubts and let's go interview the Hansons and the Goodwins."

They found Rob Hanson at the smithy, shoeing a horse. Mr. Gale was inside, pounding something out on the anvil. He gave them a curt nod and returned to what he was doing.

Rob Hanson was a man of about thirty with light brown hair and pale blue eyes. He was stocky and broad, his upper arms bulging with muscle and straining the fabric of his shirt. His skin was bronzed from years spent working outdoors, and his forehead glistened with sweat as he went about his work.

"Mr. Hanson, a word, if you please," Daniel said.

"Sure thing, guv. Just let me finish with this handsome fella here." He finished what he was doing, returned the horse to its owner, accepted payment, and turned to the two men. "How can I help?"

"You've recently returned to Upper Finchley," Daniel said. "How long ago was that?"

"'Bout three years now," the man replied. "Why?"

"You worked as a navvy?" Daniel continued.

"Yeah, I did. What of it?"

"Did your work ever take you to London or Oxford?" Daniel asked, ignoring Rob Hanson's questions.

"Neh. I worked mostly in West Yorkshire and the Midlands."

"You're obviously a skilled blacksmith. What made you leave Upper Finchley?" Jason asked.

"Thought I'd have me a bit of an adventure afore I settled down," Rob Hanson said. "It sounded glamorous to a young fool like me, but navvying is hard, thankless work that pays next to nothing. I did manage to put by a little something, but I was more than ready to come home and settle down."

"Did you have occasion to meet Mr. Slade before he arrived in the village?" Daniel asked.

Rob Hanson looked genuinely surprised by the question. "No. Where would I meet the likes of him?"

"Were you at St. Martin's last Sunday?" Jason asked.

"Sure."

"Did you enjoy the sermon?"

The man shrugged. "It were all right, I suppose. Can't say I recall any of it."

"Did anything strike you as odd?" Daniel asked.

"Like what?"

"Like anything Mr. Slade said from the pulpit, or maybe something someone did," Daniel suggested, watching the man like a hawk.

"No."

"Were there any disruptions?" Jason asked.

Rob Hanson thought about that for a moment. "Not as I noticed," he finally replied, then thought better of it. "Oh, Johnny Goodwin started crying right at the start, so Mrs. Goodwin took him outside."

"Did she return?" Daniel asked.

"No. After a time, Neil Goodwin took their daughter and went after her. I suppose the boy must have taken ill."

"Did everyone else remain in their seats?" Jason asked.

"They did."

"Thank you, Mr. Hanson," Daniel said, and strode away.

They retrieved the curricle from The Black Boar and headed toward the Goodwin farm. "A little boy acting out during a service is all we have left to go on," Daniel said morosely. "I would love to snap out of it, as you so eloquently put it, but we have no leads. Not a one."

Jason nodded. He hated to admit it, but Daniel was right. This case wasn't likely to get solved. After calling on the Goodwins, Daniel would have to return to Brentwood and inform Chief Inspector Coleridge that the investigation had hit a dead end. Jason didn't envy him. It wasn't that Daniel was vain and needed the validation of solving every puzzle put before him; it was that he was diligent and dedicated and hated to see an injustice go unpunished. He might not have approved of the man Sebastian Slade had been, but that didn't mean he could live with his failure to find his killer.

"I'm sorry, Daniel," Jason said softly, wishing he could say something to lift Daniel's spirits.

Daniel turned to him, his bespectacled gaze serious and direct. "Jason, I wouldn't have made it this far without your help. We might not solve this case, but there will be others. I hope this setback will not prevent you from assisting me in future investigations."

"Of course not," Jason replied, touched by Daniel's gratitude. "I will be there for as long as you want me."

# Chapter 29

The Goodwin farm was about two miles east of the village. It looked to be a prosperous place, the farmhouse sizeable and in good repair. There were several outbuildings, and a good number of sheep were grazing in the meadow beyond the wooden stile. Three lines of laundry hung outside, sheets and towels flapping in the breeze like canvas sails. The windows looked spotless and sparkled with reflected sunshine above the potted plants positioned on the sill to benefit from the summer sunshine.

Daniel knocked on the door and introduced himself to Mr. Goodwin, who looked less than pleased to see them.

"Come in," he said without much enthusiasm and stepped aside to let them pass.

Mrs. Goodwin was more welcoming. She wiped her hands on her apron as she stepped out of the kitchen, her face wreathed in a warm smile. "Good afternoon, gentlemen. Please, make yourselves comfortable in the parlor. Can I offer you some refreshment?" she asked. "Tea? A cup of ale, perhaps?"

"No, thank you, Mrs. Goodwin," Daniel replied politely. He was in no mood for social niceties.

"Neil, did you want something?" Mrs. Goodwin asked.

"Don't trouble yourself, Rosie," Neil Goodwin said, smiling at his spouse.

The four of them trooped into the parlor, where Daniel and Jason were invited to take the two chairs while the Goodwins settled across from them on the settee. The parlor looked just like its owners—comfortable and lived-in. The furnishings were by no means new or expensive, but they were in good condition, and there was a nice painting of a naval scene over the mantel. There were lace antimacassars on the chairs, and the carpet looked hardly worn. Daniel studied the couple before him casually, not wishing to be caught staring.

Mr. Goodwin wasn't very tall, but he had the wiry build and economical movements that gave the impression of vigor and physical strength. His dark gaze was inquisitive, and his thin moustache did little to hide sensuous lips that had formed a nice smile when the situation called for it a few minutes ago. He wasn't smiling now. Instead, he remained alert, his hands at his sides as he waited to hear the reason for the intrusion.

Rose Goodwin was dark-eyed like her husband, but her brown gaze was calm and warm rather than watchful. She had light brown hair and was a bit plump, possibly in the early stages of pregnancy, Daniel surmised. It was difficult to tell. He was just about to state their business when two children ran into the room. They appeared to be around three years of age and, despite their different coloring, may have been twins. The girl had light brown hair like her mother, but the boy favored his father.

"Hello," the little girl said, looking from Daniel to Jason and back again.

"Hello," Daniel and Jason replied in unison.

"Are you friends of my papa?" the girl asked, clearly the more outgoing of the two.

"We've only just met," Jason replied, smiling at the child. "My name is Jason Redmond. What's yours?" he asked, holding out his hand to her.

She took it shyly. "Emily Goodwin, sir."

"It's a pleasure to make your acquaintance, Emily," Jason said solemnly. He held out his hand to the boy next. "And your name, young man?"

"Johnny Goodwin," the little boy replied.

"It's an honor to meet you," Jason said, having shaken the boy's hand.

The Goodwins looked bemused, probably attributing Jason's odd behavior to his foreignness. Few adults would take the time to speak to children, especially when calling on a matter of business rather than making a social visit.

"Children, go play outside," Mrs. Goodwin said, suddenly flustered. "I'll be along in a moment, and we'll go for a walk in the meadow."

"Can we pick some flowers, Mama?" Emily asked. "We can lay them on Grandpa's grave when we go into the village."

"Yes, of course," Mrs. Goodwin said, smiling indulgently at her daughter. "Grandpa would like that. Now, go on with you. These gentlemen wish to speak to us."

"All right," Emily said, her narrow shoulders dropping. She looked like she would have liked to stay and join in the visit.

"Now, where were we?" Mrs. Goodwin asked, turning her attention back to the visitors. "How can we help you, gentlemen?"

"You left the service early last Sunday," Daniel said.

"Yes. Johnny had a bellyache and needed to be taken outside," Mrs. Goodwin replied.

"Is it a crime to miss the service?" Neil Goodwin asked, somewhat belligerently.

"Not at all. We're talking to all the parishioners to determine if anyone had seen or heard anything leading up to Mr. Slade's death. Did you happen to see any strangers outside?" Daniel asked Mrs. Goodwin.

"No, I didn't."

"Did you go back inside?"

"Johnny was unwell, so I thought it'd be best to take him home rather than disrupt the service again. Neil and Emily came out when I didn't return, and we headed home."

"I hope Johnny wasn't seriously ill," Jason said. "I'm a doctor. I can examine him if you like."

"There's no need," Mrs. Goodwin replied, clearly surprised by the offer. "He got at the gooseberries is all. We picked them on Saturday, and I was going to make gooseberry pie, but Johnny helped himself to the lot on Sunday morning before we left for church. Ate half a basket before I caught him in the act."

"Yes, too many gooseberries will have that effect," Jason replied with a knowing smile. "He looks to be a healthy boy."

"Thank you," Mrs. Goodwin said. "He's big for his age."

"Mrs. Goodwin, can you tell us about your time in London?" Daniel asked, tired of talking about gooseberries and their effect on one's bowels. He smiled encouragingly. "How did you come to leave the village?"

"Of course," she replied, looking a little taken aback by the question. "I saw an advert in a London paper and wrote to apply. Mrs. Huxley had advertised for a companion. I looked after my mother when she was ill, so I thought I might have a chance at securing the position. I was lucky to get the job," Mrs. Goodwin said.

Daniel noted that her speech was more cultured than that of an Essex farm girl, so she must have put her time in London to good use. "Please, go on. How long did you work for Mrs. Huxley?"

"Until she passed. That was four years ago now. Lord, how time flies," she said, smiling at them. "Seems like yesterday."

"Did you go on to another job?" Daniel asked.

"No. I had met Neil while I was working for Mrs. Huxley. We were going to be wed anyway, so there was no need for me to seek new employment."

"Where did you two meet?" Jason asked, smiling at the Goodwins benevolently.

"We met at Drury Lane," Mrs. Goodwin said. "I saved my wages and allowed myself a visit to the theater. I'd never seen a play," she said shyly. "That's where I met Neil."

"Did you go to see a play as well?" Jason asked Mr. Goodwin.

"No, I worked at the theater. I did some carpentry, the props and such," Mr. Goodwin supplied.

"So, it was opportune that you met your husband just as your employment had come to an end," Jason said.

"Yes, it was. We left London shortly after and moved to Brighton. That's where Neil is originally from. The children were born there. Then we came back here when my father took ill and needed help," Mrs. Goodwin explained.

"Do you like it here, Mr. Goodwin?" Jason asked.

"Yes, I do. I didn't know much about farming, but I am a quick study. We're doing all right for ourselves," he said, his pride evident.

"You have a fine place here," Jason said. "Daniel, if you don't have any further questions, I think we should get on."

"Yes, of course," Daniel said, rising to his feet. He'd asked everything he'd meant to but was surprised by Jason's desire to leave. He supposed Jason saw the futility of this interview. The Goodwins had nothing of value to add.

When they stepped outside, the children were chasing a cat, who had probably been dozing in peace until then. They waved happily, and Jason waved back.

"Charming children," Daniel said as he climbed into the curricle. "Should we bother to interview Miss Lundy or call it a day?" he asked sourly.

"There's no need," Jason replied, still smiling at the children. "We will go to Brentwood for reinforcements, and then you will arrest the Goodwins for the murder of Sebastian Slade."

# Chapter 30

"What are you talking about?" Daniel exclaimed as the curricle rolled out of the Goodwins' yard. "We were both there and heard the same answers. What did you hear that I didn't?"

Daniel had to admit that he was deeply stung by Jason's comment. He was the detective; it was his job to solve the case. How could Jason have figured it out from the brief conversation they'd had with the Goodwins and be so certain of their guilt that he believed an arrest was imminent?

Jason looked over at him, all too aware of his wounded pride. "Daniel, it wasn't anything you missed. It was just something I happened to notice."

"What?" Daniel demanded. "What did you notice?"

"Emily's face. That child is Grace Holloway."

"How do you know that?" Daniel asked, now even more stunned.

"When we interviewed Mr. and Mrs. Holloway, you sat closer to the window, but I had a clear view of the sideboard where the family photographs were displayed. There was a photograph of Iris Holloway holding Grace. Grace had a thin scar running between her right nostril and upper lip, the result of being born with a cleft palate, commonly known as harelip," Jason explained. "As far as I know, it's a hereditary affliction, and Grace had inherited it from her father. Grace's condition must have been very mild because the defect was barely visible and had been expertly stitched soon after birth, but it was still noticeable. Emily Goodwin bears the same scar, and although she shares her coloring with Mrs. Goodwin, she resembles Iris Holloway."

"Is that why you introduced yourself, in order to get closer to Emily?" Daniel asked, somewhat mollified.

"Yes. I had to be sure."

"Bernard Holloway wears a moustache," Daniel said, casting his mind back to the last time they'd interviewed him.

There did seem to be something not right about his upper lip, he thought now that he recalled the occasion.

"He does, but I noticed that beneath the moustache, his upper lip was deformed, and the moustache was waxed, the hair brushed slightly sideways to conceal a tiny bald patch. Hair does not grow on scar tissue."

"If your theory is correct, then Sebastian Slade must have recognized his niece when he saw her at the Sunday service, the realization that he was looking at Grace Holloway the cause of the momentary distraction several people have alluded to. Unsettled, he returned to his lodgings, went up to his room, and penned several letters to the people closest to him, needing to organize his thoughts without openly revealing his suspicions. At some point between Sunday afternoon and Monday night, he must have confronted the Goodwins, who murdered him to protect their secret," Daniel said. This theory fit in neatly with the facts, giving Daniel a moment of quiet satisfaction the likes of which he hadn't experienced since the body of Sebastian Slade was found on Tuesday morning.

"Emily Goodwin sat at the back of the church with her parents," Jason said. "I doubt Sebastian Slade would have been able to discern the scar from that distance and immediately recognize a child he'd last seen when she was only nine months old as his niece. It's more likely that he recognized one of the Goodwins. My guess is that Rose Goodwin's maiden name is Evans, and she had been Grace's nursemaid. Overcome with shock at seeing her daughter's uncle, she had grabbed her son, who was already fussing, according to several people we've interviewed, and stepped outside to calm herself, using the child as a decoy. When she didn't return, Neil Goodwin followed, and the two of them put their heads together on how to deal with the problem."

"So, why hit him with a shovel? As you yourself pointed out, it was opportunistic and clumsy."

"Perhaps they never meant to kill him, only to assure him that the child was not Grace and he had made a mistake. When

Slade refused to keep silent, Neil Goodwin grabbed the shovel and brought it down on his head."

Daniel shook his head in dismay. "But why would Rose Goodwin want to take Grace? She married and had another child almost immediately after."

"Perhaps she'd grown attached to Grace. It's not uncommon," Jason suggested.

"Do you think the Goodwins realized you're on to them?" Daniel asked. He had been clueless of Jason's motives, but then he hadn't known about the harelip. Now his stomach clenched with anxiety, his every instinct telling him not to leave the Goodwins at liberty while he and Jason went for reinforcements.

"I hope not, but I wouldn't count on it," Jason replied, and snapped the reins, urging the horses to go faster. "A guilty conscience is always sure to raise the alarm in one's mind."

# Chapter 31

It took more than two hours to get to Brentwood, state the case to Chief Inspector Coleridge, who was pleased to see some progress at last, mobilize Constables Pullman and Ingleby, hitch the police wagon, and finally depart for Upper Finchley. It was nearly another hour later that the two vehicles neared the Goodwin farm. The road leading up to the farm was straight as an arrow and ran through a flat, grassy stretch of land, eliminating the element of surprise that would have given Daniel the upper hand. The police wagon came first, with the two constables on the bench, followed by Jason's curricle. The horses were hungry and tired, but rest and a nice bucket of oats would have to wait until the Goodwins were in custody.

All was quiet when they pulled into the yard. The windows were closed despite the heat, the curtains now drawn. The sheep that had been grazing in the meadow were nowhere to be seen, and not a sound came from the barn, as if the animals sensed the tension and understood the need to keep their heads down. In fact, the place felt deserted. Jason briefly wondered where the farmhand, Solly Higgins, was and if his loyalty would go as far as interfering with the arrest. If he was smart, he'd be keeping his head down as well.

Constable Pullman brought the wagon to a stop in the middle of the yard but didn't jump down, waiting for the curricle to pull up. His head swiveled on his thick neck, his gaze traveling from the farmhouse toward the approaching curricle and back again. He was visibly excited, since most of his daily activities involved complaints of petty theft, impromptu tavern brawls, and countless hours of patrolling the streets of Brentwood, dressed in the thick woolen uniform that had never been designed with this August's broiling temperatures in mind. Constable Ingleby, who was hardly more than a boy, looked nervous, his neck barely visible between his hunched shoulders and the low brim of his helmet.

The first bullet pierced Constable Pullman's helmet. His head jerked back violently as the velocity of the projectile knocked the helmet off his head and pressed the strap against his Adam's apple, making him gasp. Despite the shock of being shot at, Constable Ingleby had the presence of mind to grab hold of the reins, ensuring that the horse didn't take off, although the wild neighing and rolling of its eyes were indicative of its panic and intention to flee. This was not a war horse, used to the chaos and sounds of battle, but an aging nag not suited to anything other than pulling a wagon.

Constable Pullman grabbed at the strap and tore his helmet off as he jumped down to the ground and crouched behind the wagon. Constable Ingleby gaped around in panic, looking to Constable Pullman or Daniel to tell him what to do. Neither man obliged.

Jason tightened his hold on the reins, pulling hard to keep the chestnuts from rearing and thankful that the curricle was partially obscured by a shed and not in the direct line of fire. A cacophony had erupted, every animal within hearing distance mooing, bleating, neighing, or barking in fear. Jason stared at the farmhouse, trying to determine where the shot had come from. The windows on the ground floor were firmly shut, but there was a partially open shutter on a tiny window in the attic. Goodwin was up there, and now that Jason had deduced that, he could make out the muzzle of a rifle.

"We need to get round the back," Daniel cried. "Goodwin can't man the front and the back of the house simultaneously."

"Unless Rose Goodwin or Solly Higgins is stationed by the back door with a rifle," Jason replied. Neither he nor Daniel was armed. Jason hadn't thought to take his army revolver when he left the house that morning, and as an inspector of the police service, Daniel wasn't authorized to carry a weapon.

The two constables had nothing but wooden truncheons, which were useless against a firearm. They were positioned behind the wagon, their heads pulled into their shoulders, their legs bent at the knees as they awaited instructions. Constable Ingleby held on to the reins for dear life, using both hands to keep the horse from forcibly removing the only barrier between the two constables and the pointed rifle.

"Come on," Jason cried as he jumped down from the curricle and tied the reins to a sturdy post to keep the horses from bolting. He hoped Neil Goodwin would not take it into his head to shoot the animals but had no way of knowing how far the man would go to protect his family. Wounding or killing the horses outright would not only prevent the police from escaping but keep them from following the Goodwins should they try to flee.

Was Neil Goodwin shooting to kill and had simply missed the mark, or was the shot a warning? Jason's question was answered almost immediately. Constable Ingleby, who'd foolishly peered out from behind the wagon to see what was going on, was promptly shot in the shoulder. He let out an agonized scream and crumpled to the ground, his hand pressing on the wound, blood oozing between his fingers and dripping down into the dirt of the yard.

"You damn fool," Constable Pullman growled as he crouched next to Ingleby. Constable Pullman pulled out his handkerchief and tried to force it beneath the younger man's trembling hand, but the cotton square became soaked in moments, eliciting a moan of terror from Ingleby, who rested his back against the wheel of the wagon. Jason could have sworn he heard a chuckle coming from the attic window, but perhaps that was just his imagination. Goodwin was too far away for the sound to carry.

"That son of a bitch," Daniel cried, his gaze glued to the bleeding constable. "I'll have him on attempted murder of a police constable."

*If you can get him*, Jason thought as he assessed the situation. Goodwin had the upper hand and would retain his advantage for as long as the men remained in the yard. Should they try to retreat, Jason was in no doubt that Goodwin would take the opportunity to flee, getting a head start on his pursuers, especially if he shot at the horses.

"Daniel, stay here," Jason commanded, and ducked into the nearest outbuilding before Daniel could protest.

After the glare of the midafternoon sun, the shed was dark, the only light coming through the narrow gaps between the wooden wall planks. Jason allowed his eyes a moment to adjust and looked around, pleased to find tools and pieces of wood of various sizes that Neil Goodwin had no doubt prepared for some project. Jason grabbed a stout plank, thinking to use it as a cudgel, then reconsidered. The plank was as long as his arm and would have greater reach, but it wasn't enough to cause serious damage. It might crack, leaving him defenseless. He was reaching for a hammer when he became aware of movement in the corner of the shed.

"Who's there?" Jason demanded, grabbing the hammer and wrapping his fingers around the handle.

"It's Solly," the boy cried. "I don't mean no harm. I was scared is all."

"Come out," Jason instructed. "Slowly."

"I ain't armed, sir," Solly said as he got to his feet and slowly came forward. He was no more than seventeen, but his arms were thick with muscle, his hands disproportionately large. He splayed his fingers and held his hands up to show he wasn't armed.

"Is there anyone else in the house besides Neil Goodwin and his family?" Jason asked.

"Not that I knows of, sir," Solly replied. Jason noticed the glazed look in the boy's eyes and marked his slow speech. He thought Solly might be mentally deficient, but now was not the time to ponder the question. As long as he didn't feel the need to protect his master, it didn't matter.

"Is there a back door to the farmhouse?" Jason asked. Solly nodded.

"Is there an attic window at the back of the house?"

"I don't know," Solly moaned. "I really don't know." He covered his ears with his hands and hunched his shoulders. "I'm afraid of the shots," he whispered.

"You just stay right here, Solly. No one will hurt you," Jason promised. He hoped the boy would have somewhere to go once the Goodwins were taken into custody. *If* they were taken into custody.

Jason slipped out of the shed. Daniel stood off to his left, his back pressed to the wall, his gaze fixed on the two constables. Constable Ingleby's face was a mask of agony, his forehead glistening with perspiration now that he had removed his helmet and the top of his head was visible. Constable Pullman was looking at Daniel, his eyes demanding instructions. It had only been a few minutes since the wagon had pulled into the yard, but it was a few minutes too long to remain in the line of fire. Daniel, his face set and his shoulders squared, looked as if he was set to cross the yard. Jason assumed he intended to draw Goodwin's attention to himself, therefore giving the two constables enough time to make it to the shed. Jason thought it a foolhardy plan.

"Daniel, I'm going round back. Wait till Goodwin realizes I'm there, then get the constables out of the way."

"Jason, wait," Daniel hissed, but Jason was already on the move. He darted toward the house, hoping Goodwin couldn't see him from his vantage point behind the partially closed shutters.

The back of the house looked much like the front. The door was firmly shut, the windows closed, the curtains drawn. It was impossible to tell if someone was watching. Just because Jason didn't see anyone didn't mean they weren't there. For all he knew, Rose Goodwin was a crack shot, or maybe she was the one in the attic and her husband was watching the back way. Jason pressed himself against the wall and inched his way toward the door, ducking when he passed beneath the window.

Another shot rang out at the front of the house, the sound causing Jason's stomach to clench with fear. He hoped Daniel hadn't been hit. Not being a military man or someone who enjoyed hunting, Daniel wouldn't be familiar with the range of the shots, and he was just angry enough to put himself in danger.

Jason reached out and tried the door. It was locked, as he'd assumed it would be. The house was strangely quiet, given what was happening. Children were not known for remaining silent when shots were fired. Were they inside, or had Neil Goodwin sent his family away, remaining behind to give them enough time to flee? That was what Jason would have done in his place, but he didn't know the man. To assume anything was to make himself vulnerable.

Jason risked taking a step back, then put his shoulder to the door. It didn't budge. He tried again, but the door stood firm. He did hear a cry, though. It was Rose Goodwin, calling to her husband that someone was at the back door. So, the whole family was inside, after all.

Loud footfalls echoed in the quiet that ensued. Neil Goodwin had given up his position at the attic window and come thundering down the stairs. A downstairs windowpane shattered. Jason threw himself to the ground just as Goodwin fired. Knowing he had only moments before the man reloaded, Jason sprang to his feet, raised the hammer overhead, and smashed the window.

Momentarily distracted by a shower of broken glass, Neil Goodwin did not step away quickly enough. Jason struck again, hitting the man on the head. Goodwin went down like a brick, his body thudding to the floor just beneath the window. Jason heard Mrs. Goodwin scream in terror, and then the pitiful cries of the children muffled by the cellar door. The commotion was followed by the crash of the front door. Daniel and Constable Pullman were in.

Daniel unlocked the back door and beckoned for Jason to enter. Neil Goodwin's rifle was in his hand. Inside, it was mayhem. Rose Goodwin was shrieking and kicking Constable Pullman, who was no small man but still had difficulty dodging her blows. In the end, her efforts would no more deter him than the scratching of a kitten. Daniel handed Jason the rifle and cuffed Neil Goodwin, afraid the man would come to and try to fight his way out by any means necessary. Given his willingness to shoot at the police, he might not want to be taken alive and might hope to do enough damage to give his wife a fighting chance.

Mr. Goodwin moaned but didn't wake, which was probably just as well, since his eyes were covered with blood gushing from a cut on his forehead. There were several other cuts on his face and neck, but they weren't as deep.

The children continued to cry, begging to be let out of the cellar. Daniel went to set them free while Jason found a clean towel, wet it, then wiped the blood off Neil Goodwin's face and held the towel to the cut to stem the bleeding. He gently probed the wound on Goodwin's head, hoping he hadn't fractured the man's skull. It had been his intention to stun, not kill, but he'd hit Goodwin hard, knowing he had only one chance to slow him down. The man's eyes fluttered open, and Jason saw misery in his gaze. He knew all was lost.

"Rose," he whispered. "I'm sorry, Rosie."

The spouses exchanged looks filled with unspeakable pain. Whatever they had done had been out of love, for each other and for their children.

"Can you stand?" Jason asked.

"I suppose," Neil Goodwin mumbled. "It'd have been better had you killed me."

"I wasn't aiming to kill," Jason replied. He hauled Neil Goodwin to his feet and passed him to Daniel.

Subdued at last, Mrs. Goodwin was led outside, followed by her husband, who staggered out, supported by Daniel. The two were handed into the wagon.

"The children," Rose Goodwin screamed. "Please, don't leave the children on their own."

"The children will be looked after, Mrs. Goodwin," Daniel replied calmly as Constable Pullman exited the farmhouse with the children in tow. Their faces tearstained, they called for their parents and begged them to come back inside.

Jason would have liked to comfort them, but as a doctor, his duty lay with the injured. He hurried toward Constable Ingleby, whose hooded eyes were mere slits, his lips clamped tight as he tried not to cry out. Carefully removing the constable's coat, Jason examined the wound. Constable Ingleby whimpered pitifully when Jason pulled him forward in order to see his back.

"The good news is the bullet went right through, Constable," Jason said in his most reassuring tone. "So there's no need to extract it. Once we get back to the station, I will patch you up. There are medical supplies down in the mortuary."

The constable blanched, and Jason moved back in case the man was going to be sick.

"What's the bad news?" the constable muttered.

"The bad news is that you lost a lot of blood and will probably pass out on the way back to Brentwood."

"Right," Constable Ingleby said under his breath. He didn't seem too put out by the prospect.

"Come, you'll ride with me," Jason said as he helped the man to his feet.

Constable Ingleby sagged against him, panting with exertion as Jason maneuvered him toward the curricle. "This is a nice carriage," he said weakly, still able to admire the expensive conveyance despite his obvious pain. "Always wanted to ride in one." His voice was barely audible.

"Thank you," Jason said absentmindedly. His attention was on the children, who looked bewildered. They were no longer crying but huddling together, their fingers intertwined as they held on to each other. Daniel lifted them into the wagon one by one so they could ride with their parents. There was no need to frighten them further, although what would become of them once the prisoners were brought to the station was yet to be determined.

"Perhaps we should ask the vicar and his wife to look after them," Daniel said as he approached the curricle.

"Yes, that seems a good idea," Jason said. "The children know the vicar, so they won't be as frightened. But what will happen to them if the parents are sent to prison, or worse?" Jason asked.

"If Emily Goodwin proves to be Grace Holloway, she will be returned to her family, and Johnny will most likely go to a workhouse if there are no relatives to take him," Daniel said. He wasn't indifferent to the suffering of the children. Compassion for them was right there in his eyes.

Daniel turned to Constable Ingleby. "All right, Constable?" he asked, a rather inane question given the constable clearly was anything but.

"Yes, sir," Ingleby moaned. "Right as rain."

"If you are up to sarcasm, clearly you'll live," Daniel replied. "Let's get back to the station. We have suspects to interview."

Given Constable Ingleby's condition, Jason made sure to go slowly so as not to jolt the poor man and cause him more pain. The police wagon, being a cumbersome vehicle to start with, followed, Neil Goodwin's repeated demands that his wife be released ignored by all involved.

Once the children were dropped off at the vicarage and Mrs. Goodwin finally quieted down, they turned for Brentwood, a ride that would take at least an hour at their current speed. Jason kept a close eye on Constable Ingleby as he drove, surprised that the young man was still lucid. The wound wasn't grave, but the shock, pain, and stifling heat were making Ingleby woozy. He vomited over the side of the curricle twice before they finally got to the station, which was quiet now that everyone except Sergeant Flint and Chief Inspector Coleridge had gone home for the day.

"Well, well," CI Coleridge said as Daniel and Constable Pullman brought Mr. and Mrs. Goodwin inside. "Separate rooms, I think," he said, relishing their obvious misery.

"Good man, Ingleby," CI Coleridge boomed, correctly assuming that the constable had been injured in the line of duty. "Will you see to him, Lord Redmond?"

"Of course."

Jason took Constable Ingleby down to the mortuary and sat him down in a chair, choosing not to help him to the table where the cadavers were normally autopsied. "Let me get you a glass of water," Jason said, noting the beads of sweat sliding down the man's face.

Once Constable Ingleby had downed the water and allowed Jason to strip him to the waist, he sat quietly, letting Jason tend to the wound. Jason cleaned it with alcohol, dabbing generously despite the constable's sharp intake of breath, then threaded a needle and sewed up both the entry and exit wounds to keep them from becoming infected. He swabbed the area with alcohol again and covered the wounds with a bandage that he wound beneath the constable's arm and over his shoulder. "That should do it," Jason said as he tied off the bandage. "Now, why don't you lie down for a little while, and then I will take you home."

"I ain't lying in here," Constable Ingleby said, eyeing the table with horror.

"I wasn't suggesting you should," Jason replied, a smile tugging at his lips. "You can use one of the empty cells."

Constable Ingleby looked like he was about to argue but seemed to change his mind. "I think I'll need some help," he said instead.

Jason helped him to stand and walked him to the nearest cell, setting him down gently. "It's all right, Constable," he said. "You'll feel much better in a few days. Is there anyone to look after you once you get home?"

"My mother," the young man said. "She'll have something of a shock when she sees me."

"Don't worry. I will speak to her and tell her how brave you were today," Jason promised.

Constable Ingleby smiled woozily, then laid his head down on the cot. His eyes fluttered closed as he allowed himself to relax.

When Jason came back upstairs, he was met by Sergeant Flint at the front desk. "Nice job out there, your lordship," he sneered. "Always the hero."

"Where's Inspector Haze?" Jason asked, ignoring the man's sarcasm.

"Interviewing the suspects."

Jason took a step toward the corridor where the interview rooms were, but Flint called out to him. "I think it's time you went home, Lord Redmond. Your presence is no longer required. If there's someone as needs butchering or stitching, I'll be sure to let you know."

Jason fixed Sergeant Flint with a derisive stare. The man had been growing progressively more hostile, possibly because he rarely left his position behind the desk, reading penny dreadfuls and drinking endless cups of tea to pass the time between the few individuals who visited the station to report a crime or file a complaint. Despite his rank, he was rarely out in the field. Jason had never asked why that was, nor did he care. The running of the station or the use of its resources had nothing to do with him.

To some degree, Sergeant Flint was correct. In his capacity as on-call police surgeon, Jason had no business interviewing the suspects. He was neither a policeman nor a private investigator. He was what some would refer to as an amateur sleuth. He wasn't sure he liked the classification, nor did he care for Sergeant Flint's insinuation that he wasn't welcome. If neither Chief Inspector Coleridge, who was Daniel's superior, nor the Commissioner had expressed a desire for him to leave, he was sticking around.

"Thank you for your suggestion, Sergeant Flint. When I have a mind to take orders from a lowly clerk with ideas above his station, I'll be sure to let you know. Now, if you don't mind, I'll join Inspector Haze." Perhaps the retort had been too cutting, but Jason was in no mood to play games. He was too eager to hear what the Goodwins had to say.

# Chapter 32

Jason found Daniel in the corridor, looking tired and anxious. Now that the Goodwins were safely ensconced in interview rooms, the full extent of what had taken place at the farm was beginning to sink in. Had the curricle pulled into the yard first, Neil Goodwin might have decided to eliminate the one person who had the authority to make an arrest, and then pick off the rest of them one by one until there was no one left to stand in the way of the Goodwins' escape.

"How's Constable Ingleby?" Daniel asked.

"As well as can be expected. He's resting in one of the cells," Jason replied. "Have you spoken to either of them yet?" he asked, referring to the Goodwins.

"No. Mrs. Goodwin is weeping, and her husband is pacing the room like a caged animal and spewing threats. I think I'll let him cool his heels overnight and then try to speak to him in the morning. At any rate, Mrs. Goodwin seems a better bet. She's frightened, heartbroken at being separated from her children, and furious with her husband for turning what could have been a peaceful arrest into a shootout worthy of the Wild West. Had Neil Goodwin climbed onto the roof and shouted that he'd murdered Sebastian Slade, he'd look less guilty than the option he settled upon."

"Shall we speak to Mrs. Goodwin, then?" Jason asked. He reached for Daniel's arm when he turned toward the door. "Daniel, it's all right that I'm here, isn't it?"

"Of course. Why do you ask?"

"Seems Sergeant Flint has other ideas. He just told me I have no right to be here and suggested I make myself scarce."

"Sergeant Flint has no authority here," Daniel replied. "CI Coleridge, however, does, and he takes no issue with your presence. As our police surgeon, your involvement is justified, and all the more appreciated because you're not a salaried policeman, nor do you make any demands for compensation and perform the autopsies pro bono. Now, are you ready to question this suspect, or do you require further reassurance?" Daniel asked with a tired smile.

"Lead the way."

Rose Goodwin looked a fright. Her eyes were puffy from crying, her face blotchy, and her nose red and moist. She held a crumpled handkerchief in her hands and sniffled loudly.

"My children," she moaned as soon as Daniel walked in. "They'll be frightened."

"Your children will be well cared for, Mrs. Goodwin," Daniel assured her. "The vicar and Mrs. Hodges will do their best to explain the situation to them."

Mrs. Goodwin looked dubious. She'd seen the look on the Hodges' faces when Daniel had delivered the children to their door but had not flinched in the face of their disapproval and shock, all her thoughts for her children.

"And my husband?" she asked warily.

"Shouting obscenities at anyone who comes near," Daniel replied, his voice taking on a sharp edge.

"I'm sorry about that. I tried to reason with him; you must believe me. I didn't want anyone to get hurt."

"But hurt they were, Mrs. Goodwin, so let's talk about what happened, shall we? First, I'd like to ask you a question. Is your daughter Emily Grace Holloway?"

"No," Rose Goodwin cried. "No, she's not."

Daniel sighed with impatience. "Mrs. Goodwin, I have been up since dawn. I haven't eaten, and I'm so hot, I feel like I'm being roasted alive. In other words, I don't have the patience for your lies. I can lock you up in a cell and go home. So, let's try this again. Is Emily Grace Holloway?"

"Why do you think she is?" Rose Goodwin asked, her shoulders sagging in defeat.

"Because your maiden name is Evans. Mrs. Hodges was happy to confirm that when I delivered the children to the vicarage. Grace Holloway's nursemaid was named Evans. Quite a coincidence, as is the fact that Emily shares a familial defect with Bernard Holloway, who's her biological father."

"What defect?" Rose Goodwin asked, looking genuinely taken aback.

"Grace was born with a harelip, which was repaired shortly after birth. Her father is similarly afflicted."

"I never noticed," Rose whispered. "He always wore a moustache."

"Emily is also about the same age as Grace would now be and bears a striking resemblance to her mother."

Rose Goodwin didn't say anything but seemed to grow smaller, sliding down in her chair as if she wished to disappear altogether.

Daniel continued. "Grace Holloway was in your charge at the time of her kidnapping, and the police only had your word for what occurred."

"There were witnesses," Rose Goodwin protested meekly.

"Yes, but what they saw and what actually took place are two very different things, aren't they? Now, I ask you again, and if you lie to me, down to the cells you go. Is Emily Grace Holloway?"

"Yes." The word sounded like an exhalation, the final breath of a dying person.

"Why did you take her?" Daniel asked, his gaze boring into the cowering woman.

Rose shook her head miserably. "I can't tell you," she whispered, her cheeks and neck turning a mottled red. "You're a man."

"Will you tell me, Mrs. Goodwin?" Jason asked softly. "I'm a doctor."

Rose Goodwin considered that for a moment. "All right," she said at last.

"Inspector Haze, please give us a moment," Jason said.

Daniel stood and left the room.

"Go on, Mrs. Goodwin. Please, don't be embarrassed."

Rose took a moment to work up the courage to speak. "My mother died when I was twelve," she said quietly. She stared at the handkerchief in her hand, unable to meet Jason's gaze. "I had no sisters or aunts to talk to. It was just me and my dad. He was a good man, but he wasn't much of a talker, not that he would have spoken to me of such things. I was eighteen when I took up the position with Mrs. Huxley. She was a kind woman, and as much a companion to me as I was to her. She liked to talk, and not only about herself."

"Go on," Jason said, wondering where this was heading.

"She was quite wealthy. Her late husband made a fortune importing Indian textiles and spices and such." Rose drew a shuddering breath. Jason thought she was stalling, but she had to tell her story in her own time.

"There was a parlor and an upstairs maid, a cook, a scullion, and a lady's maid, so for the first time in my life, I was surrounded by women. I didn't realize it right away, but as the months passed, I became aware that something was different about me." Rose Goodwin started crying again, silent tears sliding down her cheeks. "Shelly, the upstairs maid, kept asking if I needed rags, and said I didn't need to see to them myself. She'd wash them. It was part of her duties to see to the laundry. I had no idea what she meant. Eventually, I worked up the courage to ask."

"You don't menstruate," Jason said, feeling immense sympathy for this woman, who must have been frightened out of her wits to discover there was something profoundly wrong with her.

"No."

"Did you ever see a doctor?"

"Mrs. Huxley sensed that something was wrong, so I confided in her. She called in her own physician to examine me," Rose said. She bowed her head and fixed her gaze on her folded hands, working up the strength to tell him the rest. "The doctor said I didn't have a womb and would never have children of my own. Until that day, I never really thought about having children. I was eighteen. I wanted to save my wages and maybe open a shop one day or see something of the world, but the moment he said it, it was like my whole being was overcome with longing. It was all I could think about. I fretted about it for weeks, trying to come to terms with this new reality, but I just couldn't. If I couldn't have children, no man would ever want me, I thought. I would be forever alone, left to wither and die like an unpicked fruit."

"I'm sorry. That must have been a very difficult time for you," Jason said.

"It was. After a time, I decided that one day I would take a baby from an orphanage and raise it as my own. That made me feel a little better, just knowing that not all was lost. When Mrs. Huxley died, she left me a small bequest, but I didn't want to spend it, so I found another position. The Holloways had known Mrs. Huxley, so a character reference she'd been kind enough to write before she died was enough to get me hired. I wanted to see how I would feel taking care of an actual baby. Maybe I wouldn't like it at all, I thought. Maybe I'd find it burdensome to look after a child. But I didn't. I loved Gracie with all my heart. I pretended she was mine," Rose said softly.

"So you decided to take her?" Jason prompted.

Rose nodded. "When Neil started talking marriage, I told him the truth. I would never be able to give him children of his own. Not ever. But he didn't seem to mind. He said if it meant so much to me to have a child, we could always get one. I thought he meant we could take on an orphan or even buy some unwanted mite from a baby farm, but he knew how much Gracie meant to me."

"So it was his idea?"

"At first, yes. But the more I thought about it, the more it made sense. Gracie was so lovely, so sweet, but her parents paid her no mind. Mrs. Holloway saw her for a few minutes in the morning and then again in the evening before I put her to bed. Mr. Holloway saw her maybe twice a week. They took no interest in her and were embarrassed by the defect she'd been born with, fearful it would ruin her chances of a good marriage once she came of age. They didn't love her, but I did," Rose exclaimed. "I knew her every expression, her every mood. I rocked her and sang to her and walked all night with her when she was cutting her teeth. I bathed her and changed her and talked to her. She was my baby."

"Was it Neil who snatched Gracie in the park?" Jason asked.

Rose nodded again. At this stage, there was no use denying anything. "Yes. He knocked me to the ground, like I told him to, took the baby, and ran. He handed Gracie off to a mate of his as soon as he reached the trees, so when the men from the park caught up to him, he was empty-handed. They thought they got the wrong bloke, so they had to let him go. The police never even questioned him. Neil's friend's wife took care of Gracie until I was able to leave my position with the Holloways, and then we left for Brighton the very next day."

"I'm going to call in Inspector Haze now," Jason said. He stepped out into the corridor and quickly filled Daniel in on what had been said.

"She doesn't have a womb?" Daniel questioned, his brow knitting in confusion. "Is such a thing even possible?"

"In nature, anything is possible. I've never come across a woman who was born without a womb myself, but I've heard of such things. There are many reasons for infertility; this just happens to be one of them."

Daniel nodded, the truth of the situation making itself known. "That would mean that the boy isn't hers either."

"Precisely."

"What a kettle of fish this turned out to be," Daniel said. "Kidnapping, murder, and an attempt on a constable's life. They knew there was no way out for them the minute you spoke to that child."

"They had time to flee," Jason pointed out, but he understood the ramifications of such a decision.

"Yes, but they'd be forced to leave everything they own behind. That farm is worth a fair bit, and they'd always be looking over their shoulders, since disappearing that way would be an admission of guilt."

"As soon as Sebastian Slade showed up in Upper Finchley, there was never an out for them, was there?" Jason agreed.

"No, I don't suppose there was, but I'd still like to hear how it happened."

"Let's find out, then," Jason said, and the two men returned to the interview room.

"Mrs. Goodwin, you do understand that Grace Holloway will be returned to her parents?" Daniel asked once the two men took their seats.

Rose Goodwin didn't reply. She was no longer weeping, her demeanor reminiscent of a rag doll, a boneless dummy devoid of all human emotion. She was spent, but Daniel wasn't finished with her, not by a long shot.

"Did you take Johnny from a family in Brighton?" Daniel continued, ignoring Rose Goodwin's blank stare. "Mrs. Goodwin," Daniel prompted when she failed to respond.

"Would you like a glass of water?" Jason asked.

"Yes, please," she finally replied.

"I'll call Constable Pullman," Daniel said.

"I'll get it," Jason said.

The water was lukewarm at best, but Rose Goodwin downed it in seconds and set the cup on the table before her. Her hand trembled violently.

"Mrs. Goodwin, where did your son come from?" Daniel asked again.

"His mother left him alone for hours while she charred for the neighbors. He cried and cried, the poor mite," Rose said, her voice so low, the men had to lean forward to hear her. "I could hear him through the window."

"Do you know her name?" Daniel asked.

Rose nodded. "Gladys Motte."

"And what was Johnny's given name before you took him?"

"Silas. Silas Motte. It wasn't a nice name." Rose's head snapped up, her gaze filled with desperation. "I was a good mother to him, to them both. I love them with all my heart and always will."

"I'm sure you do, Mrs. Goodwin," Daniel said in his most soothing tone, "but you had no right to take those children. Not even if you thought their parents were neglectful or even cruel."

"I know that, Inspector Haze. Don't think that I don't," Rose said wearily. "What will happen to us now?" That last bit was said with no emotion, as if she'd already made peace with the outcome.

"That largely depends on how honest you are prepared to be," Daniel replied.

Rose Goodwin's head lifted, her bleary gaze fixing on Daniel. "What do you mean? I have been completely honest."

"What happened with Sebastian Slade?" Daniel asked.

"I don't know, Inspector. That had nothing to do with us. Neil and I thought you'd figured out about Emily and that's why you'd come."

"I don't think that's entirely true, Mrs. Goodwin. As soon as you saw Sebastian Slade at St. Martin's, you knew you were in danger. Mr. Slade wasn't likely to recognize Grace, not after all that time, but he was sure to remember you. After all, he'd lived at the house while you were employed by the Holloways. He would have seen you every day."

"So what?" Rose Goodwin asked, a note of defiance creeping into her voice. "I left their employ, got wed, and had me a child. Nothing sinister about that. And you can be sure he never looked at Gracie close enough to notice the scar. He had no interest in her. He held her maybe once the whole time I was there," Rose fumed. "The man was too preoccupied with his own fine self, strutting around like a peacock and harassing the servants. I was too plain to catch his roving gaze, so I was safe, and to someone like him, invisible."

"According to those who knew him, Mr. Slade was quite upset by Gracie's abduction. It had weighed on his mind. Seeing a woman who'd been her nursemaid with a little girl of a similar age who bears a more-than-passing likeness to his sister was sure to raise his suspicions."

"He never noticed her, I tell you. We came in just before the service began and left before it ended. He hardly saw us."

"He would have made the connection sooner or later, Rose," Daniel pointed out.

"Maybe so, but I didn't think he'd be around long enough to figure out the truth of the matter."

"Why was that?" Jason asked.

"Because I'd overheard Mrs. Holloway talking about him to her husband. She said he was fickle, spoiled. Couldn't settle to anything. He was in debt too. Lost every penny his parents had settled on him. She was afraid they'd have to support him for the rest of their days. So I knew he wasn't a man of fine character. I didn't think he'd last long in a place like this. All we had to do was wait a while, and he'd be gone."

"So, you have no knowledge of what happened to Mr. Slade?" Daniel asked.

"I do not."

"Thank you, Mrs. Goodwin," Daniel said.

"Please, can I go home now?" Rose Goodwin pleaded. "Can I see my children?"

"I'm afraid not. You'll be spending the night in the cells."

"But I told you the truth," she cried. "I was honest about everything. I know I did wrong, but I didn't kill no one."

"Mrs. Goodwin, you are guilty of two counts of kidnapping. That's not a charge you can walk away from. It carries a lengthy prison sentence."

"Prison?" Rose Goodwin echoed, as if she'd never considered the possibility of being tried for her crimes.

"That's right. We'll talk more tomorrow," Daniel said. "It's been a long day for all of us."

Daniel summoned Constable Pullman, who took Rose Goodwin down to the cells. She shuffled along like an automaton, her gaze unseeing as she was led away.

"Why do I feel pity for her?" Daniel asked once they had taken Constable Ingleby to his mother and left him to her tender care.

"Because you are a compassionate man, and anyone can see that she genuinely loves those children."

"Which is absolutely no excuse," Daniel replied.

"I didn't say it was. As she herself pointed out, there are plenty of children in need of a home. She could have had a family without destroying someone else's. Had she never met Neil Goodwin, she likely never would have had the courage to take Gracie."

"No, she wouldn't," Daniel agreed. "Perhaps if Goodwin admits to the actual kidnapping, his wife can be tried on a charge of accessory. She'll still go to prison, but for a shorter time."

"Either way, her life is ruined," Jason said.

"Do you think she told us the truth about Slade?" Daniel asked.

"She seemed sincere enough," Jason replied. "But this is a woman who's played a part for the past three years. She could just as easily be playing one now. The Goodwins have a rock-solid motive for killing Slade, and they would have had the opportunity."

"That's true, but why leave him where he could be found? They have a sizeable farm. Had they buried him on their land, no one would have been the wiser."

"Just bad luck, I suppose," Jason said. "Not many gravediggers take their duties as seriously as Arthur Weeks. Had he not examined the grave so closely, Slade would have spent eternity resting beneath Mrs. Crowe's coffin."

Daniel sighed. "Truth be told, I'm not looking forward to questioning Neil Goodwin tomorrow. The man is volatile."

"Yes, I think you'd better have Constable Pullman in the room with his truncheon and keep Goodwin handcuffed throughout. He will not go down without a fight."

# Chapter 33

## Tuesday, August 13

Morning came all too soon, and Daniel found himself heading back to the station. He was glad that Jason had agreed to come as well, despite Sergeant Flint's nasty comments. He would have to speak to Chief Inspector Coleridge about that and see what his superior had to say. Perhaps Sergeant Flint had only been repeating what he'd overheard and felt confident in belittling Jason's contribution, safe in the knowledge that his viewpoint was supported by those above. But Daniel couldn't allow such an injustice to go unacknowledged.

The men at the station might not be aware of it, but he knew that Jason had solved the case singlehandedly, and Daniel felt both grateful for and embarrassed by the outcome. Even if the Goodwins hadn't killed Sebastian Slade, which was a big if, Jason was responsible for two families getting their missing children back. Daniel was sure the newspapers would make much of the story, especially if they got wind of the fact that the case had been cracked by an outsider and not a member of the police service.

The Brentwood Constabulary would likely never live down the humiliation. And neither would Daniel, not because he'd failed to solve the case, but because in the small hours of the night, he'd admitted to himself that he was quite shaken and maybe a tiny bit jealous of Jason, and the acknowledgement of those feelings had made him burn with shame. He had to do better, had to be better, not to impress Jason or remain on the police service, but for himself, and for Sarah. His dreams had come true, but now he had to work hard to hold on to the results. He'd finally fallen asleep just as the sky turned a lighter black in the east, feeling slightly more at peace with himself now that he'd confronted his deepest fears.

"Did you tell Katherine about the case?" Daniel asked as the curricle chewed up the miles and sped toward Brentwood.

"No. I didn't want to upset her," Jason replied. "Anything to do with mothers and babies is very close to her heart, particularly at the moment."

"You mean because she's expecting?" Daniel asked.

"Yes, and also because we now find ourselves responsible for Liam, an arrangement that has been foisted on us without our consent, more so on Katherine, since she has no ties to the Donovans beyond my involvement with them. We both love the boy, but it still rankles that Mary would simply walk out and leave her son."

"She trusts you to look after him," Daniel said.

"Yes, I know," Jason replied. "But that doesn't make it okay."

Daniel never had understood that odd American expression, but he got the gist. No, it wasn't *okay*, just as his bout of resentment hadn't been okay.

"Would you like to interview Neil Goodwin?" Daniel asked, hoping to make it up to Jason in some small way.

"No, Daniel. Neil Goodwin is yours."

"Jason, I—" Daniel began, but Jason cut him off.

"Daniel, forgive me for saying this, but I don't think pride and police work go hand in hand."

"What on earth do you mean?" Daniel demanded, suddenly wondering if Jason could see right through him.

"I mean that what matters is the result, not how you got there or who helped you along the way. As long as the methods are honorable and you have nothing to be ashamed of, you must take the good with the bad. Stop beating yourself up about missing the Emily Goodwin/Grace Holloway connection and solve Sebastian Slade's murder. Today, that's what matters."

Daniel nodded, unable to speak. It pained him that Jason could so easily see through him, but he was right. Today was all about Sebastian Slade.

Jason left the curricle at a nearby livery, and the two men entered the police station. Sergeant Flint's gaze lingered on Jason a moment longer than necessary, but Jason didn't seem to notice, or if he did, he didn't acknowledge the sergeant's displeasure.

"How were things last night?" Daniel asked.

"All quiet, guv. The prisoners attempted to communicate, but Constable Pullman put an end to that right quick. He moved the woman to the furthest cell, so they'd have to yell pretty loud to get themselves heard."

"Was Constable Pullman here all night?" Daniel asked.

"Nah. He went home around eleven and was right back here at the crack of dawn. He's taking this case very personal-like, on account of Ingleby."

"Do we know how he is this morning?" Daniel asked.

"I stopped in on the way to the station. I expect he'll be back before you know it," Sergeant Flint said with a sly smile.

"Why's that?" Daniel asked.

"Have you met his mother?" Flint replied, his sarcasm obvious.

"Yes, I have, and if she gets him back to us quickly, I'll be grateful," Daniel replied. Sergeant Flint grated on him at the best of times, and this was hardly that. "Please have Constable Pullman bring Neil Goodwin to the interview room. And tell him to handcuff the man before taking him out of his cell."

"Right, guv," Sergeant Flint said, and headed downstairs, while Daniel and Jason proceeded to the room.

Daniel had expected much the same behavior as the day before, but Neil Goodwin looked like a man who hadn't slept a wink, and his lean jaw was dark with a day's worth of stubble, the bandage on his forehead crusted with blood. Given the blow on the head he'd sustained the day before, his head had to be hurting like the devil. Neil Goodwin sat behind the table, his cuffed wrists visible as he rested his hands on the tabletop, his gaze traveling from Daniel to Jason in the dispassionate way of someone who no longer had anything to lose. But despite his subdued demeanor, there was a coiled strength in him, a suppressed violence Daniel could only guess at. Constable Pullman was positioned behind Goodwin's chair, his truncheon at the ready should the man decide to put up a fight.

"Mr. Goodwin," Daniel greeted him as he took a seat. Jason sat down next to him, his expression wary. Goodwin didn't reply.

"Mr. Goodwin—" Daniel began, but the man interrupted him.

"I did it. I'll sign a confession to that fact, if ye like."

"Did what, exactly?"

"All of it. I talked Rose into taking Grace Holloway 'cause I knew how much she loved that girl. It were all my fault. And I killed Slade."

"Why? Did he threaten to expose you?" Daniel asked.

"Aye, he did, when we met to talk things over."

"Human life doesn't mean much to you, does it, Mr. Goodwin?" Daniel asked. "You killed Sebastian Slade and would have probably killed all four of us if you'd had the chance."

"I have as much respect for life as any man, but I will do what I must to keep my family safe."

"You mean to keep your family from undue scrutiny?" Jason interjected, unable to remain quiet.

Mr. Goodwin turned his head slowly and looked at Jason, his gaze misted with unshed tears. "I love Rose. I've loved 'er since the day I saw 'er at Drury Lane. She's a wonderful woman, kind and gentle and loving, and too good for the likes of me. All I ever wanted was to make 'er 'appy, and she was 'appy for a time, and would 'ave continued to be 'ad that nosy curate not shown up and ruined everything."

"How did you get him to meet you at the graveyard?" Daniel asked.

"I sent round a note asking 'im to come."

"Why did you wait nearly two weeks to confront him?" Jason asked. "Were you hoping he hadn't made the connection?"

Neil Goodwin sighed. "We hadn't been at church that first Sunday, when 'e were introduced to the congregation, but when we came last Sunday, that's when we knew it were all over for us. 'E recognized Rose as soon as 'e laid eyes on 'er. 'E stopped speaking midsentence, 'is mouth opening like a fish. She were so unsettled, she 'ad to leave. Just grabbed Johnny, since 'e were grizzling anyway, and fled. I didn't know what 'ad 'appened at first, but once she told me 'e were our Emily's uncle, I knew it were time to act."

"Whom did you send this note with?" Daniel asked.

"Solly. 'E's a bit slow, so everyone just ignores 'im. Treats 'im like 'e's invisible. I told Solly to wait till 'e saw the curate come outside, not go to the door and ask to see 'im. Solly gave 'im the note on Monday afternoon."

"So, you met at the graveyard, then what?" Jason asked.

"Slade threatened to call the authorities on us, said 'e'd see us 'ang for what we'd done, so I grabbed the shovel and struck 'im on the 'ead. I thought 'e were dead, so I buried 'im. Then I went 'ome."

Daniel and Jason exchanged long looks before Daniel turned back to Neil Goodwin. "Mr. Goodwin, you didn't kill Sebastian Slade. Your wife did," Daniel said, never taking his eyes off the man.

"No!" he cried. "I tell ye, it were me. I did it. Rose never knew nothin' about it. She were asleep."

"Take him to his cell, Constable, and bring up Mrs. Goodwin," Daniel said.

Neil Goodwin allowed himself to be led away, his head hanging low, his whole posture that of a man defeated by life, or a man who wished to give that impression.

"She lied to us," Daniel said to Jason as soon as they were alone.

"Yes, I believe she did," Jason replied sadly. "And her husband is willing to hang for her."

Daniel nodded. "Sebastian Slade was many things, but a fool wasn't one of them," he said, needing to verbalize his reasoning. "He would not have agreed to meet Neil Goodwin in the graveyard at night. Lord knows I never would. The man radiates violence, even when he's seemingly calm. But Slade would have felt safe enough to confront Rose on her own, thinking she wouldn't have what it takes to do him harm. Although I can't see what such a meeting would have accomplished. If Sebastian Slade was set on alerting the authorities, nothing Rose could say would have changed his mind, not if he was certain Emily was Grace Holloway." Daniel sighed. "I almost admire Neil Goodwin for willing to take the blame, but I bet Rose isn't aware that's what he tried to do."

"He adores her, and he loves those children," Jason said. "His sacrifice can't undo what's come to pass, but it can save Rose's life and give her another chance at a family, if she's willing to risk it again."

Constable Pullman returned with Rose Goodwin. She looked exhausted and unkempt, her hair hanging around her face like limp curtains and her dress soiled with sweat and snot. She wasn't crying, but her eyes were red-rimmed, her face puffy and pale. She fell into the chair as if her legs had suddenly gone out from under her.

"Mrs. Goodwin, your husband has confessed to the murder of Sebastian Slade."

Rose grew even paler, her eyes widening in shock, but she remained silent, saying nothing to give herself away.

"I don't think he did it," Daniel went on. "It was you, wasn't it?"

Rose Goodwin refused to meet his gaze, but her lower lip trembled, and she bit it, drawing blood.

"Are you willing to allow the man you love to hang for your crime?" Daniel pushed.

Rose bowed her head and gave it a minute shake. She looked like a woman about to come undone. Perhaps she already had.

"Rose Evans Goodwin, I charge you with the murder of Sebastian Slade, two counts of abduction, and obstruction of a police inquiry."

Rose Goodwin nodded dumbly. "What will happen to Neil?" she asked at last, her voice low and hoarse. "He was only trying to protect me."

"Your husband shot at and wounded a policeman. He will go to prison. He's lucky Constable Ingleby didn't die. The penalty for murder is death by hanging."

She nodded again and wrapped her arms about her middle for support.

"Mrs. Goodwin, why did you kill Sebastian Slade?" Daniel asked. The answer was obvious, but he needed to hear her say it, to have it on record that she had done the deed.

"Because he blackmailed me," Rose Goodwin replied, surprising both men.

"He threatened to turn you over to the police because he realized Emily was his niece?" Daniel asked.

Rose Goodwin's head shot up, her red-rimmed eyes blazing with anger. "He cared nothing for Emily, or Grace, if that's what you prefer to call her. Nor did he care about his sister's suffering. He wanted money. He always had. Slade knew I had Grace all along. He'd seen me with Neil when he walked me home on my afternoon off, and Slade was at the park when Neil snatched Grace that day. Slade recognized him, but he didn't say anything to his sister or to the police.

"Instead, he told me I could keep Grace as long as I paid him off. Neil and I gave him everything we had, but then we left London and changed our surname to Goodwin, and he lost track of us. Everything was all right. We were happy. Imagine my surprise when we came to church last Sunday to find that the new curate was the one person who had the power to ruin our lives." She raised her head defiantly.

"I didn't tell Neil it was him, not at first. The two had never met face to face, so Neil was none the wiser. But Slade recognized me immediately when he saw us before the service, and made a point of speaking to Emily, asking her name and such. Much as you had," she said, turning to Jason. "As soon as Neil walked on ahead, he told me to meet him at the graveyard at midnight and to bring money."

"So you went," Daniel said.

"No, I didn't. We left halfway during the service. You should have seen the look on Slade's face when he saw me walk out. Probably thought we meant to flee, and he'd lose his chance to squeeze us again. Once we were home, I told Neil I wasn't well. I spent the rest of the day in bed, wrestling with myself, trying to figure out what to do. We could run, change our names again, start someplace else, but we would lose everything we'd worked for. We'd lose the farm, our friends and neighbors. So I decided to meet with him. I thought maybe I could reason with him, plead with him to leave us alone if I paid him one last time. I went round to Mrs. Monk's on Monday to bring her some eggs. I'd written a message for him and was going to leave it with her, but there was no need. I met him on the way; he was coming out of the post office. I said, 'Graveyard at midnight,' and walked past."

"What happened when you met?" Daniel asked.

"I sneaked out after Neil fell asleep and walked to the village. Slade was already there, waiting for me, sitting on the plinth of an angel gravestone, looking up at the stars. He smiled, as if we were old friends. I told him I'd brought the money—this was what was left of Mrs. Huxley's bequest to me. He took the money, counted it, and put it in his pocket. Then he said that I still owed him for the three years I'd skipped out on and that he expected a payment every month from now on. If I failed to pay, he would go straight to the police and tell them he'd recognized his niece. I knew Neil and I would never be safe, not ever. So I grabbed the shovel and struck him. He sank to his knees and grabbed his head, but then he managed to stand and began to stagger away. I hit him again with all my might and he went down on his knees and then fell over, his eyes rolling into the back of his head. I thought he was dead, so I pulled the money out of his pocket, shoved him into the open grave, and shoveled dirt over him. I was sorry for what I had done, but there was no going back. All I could do was make sure he was never found. And had that dolt of a gravedigger not come round the next morning, I'd have gotten away with it. I'd have saved my family."

Rose Goodwin's expression changed from one of defiance to desperation. "Inspector Haze, please, may I say goodbye to my children?" she asked. "May I explain to them that what I did, I did for love of them? I just need them to know that."

"I'm sorry, Mrs. Goodwin, but I'm afraid I can't allow you to see the children. You and your husband will be transported to the nearest prison, where you will await trial. The children will be returned to their parents."

"Please," Rose Goodwin wailed. "I beg you."

"The best I can do is allow you to write a letter to them. I will pass the letters on to their families and ask them to allow the children to read them when they are older. Whether they agree or not is entirely up to them."

She nodded. "Thank you. I appreciate that."

"Take her away, Constable," Daniel said, and watched as the woman was led away.

# Chapter 34

"Why do I feel no satisfaction at having apprehended the murderer?" Daniel asked once Rose Goodwin was gone and he and Jason were left alone.

"Because you know what it's like to lose a child," Jason replied. He hated to admit it, but he felt pity for Rose Goodwin as well. "What Rose Goodwin did is reprehensible, but in some instances, it's impossible not to feel some compassion for the perpetrator, especially when the victim is not worthy of sympathy. I must admit I didn't see that coming. To think that Slade had known about Grace all along," Jason said. "That's diabolical, so much more so in a man of God."

"Yes," Daniel said. "I do feel sorry for her, even though I shouldn't. And I do feel sympathy for her husband. Just don't tell Constable Ingleby that," Daniel said with a small smile. "I'll never live it down."

"I wouldn't dream of it," Jason replied.

"All this time, we thought Sebastian Slade had been distressed by something that had happened during the service, because everyone said he had seemed distracted and unsettled, but he was probably worried that the Goodwins would outwit him again and flee before he had a chance to blackmail them. He hadn't been shocked by the sight of his niece, as one might expect, only fearful of losing out on the money he could make and annoyed by Mr. Gale's attempt to speak to him after the service when all he'd probably wanted to do was consider how to best proceed without compromising his new position," Daniel said, obviously still needing to understand Sebastian Slade's state of mind.

"When he'd written the letters to his sister and friends, he must have felt as if God himself had sent him to Upper Finchley, the one place he'd never expected to find Rose Evans. No wonder he'd felt as if he suddenly understood his true purpose. It wasn't to help Reverend Hodges or become worthy of his position; it was to squeeze the Goodwins dry."

"Will Rose Goodwin hang, do you think?" Jason asked.

"Most likely. There are no mitigating circumstances that can appeal to a judge's sense of pity. She took the children, and she killed Slade. It's an open and shut case."

The two men stood and left the room, Daniel to report to CI Coleridge and Jason to retrieve the curricle.

"Would you like me to wait for you?" Jason asked.

"No, you go on home. I've taken up enough of your time this week, and you have your own life to attend to. When's Micah leaving for school?"

"Two weeks," Jason replied. "And now we must find a nursemaid for Liam. Perhaps Katherine knows of someone local who'd like a job."

The men approached CI Coleridge's office, and Jason raised his hand in greeting before walking off.

"Lord Redmond, a word before you leave," CI Coleridge called out just as Daniel was about to enter his office.

"Go on," Daniel said. "You go first."

Jason entered the office and accepted the offered seat.

"Well spotted on the Holloway girl," CI Coleridge said. "Couldn't have solved this case without you."

"Thank you, sir," Jason replied.

"I hear Neil Goodwin has confessed."

"Inspector Haze will fill you in on the details," Jason said, not wishing to steal Daniel's thunder. His confidence had taken a beating over the past few days. He needed to be the one to tell his superior of the outcome of the case and receive the praise. Sometimes, Daniel was his own worst enemy, but it was his vulnerability that made Jason feel close to him. He was real, and as an American, Jason valued that above all else.

"Was that all, sir?" Jason asked when CI Coleridge failed to continue.

"Eh, no. There have been some rumblings from the men."

"Meaning?"

"Meaning that there's some resentment that Inspector Haze is relying on you to assist him on his cases when he could be training up one of them. Constable Pullman is a competent young man. He'll go far if paired with the right mentor."

Jason felt a pang of sadness. He loved working a case, thinking it through, testing out his theories, and sharing them with Daniel. He would miss detective work, but he could understand why the constables would feel resentful toward him. For Jason, this was a bit of fun. For them, it was their livelihood.

"Are you asking me not to involve myself in any more cases, sir?" Jason asked, just to be clear.

CI Coleridge chuckled. "No, your lordship. I'm asking you to come aboard. Look, I know you're not looking for paid employment. You said so yourself when I asked you to act as permanent police surgeon, but I know you enjoy police work, and you're damn good at it."

"So, what are you suggesting, exactly?" Jason asked, suddenly feeling lighter than he had only a moment ago.

"I suggest we give what you do for us legitimacy. How about becoming Special Advisor to the Police? What do you think of that? You will be paid for your time and expertise." CI Coleridge raised a hand before Jason had a chance to protest the monetary aspect of this solution. "If you don't want the money, give it to a charity. Use it to buy goodwill from the men by buying them a round at The Bells. It's entirely up to you, but if you wish to continue to involve yourself, it must be in a more official capacity. What do you say?"

"I say yes," Jason replied, smiling happily. "Special Advisor to the Police," he repeated. "I like that. Just don't call me a SAP."

CI Coleridge nodded, not quite getting the joke. "I'll inform the men. Good day, your lordship."

"Sir, if I may. As my first official assignment, I'd like to ask permission to be the one to return the Goodwin children to their real parents."

"Good idea. That will require sensitivity, and you are just the man to do it. I don't expect it will take long to locate the boy's family."

Jason left the office and grinned at Daniel. "I'll wait for you. I have some news."

"All right. I won't be long," Daniel replied, and went in to update his superior.

Jason stepped outside into the muggy afternoon and looked up at the sky. He wasn't sure how Daniel would take his news or how the other men would react to his new legitimate role, but he didn't care. He'd earned this, and it made him surprisingly happy to feel acknowledged. He had no wish to become a full-time detective, nor to take too much time away from his life with Katherine, but he needed something to occupy his mind and give him a sense of accomplishment. Had they lived in London or Edinburgh, he might have approached one of the medical schools and offered his services. Surgery was a growing field, and there was a demand for teachers to train the younger generation. Maybe in time, Jason thought.

"What did Coleridge want?" Daniel asked once he exited the station and came to stand beside Jason.

"He made me Special Advisor to the Police," Jason said, not bothering to hide his elation.

"I think this news deserves a drink. The Bells?" Daniel asked as he clapped Jason on the shoulder. His reaction seemed genuine, and Jason breathed a sigh of relief, glad Daniel didn't see his new status as a reflection on his own abilities.

"The Bells," Jason agreed, and followed Daniel to the tavern.

# Epilogue

## December 1867

A dusting of snow covered the front lawn and coated the trees of the park, making them sparkle silver in the moonlight. The night was quiet and peaceful, a merry fire crackling in the hearth and the glow of the gas lamps casting a mellow pool of light over Katherine's hair. She was already in bed, a book propped up on her belly. She set the book aside and smiled at Jason as he joined her in bed, his hand instinctively resting on the growing mound that was his child.

It had taken time to grow used to the silent house once Micah started school and Shawn Sullivan departed for London, but Jason couldn't complain. Life had been good. Katherine's pregnancy was progressing normally, Liam was thriving with his new nursemaid, and Mary was well, or at least that was what her letter said. She was in Boston, working in a shop and seeing a young man she'd met soon after returning stateside. Micah was enjoying school and making new friends.

But Jason was restless and bored. He'd worked on a few cases since the arrest of the Goodwins, but nothing that had required any great detective skill. The perpetrators had been so careless, they'd practically left a trail of crumbs for the police to follow. Jason and Daniel had not worked together since August, and their interaction had been limited to social occasions and brief meetings at church. They had seen each other only that afternoon, though, and the meeting had left Jason feeling unbearably sad.

"What is it?" Katherine asked softly as she lay her hand over his. "You've been prowling the house like a caged tiger all day."

"It's nothing, Katie," Jason replied, not wishing to upset her. "Everything is perfect."

Katherine gave him a knowing look. "If it has something to do with the newspapers you've tried to hide from me, then I'll find out anyway," she said. "I only have to ask someone in the village. I'm sure Moll Brody will be happy to fill me in. She's always up on the latest gossip."

"I didn't want to distress you. Please, let's not talk about it."

"Just tell me," Katherine said. "Whatever it is, I'd rather know the truth."

Jason sighed. There was no sense in arguing with her. She would find out anyway, and whoever told her would be sure to lay on the gory details.

"Rose Goodwin was hanged yesterday," Jason said, an image of Rose's sweet, round face before his eyes. She hadn't died easily. The fall hadn't broken her neck, and it had taken her a good twenty minutes to suffocate to death, her suffering witnessed by a bloodthirsty mob who had jeered at her and called her names. Daniel had been present at the hanging, since he had been the arresting detective and felt it his duty, but Jason had refused to attend. He'd seen enough violent death to last him a lifetime.

"May God have mercy on her soul," Katherine said. "But there's more, isn't there?"

There was. "Neil Goodwin used his shirt to hang himself last night. He tore it into strips and braided the strips into a rope. They found him this morning. He left a note asking for the farm to go to Johnny, since neither he nor Rose had any living relatives and Grace's family is well-to-do, so Grace will be looked after."

"I expect Johnny's parents will sell it, but the proceeds will give the boy a good start in life," Katherine said sadly. "Neil was thinking of his children until the very end. What a sad ending for that family. I hope the children will be able to forget Rose and Neil in time and accept their new situation." Katherine suddenly raised her head, her gaze flying toward the window. "Someone's coming," she said. "I heard hoofbeats."

Jason jumped out of bed and went to the window. He couldn't see the man's face, but the tall helmet was easy enough to recognize, as was Constable Pullman's distinctive gait, and the wagon that stood in the middle of the drive was the police wagon Constable Pullman usually brought to a crime scene. Jason hastily dressed, ran a hand through his hair, and stopped by the bed to plant a kiss on his wife's forehead.

"It's Constable Pullman. Don't wait up, darling," he said, his heart beating just a little bit quicker than it had five minutes ago.

"Please be careful," Katherine said. "Oh, I do hope it's nothing dreadful."

Jason arrived in the foyer to find Constable Pullman pulling rank on Dodson. "I don't care what time it is. His lordship is needed," Pullman was saying. His coat was dusted with snow and his face was red with cold beneath the bulky helmet.

"What's happened, Constable?" Jason asked.

"I'm sorry to disturb you so late in the evening, sir, but there's been a suspicious death."

"Tell me," Jason said as he absentmindedly held out his hand for the medical bag Fanny had just brought down.

"Seems the Tarrants, the new owners of Ardith Hall," Pullman clarified, "held a séance tonight. All was going according to plan and everyone was in high spirits," Constable Pullman couldn't help but grin at his own little joke before continuing, "when one of the guests was taken by a coughing fit. Next thing you know, he was spewing blood, and was dead as a doornail a few minutes after. Dr. Parsons was called in. He reckons the man was poisoned."

"Dr. Parsons was called to a séance?" Jason asked as he shrugged on his coat and followed Constable Pullman out the door. He couldn't imagine the uptight country doctor involving himself in such goings on, even as a medical professional, if he could be referred to as such.

"Indeed, he was," Constable Pullman said, his gaze sliding away from Jason in a way that made Jason suspect he wasn't telling him the whole story.

"Constable?" Jason asked. "What's troubling you?"

Constable Pullman seemed to draw in his head, his shoulders hunching as he held the reins. "It's Mrs. Haze, sir."

"What about her?"

"She was there, at the séance," Constable Pullman said, his voice barely audible.

"What?" Jason cried. "Are you certain it's her?"

"Yes, sir. Seems she was hoping to contact her little boy."

"Where's Inspector Haze?" Jason asked as he climbed onto the bench of the police wagon.

"He's been summoned. I reckon he'll meet us there. If you're ready, sir," Constable Pullman said.

"Let's go," Jason said warily. This case promised to be a tricky one.

**The End**

**Please turn the page for an excerpt from**
**Murder at Ardith Hall**
**A Redmond and Haze Mystery Book 6**

# Notes

I hope you've enjoyed this installment of the Redmond and Haze mysteries and will check out future books.

I'd love to hear your thoughts and suggestions. I can be found at irina.shapiro@yahoo.com, www.irinashapiroauthor.com, or https://www.facebook.com/IrinaShapiro2/.

If you would like to join my Victorian mysteries mailing list, please use this link.

https://landing.mailerlite.com/webforms/landing/u9d9o2

# Excerpt from Murder at Ardith Hall

# A Redmond and Haze Mystery Book 6

# Prologue

A single candle in a silver holder glowed in the center of the table, casting a golden halo of light onto the tense faces of the people seated around it. The velvet tablecloth felt smooth and rich beneath her exposed wrists as Sarah joined hands with the guests on either side of her. The gold fringes of the cloth brushed against her thighs, sharpening her already heightened awareness.

The psychic, Mrs. Lysander, sat directly across, her dark eyes wide and her lips slightly parted as she took in the subdued group. She was younger than Sarah had expected, and more beautiful, her face and manner radiating an ethereal quality further enhanced by a low, melodious voice that Sarah found strangely soothing.

There were four others at the table: Mrs. Tarrant, their hostess, Lord Julian Sumner, Mr. Roger Stillman, and Mr. Nathaniel Forbes, a businessman from Barbados, all of whom had been introduced when they'd gathered in the drawing room before adjourning to the little parlor Mrs. Tarrant had designated for Mrs. Lysander's use.

Sarah shivered with anticipation, her reservations about coming tonight forgotten, as Mrs. Lysander asked them to close their eyes and remain silent for the duration of the séance. Mr. Forbes was on Sarah's right, his hand large and warm on hers. Mr. Stillman sat on her left, his fingers long and elegant but cold and unsteady as he took hold of her hand. It felt odd to hold hands with men who were virtual strangers, and uncomfortably intimate without the benefit of gloves to prevent such personal contact.

She had lied to Daniel, telling him an old acquaintance had invited her to an evening of cards. He'd been surprised, since she rarely went out on her own, especially in the evening, but made no move to dissuade her from coming. Daniel wouldn't understand, nor would he approve, but this was something Sarah felt she had to do. And so here she was, trying to contact her darling Felix, who'd died four years ago at the age of three.

Mrs. Lysander closed her eyes and began to speak, summoning the spirits of the departed and urging them to show themselves. Sarah wondered if they were all meant to come at once, or would they take turns appearing to their loved ones? She shivered, suddenly frightened. Her earlier excitement had been replaced by gnawing fear, and she wished she could leave, but it was too late. The psychic's voice grew louder, turning into an almost inhuman wail as she called out to the deceased.

"Show yourselves," she implored.

Sarah allowed one eyelid to lift marginally. Mrs. Lysander sat with her eyes closed. Her head was thrown back, her face contorted with raw emotion as she opened herself up to the otherworldly presence that she claimed had entered the room and was ready to speak to them. By this point, everyone had opened their eyes. Their expressions were rapt, their gazes bright with longing, each one holding their breath in the hope that it was their loved one that was about to make themselves known.

"What is your name?" Mrs. Lysander moaned. "Tell us, O spirit."

As she sat frozen, listening intently for the spirit to fulfill her request, Mr. Stillman yanked his hand out of Sarah's grasp. His fingers clawed at the starched collar of his shirt, his eyes bugging out as his face turned a mottled red, the flush spreading to his neck. He opened his mouth, a croaking sound that might have been a call for help bubbling forth.

"Mr. Stillman!" Mrs. Tarrant cried. She sprang to her feet and rushed toward the man, although Sarah wasn't sure what she planned to do.

A torrent of blood erupted from Mr. Stillman's open mouth, the dark red fluid pooling on the velvet tablecloth and soaking into the fabric. He gasped for breath, his fingers desperately yanking at his blood-soaked cravat. When the noxious smell of loosened bowels wafted from the afflicted man, the other guests pushed back their chairs in shocked disgust, their horrified gazes flitting from one person to another as they tried to decide what to do. In his distress, Mr. Forbes knocked over the candleholder, extinguishing the flame and plunging the room into darkness.

Sarah heard a shrill cry, then realized it was coming from her. She was terrified, her hands trembling violently as she pushed away from the table, desperate to leave. Mr. Forbes grabbed hold of her hand, and together they groped their way toward the door, flinging it open to let in a faint shaft of light from the gas lamps in the corridor.

Despite her terror, Sarah turned back to see what was happening. Mrs. Lysander was on her feet, her beaded reticule in her hands. Lord Sumner seemed transfixed by the tableau playing out before him, his eyes wide with shock. Mrs. Tarrant was still working to loosen Mr. Stillman's cravat and unbutton his collar, but it was too late. His hands stilled and his gaze clouded as a soft sigh escaped his open mouth, his head tipping forward. Sarah's hand flew to her mouth as she realized the man was dead.

"Send for Dr. Parsons and the police," Mrs. Tarrant cried, her voice shrill with horror.. "And don't touch anything!"

# Chapter 1

## Wednesday, December 18, 1867

Jason Redmond gazed at the imposing façade of Ardith Hall as the carriage rolled through the wrought-iron gates and made its way up the sweeping drive. Moonlight filtered through a flotilla of clouds that sailed lazily just above the twin peaks of the roof, illuminating the scene for several moments before plunging it into semidarkness once again. The house stood solid and stark at the edge of a snow-covered lawn and was surrounded by extensive parkland. According to Constable Pullman, who was driving the police wagon, the estate had belonged to the Ardith family for more generations than anyone could recall, but for reasons known only to himself, the last descendant of the proud old family had sold the house to a wealthy merchant from London about a year ago and decamped to the south of France with his mistress.

Jason had not had the pleasure of meeting Lord Ardith before his flight to France, but he had met the new owners last August at the annual fete in Birch Hill, the closest village to the Ardith estate. Mr. Tarrant had chatted to Jason for a few minutes and drifted away to greet someone he knew, but Mrs. Tarrant had talked his ear off until he finally found an excuse to extricate himself and go find his new wife in the tea tent, where she was lending a hand.

The carriage finally pulled up before the house, and Jason hopped down and strode across the frost-crusted gravel toward the front door, not waiting for Constable Pullman to join him. He'd be along in a few minutes, once he surrendered the horse and wagon to the groom. The butler silently took Jason's things and pointed him toward the library, where Mrs. Tarrant was pacing like a caged tigress in her distress.

She was in her mid-forties, a slight, nervous creature who reminded Jason of a magpie. Her dark curls bounced as she looked up at him, her cheeks and neck flushed above the lace-trimmed bodice of her mauve gown. She wore a necklace of jet beads and matching earrings that swung like two tiny pendulums, the black stones reflecting the light of the fire. Her attire proclaimed her to be in half mourning, but Jason didn't know whom she'd lost or how recently.

"Thank the good Lord you've come at last, your lordship," Mrs. Tarrant gushed. "I really am at a loss. I sent word to Dr. Parsons, but he refused to come. Told my man to summon you, since you are more knowledgeable in these matters and there was nothing he could do for the deceased. Such a tedious man," she complained. "Utterly inept at social discourse. Not that this is a social occasion, of course, but he could have been more considerate of my guests. Mr. Stillman might be beyond his help, but my guests are in a state of shock and might have needed seeing to." She took a deep breath. "I pride myself on being a practical woman, Lord Redmond, but this is too much. Really it is," she blathered on. "To have a guest die in such shocking circumstances. The poor man. I can only hope I made his final moments a bit less frightening than had he been on his own. And John is not here," she moaned. "He's in Manchester on some wretched business. Always business," she said bitterly. "Even with Christmas right around the corner. I can't begin to imagine what Mr. Stillman's death means for the rest of us. Will we be able to continue, do you think?"

"I'm sure you did everything in your power to help Mr. Stillman and look after your guests, Mrs. Tarrant," Jason said, interrupting the flow of words. "Can you tell me what happened, and what is it that you wish to continue?"

"Yes, of course," Mrs. Tarrant said. "We were in the middle of a séance. The spirit had just made its presence known to Mrs. Lysander when Mr. Stillman went red in the face and began to cough. I was irritated at first, I don't mind telling you, since his coughing might have driven the spirit away. But this was no ordinary coughing fit. He was gasping for breath, his chest heaving as he struggled to draw air into his lungs." Mrs. Tarrant's hand flew to her breast as if she had trouble breathing herself. "And then the blood came," she whispered. "So much blood. It just erupted from his mouth, like a waterfall. Have you ever seen a waterfall, Lord Redmond?"

"Yes, I have. What happened then?" Jason asked.

"Well, he tried to say something, but it was impossible to make out the words, with the blood pouring out of his mouth. I suppose he was asking for help. He struggled in vain for a few more moments, then died. Just slumped in his chair, his eyes staring and his mouth open, blood dripping from his lips. It was horrid," she said, her eyes filling with tears. "And violent."

"Where's the deceased now?" Jason asked, hoping the dead man hadn't been moved. He wished to see him in situ.

"I left him just where he died. I knew we shouldn't disturb the scene, just in case there's something to be learned from the position of the body and the like. He's just this way. In the parlor. I had no idea you worked with the police, your lordship," Mrs. Tarrant said as she led him toward the room. "Imagine that, a man in your position assisting the police. Why, I don't quite know what to make of it. It's charitable of you, I suppose," she mused as she pointed toward the closed door. "I'll remain out here, if you don't mind. Lord knows, I won't be able to sleep tonight, not after what I've seen," she said. "Oh, I do wish John were here."

"When is Mr. Tarrant due back?" Jason asked.

"Not till the twenty-fourth, I'm afraid. You will take the body away, won't you?" she asked, her gaze pleading with Jason to say yes.

"Of course, Mrs. Tarrant. The body will be moved to the mortuary tonight."

"Well, that's something, I suppose," Mrs. Tarrant said. "I'll leave you to it, unless there's something you require."

"My colleague and I will need to speak to everyone who was present, but first, I would like to examine the body."

"Be my guest," Mrs. Tarrant said, and gestured toward the door.

Jason opened the door and entered the parlor. The curtains had been drawn, and a candle, which must have been used during the séance, lay overturned on the table, a solidified blob of wax stuck to the velvet tablecloth and the wick. The deceased sat in solitary silence, his face waxy in the light from the open door. Jason found the switch and turned on the gas lamps, flooding the room with mellow light. Setting his medical bag on the chair nearest the door, he approached the dead man gingerly, his gaze sweeping the floor and his nose wrinkling at the awful smell that emanated from the deceased. His bowels had let loose at the moment of death, and there was a noxious brown puddle beneath the chair.

The tablecloth was soaked through with blood, the stain nearly black on the burgundy velvet. Aside from smears of blood on the man's chin, cravat, and cuffs, there were no visible marks on the body. Jason studied the man before conducting an examination. Roger Stillman was in his mid-thirties. He had a thick head of fair hair and very blue eyes fringed by dark-blond lashes. His high cheekbones, fair skin, and straight nose put Jason in mind of the pillaging Norsemen he'd seen in history books. He had been an attractive man and, with his lean frame and toned muscles beneath his well-tailored suit, a physically fit one. Whatever had killed this man had not been an ongoing illness, Jason concluded.

He carefully combed the surrounding area, searching for any signs of poison or a concealed weapon, then maneuvered the dead man to the floor, carefully undressed him, and performed a thorough examination before dressing him again.

Jason left the body on the floor and exited the parlor to find Mrs. Tarrant waiting outside with a young maidservant, who had a folded towel slung over her arm and was holding a basin of warm water. Jason cleaned his hands, retrieved his medical bag, and turned toward the drawing room, where the remaining guests were assembled. It was at that moment that Daniel arrived with Constable Ingleby, who had been sent to fetch him.

Daniel's shoulders were dusted with snow, his face red from the cold, but his eyes were bright with anticipation, the question uppermost in his mind obvious as his gaze locked with Jason's. "Was he murdered?" Daniel asked.

"I won't know for certain until I perform the postmortem," Jason replied. "But the symptoms are consistent with arsenic poisoning. Given the man's violent reaction, I'd say that the arsenic was administered shortly before death rather than over a prolonged period."

Daniel nodded. "Let's interview the guests and see what we can learn," he said as he shrugged off his coat and handed it, together with his hat and gloves, to the butler hovering at his elbow. "Constable, make sure none of the guests leave," Daniel said to Ingleby. "I think it's best if you take up a position in the drawing room so you can keep an eye on the suspects while we interview them."

"Yes, sir," Constable Ingleby said.

Constable Pullman, who'd been standing near the drawing room door, his helmet under his arm, approached Daniel, ready to receive instructions from his superior.

"Constable Pullman, speak to the staff. Find out where everyone was this evening, if anyone had come in contact with the deceased, and who had been in the drawing room and parlor today. Were they privy to the identities of Mrs. Tarrant's guests? Also, I need to know who would normally be responsible for filling the decanters. Take everyone's statement, and let us know if there's anyone we need to interview in person."

Constable Pullman drew himself up, his eyes glowing with pride at the responsibility he'd been given. It was common knowledge around the Brentwood station that Constable Pullman was gunning for a promotion and hoped to be made inspector in the near future. He had been taking on more responsibility and was proving to be an invaluable asset to both Daniel and Inspector Peterson, who'd taken Constable Pullman under his wing and was teaching him the ropes.

"Oh, and Constable," Daniel said just as Constable Pullman made for the green baize door that separated the rest of the house from the servants' quarters. "Question Mr. Stillman's coachman. If he has nothing of value to impart, send him home. No sense keeping the man waiting in the bitter cold."

"Will do, sir," Constable Pullman said, and disappeared through the door.

Daniel walked toward the drawing room and opened the door. The four witnesses were spread about the room, the women sitting by themselves, the men engaged in quiet conversation, which ended abruptly when Jason and Daniel walked in. Jason had been curious to meet Mrs. Tarrant's guests, but the only person he saw was Sarah Haze, who sat staring at her hands folded in her lap.

Daniel froze when his gaze settled on his wife. He opened his mouth to say something but changed his mind, turning to Jason for help. Jason nodded his understanding and stepped in, giving Daniel a moment to compose himself.

"Ladies and gentlemen," Jason began. "This is Inspector Haze of the Brentwood Constabulary, and I am Jason Redmond, special advisor to the police. We would like to speak to each of you in turn to learn what transpired tonight. Once we are finished, you will be free to leave." His gaze slid toward Sarah, who looked like she wished the chair would swallow her whole. Jason would have dearly liked to speak to her first and send her on her way, but this was Daniel's investigation, and he would have to determine the order in which the suspects were interviewed.

Jason glanced at the men but didn't linger, allowing his gaze to settle on Mrs. Lysander instead. He'd heard of her, of course. There had been an article in the *London Times* about the renowned psychic and her uncanny ability to summon the most reluctant of spirits. Few people came away from her séances disappointed, and several past participants had been quoted gushing about Mrs. Lysander's sensitivity and discretion. She never discussed her clients nor her methods for contacting the dead. There had been a grainy photograph of the psychic in the *Essex Standard* about a week ago, but it had failed to accurately depict the woman seated before him.

Mrs. Lysander was younger than Jason had expected, around twenty-five, if he had to guess. Her jet-black hair was artfully arranged about a face that was exotic and arresting in its beauty. Almond-shaped black eyes fringed with thick lashes stared back at him, challenging him to discredit her, and a ghost of a smile tugged at her sensuous lips, as if she were amused by what had taken place during her séance rather than horrified by Roger Stillman's sudden and violent death. Jason had to admit that he looked forward to speaking with her, if only to learn more about her origins. Few people aroused his curiosity, but Mrs. Lysander was without question one of them.

Jason suddenly realized that a pregnant silence had fallen over the room as the four witnesses awaited instructions. No doubt flustered by Sarah's presence, Daniel had yet to speak.

"Daniel," Jason prompted softly.

"Right," Daniel said, as if waking from a bad dream. "I'd like to speak to Mrs. Tarrant first. Is there somewhere we can talk in private?" he asked, his gaze still glued to Sarah's panicked face.

"We can use the library," Mrs. Tarrant said, and stepped forward to lead the way.

"Did you know Sarah was here?" Daniel asked under his breath as they made their way down the silent corridor.

"No. I'm as surprised as you are. Did you not know where she was tonight?" Jason asked softly.

Daniel didn't reply, but his expression said it all.

# Chapter 2

The library at Ardith Hall was most impressive, with shelves upon shelves of books, a vaulted ceiling, and stained-glass windows that gave the room an almost church-like appearance. Several chairs were grouped around a low table before the hearth, and there were also discreet alcoves for those who wished not to be disturbed while reading.

No one had been using the library, but a fire blazed in the great fireplace, the room pleasantly warm and cozy despite its size. Mrs. Tarrant dropped into a seat and gestured for the two men to do the same. Daniel took the armchair closest to the hearth and pulled out his notebook, but his mind wasn't on the case. Sarah hadn't been at home when he'd returned from the Brentwood police station a few hours ago, and her mother had said that Sarah had been invited to an evening of cards at Chadwick Manor.

Daniel had been surprised, since Caroline Chadwick didn't normally make overtures of friendship to his wife, but had thought nothing of it, sitting down to an early dinner with his mother-in-law and then spending an hour in the nursery with his darling Charlotte before her grandmother put her to bed. He had assumed that Sarah had told him about the invitation and he'd simply forgotten, but now realized that she hadn't, probably because she preferred not to lie to him about where she was going. To think that she had made secret plans to attend a séance with the famed Mrs. Lysander left him not only speechless but deeply hurt.

Daniel flipped the notebook to a fresh page, wondering angrily why Sarah had felt the need to withhold the truth from him. Had she thought he wouldn't approve? Or he'd try to forbid her from going? Perhaps he would have. He didn't believe in the occult, nor did he condone the practice of trying to contact the dead. Psychics had sprung up like mushrooms after rain in the last few years. Feeding on the desperation of the bereaved and relieving them of their hard-earned money, they used obvious parlor tricks to convince participants at their séances that they had made contact with their departed loved ones. The psychic might go on to ask the spirits questions, instructing them to knock once for yes, twice for no. It was easy enough to counterfeit a knock, either with a foot or with a piece of wood tied to the psychic's knee. They'd raise the knee beneath the table and strike the underside, answering in place of the spirit. How gullible did a person have to be to fall for such claptrap?

Daniel refused to acknowledge the other reason desperate people waited for weeks to attend a séance with the psychic of their choice. They were heartbroken, unable to let go. He felt a dull ache in the vicinity of his heart but set his personal feelings aside and turned his attention to Mrs. Tarrant, who seemed to be vibrating with nervous energy.

"I really can't believe it," Mrs. Tarrant exclaimed. Now that the initial shock had worn off, she was as petulant as a child. "You don't know what it took me to secure Mrs. Lysander for this evening, and now everything's been ruined, and I'll never get another chance to make contact with my darling Hector. This really is unfair. I had such hopes for tonight," she moaned.

"Mrs. Tarrant, can you please tell us what happened? From the beginning," Daniel invited.

The woman sighed tragically. "Once everyone arrived, we proceeded directly into the parlor. Some hosts serve supper before, but I thought it would only delay what everyone had come for and asked Cook to prepare a light repast for those who wished to linger after the séance. Truth be told, I hoped they would leave so I could be alone with my thoughts. Who wants to make small talk after such an emotional experience?"

"When did Mr. Stillman arrive?" Daniel asked, trying to steer Mrs. Tarrant back to the events of the evening.

"He was the third to arrive. Mr. Forbes was the first, and then Mrs. Haze joined us. I invited them to have a drink in the drawing room whilst we waited."

"Did Mr. Stillman have a drink?" Jason asked.

"Yes."

"What did he drink?"

"Scotch whiskey. He had a glass when he arrived and then accepted a refill once Lord Sumner had joined us."

"Did Mr. Forbes have a drink as well?" Jason asked.

"Mr. Forbes prefers rum, which I didn't have, so he settled for a glass of sherry."

"Did anyone else have Scotch?" Daniel inquired.

"No, only Mr. Stillman," Mrs. Tarrant said.

"I would like to examine Mr. Stillman's glass and the decanter," Jason said.

"The glass has already been removed, but the decanter is still in the drawing room," Mrs. Tarrant said. "I'll be sure to give it to your man as soon as I'm done here."

"Thank you. How did Mr. Stillman seem?" Jason asked. "Did his demeanor change after he drank the whiskey?"

Mrs. Tarrant thought about that for a moment. "He was a little pale when he arrived, but I assumed he was just nervous. The whiskey did seem to calm him somewhat, but then he grew anxious again and accepted another drink when I offered it."

"Whom was he trying to contact?" Daniel asked.

"I don't know. It's not customary to discuss such things before a séance," Mrs. Tarrant said with a small shake of her head, as if the men should really know better than to ask such questions.

"Who's Mr. Stillman's next of kin?" Daniel asked, his pencil poised to make a note.

"He lived with his mother. In Mayfair. I'll get you the address."

Daniel nodded his thanks. "And how do you know the people you invited tonight?" he asked, trying to sound nonchalant.

He tried to recall if Sarah had ever mentioned the Tarrants couldn't bring up any memory of such an occasion. He'd heard of them, of course. There had been much talk when Lord Ardith absconded with his seventeen-year-old mistress and sold the family seat to a trumped-up merchant, but Daniel had never known them socially and assumed Sarah didn't either. The Tarrants had attended the church fete last August, as reported by his mother-in-law, but Sarah had been unwell that day, and she and Daniel had skipped the event.

Mrs. Tarrant smoothed down her skirts, even though there wasn't a wrinkle in sight. "I know the gentlemen through my husband. He's done business with them for years, and I've had the pleasure of receiving them at our London house."

"And Mrs. Haze?" Daniel asked, nearly choking on the name.

"I met Mrs. Haze several years ago, when we both belonged to a charitable organization for the improvement of London's orphanages. Those places are woefully overcrowded, and the conditions in which the children live are appalling," Mrs. Tarrant exclaimed. "Mrs. Haze and I had a lengthy discourse on the subject when I invited her to tea."

"In London?" Daniel asked. He couldn't recall Sarah taking tea with a Mrs. Tarrant, but then he had been busy with his work and hadn't paid as much attention to Sarah's needs as he should have. Nor had he been the best father he could have been, taking it for granted that his son would always be there when Daniel had time to spend with him.

"Yes, in London," Mrs. Tarrant replied. "It was only recently that I discovered that Mrs. Haze lives not too far from Ardith Hall. I wrote to her immediately, hoping to renew our acquaintance. You see, I had heard that she lost her precious boy several years ago. That's why she'd stopped coming to the meetings. I had sent a note of condolence but didn't wish to intrude on her grief. It wasn't long after that I lost my Hector," Mrs. Tarrant said, covering her mouth to stifle a sob. "I know Hector was practically a grown man, but a child always remains small and vulnerable to its mother. I suppose I was looking for someone who'd share my grief."

"Have you and Mrs. Haze been in contact long?" Daniel asked, afraid his chagrin was obvious. How had he not known that Sarah had belonged to the organization Mrs. Tarrant had mentioned and recently renewed their acquaintance? Why hadn't she told him?

"A few months. John and I came to Essex to escape the Season. It'd been more than a year since I'd come out of full mourning for my boy, but I simply couldn't bear the thought of attending anything more spirited than a musical evening or an intimate supper. And wild horses couldn't drag Flora to a ball," she added. "So, it's not as if we're doing her a disservice by keeping her away from all that rigamarole."

"And who is Flora?" Daniel asked.

"Our daughter. She's under the weather, so she remained upstairs tonight," Mrs. Tarrant explained. "Anyhow, Mrs. Haze and I had much to talk about, and when I put forward the idea of a séance, she agreed after a period of consideration. She did ask me to keep our plans confidential, since she didn't want her husband to know. Didn't think he'd approve."

"Mrs. Tarrant, you do realize that Inspector Haze is Mrs. Haze's husband," Jason said, clearly unable to keep silent any longer.

"What?" Mrs. Tarrant screeched, staring at Daniel with undisguised horror. "Oh, I do beg your pardon. I was so distraught, I completely missed your surname, but I thought it was all right, as long as I referred to you as Inspector." She cocked her head to the side, her dark eyes bright with glee as the implications of Daniel's presence sank in. "Do you not wish to speak to your wife, Inspector? Surely she'd be able to tell you everything you need to know."

"I'll speak to my wife in due course," Daniel replied stiffly. "Right now, I'd like to hear your version of events."

"Well, as I was saying, we all met in the drawing room. Mrs. Haze and Mr. Forbes had a glass of sherry, and then we adjourned to the parlor once Lord Sumner arrived."

"Where was Mrs. Lysander?" Jason asked.

"Mrs. Lysander arrived a few minutes before Lord Sumner and was escorted directly to the parlor so she could set up."

"Did she come alone?" Jason asked.

"She has an assistant who sees to her schedule and acts as chaperone when the situation calls for it, but he didn't come inside. He took himself off to the Hound and Partridge to have a pint or two. He is due to collect her after the séance."

"And how does Mrs. Lysander normally conduct her séances?" Daniel asked. "I didn't see any implements, such as a crystal ball or a board for receiving messages from the dead."

"You see, Inspector Haze, that is the uniqueness of Mrs. Lysander's gift. She doesn't rely on any gimmicks. When a spirit makes an appearance, Mrs. Lysander goes into a trance and the visiting spirit speaks directly through her to their loved one. They hear the message, and so does everyone else, so there's no disputing the fact that a spirit has made contact."

"And does Mrs. Lysander bring forth the dearly departed of every person in the room?" Jason asked, sounding dubious.

"Oh no, my lord," Mrs. Tarrant replied. "If the attendees are lucky, then maybe two spirits will part the veil between this world and the next and speak to their loved ones."

"But from what I've read, no one ever leaves disappointed," Jason pointed out.

"Hearing the messages meant for others helps those who weren't as lucky to feel more at peace. They see for themselves that it is possible to contact the dead and that none of them appear to be suffering. That knowledge lessens their grief and gives them hope for the future. There are some who follow mediums like Mrs. Lysander from place to place, managing to secure an invitation to a séance more than once in the hope of their loved one coming to them at last."

"Did any spirits manifest tonight?" Daniel asked.

"We had just started when Mr. Stillman's coughing fit interrupted the séance, but Mrs. Lysander did say she felt a presence in the room. She never said who it was," Mrs. Tarrant said wistfully.

"Were you not supposed to keep your eyes closed during the séance?" Jason asked.

"Yes, Mrs. Lysander did instruct us to hold hands and keep our eyes closed, but I peeked just a little. I was curious to see what she'd look like when a spirit entered her body."

"And how did she look?" Jason asked.

"Blank," Mrs. Tarrant replied.

"Blank?" Jason asked in surprise.

"Well, of course," Mrs. Tarrant said, sounding exasperated. "She is a conduit, an empty vessel for the spirit to inhabit. How would you expect her to look?"

"Thank you, Mrs. Tarrant," Daniel said with a sigh. He dreaded working on this case, and not just because of Sarah's unexpected involvement. It was hard enough to get people to tell the truth and admit to their motives without dealing with restless spirits, heartbroken relations, and clever mediums. And Mrs. Lysander had to be clever, or she wouldn't be as sought after as she was. Empty vessel or massive fraud, she had found a formula that worked and would milk it until she either made enough money or was exposed as a charlatan.

"Would you kindly send in Mrs. Lysander now?" Daniel asked, bracing himself for the conversation with the psychic.

"Of course. Oh, I do hope she agrees to come back," Mrs. Tarrant lamented as she stood to leave, her small hands clasped before her. "I so want to speak to my darling Hector one more time."

# Chapter 3

To say that Mrs. Lysander walked into the room would be like saying that a train exploded into the station or that an ocean liner crashed into port. Alicia Lysander's feet didn't appear to touch the floor. She glided. And when she took the seat Mrs. Tarrant had just vacated, she seemed to settle into it with the softness of a snowflake landing on one's tongue. She wore all black, but the absence of color did not take away from her beauty. If anything, it enhanced it.

"Mrs. Lysander, tell us about yourself," Daniel invited as he took in the woman before him. It was obvious to Jason that he felt uncomfortable, and if Mrs. Lysander was any sort of psychic, it had to be evident to her as well.

"What would you like to know, Inspector?" she asked softly, her gaze never leaving his face, which seemed to be turning pinker with every passing moment.

"Where do you come from? Where's your husband? Where do you make your home?" Daniel clarified, more forcefully than necessary, in Jason's opinion.

Mrs. Lysander smiled sadly. "I was born and raised in India, the daughter of a British major and a native woman he'd taken as his mistress. I never really knew my mother, since my father tired of her and sent her away, nor did I ever figure out why he didn't allow her to take me, since he never showed much interest in me. An English governess was engaged for me in accordance with my father's wishes and spent the next decade trying to turn me into a proper English miss, while my Indian *ayah* worked hard to help me retain something of my Indian roots. I married Captain John Lysander when I was eighteen and was widowed at twenty, shortly after arriving in England. I keep rooms in London, but I travel all over the country, helping those who can't come to terms with their bereavement contact their departed loved ones."

"And when did you realize you have this rare gift?" Jason asked, feeling an irrational desire to needle her.

"I can see you're skeptical, Lord Redmond, and I don't blame you. There's many a charlatan in my profession, but I assure you, I'm the real thing. I've been able to relay messages from the dead since I was a child. The first one was for my father from my mother, who passed when I was five. Her spirit couldn't rest because he'd separated her from her daughter. She urged him to love me and legitimize me so that I would have a chance at a respectable marriage."

"Indeed?" Jason asked, trying in vain to hide his amusement. *How convenient.* "And did he?"

"He did legitimize me, since he didn't have any other children, but asking him to love me was going a step too far."

"So, this appeal from the dead proved highly beneficial for you," Jason remarked.

"Yes, but had my mother wished for him to send me away, I would have passed on the message all the same."

"Would you have?" Jason taunted.

"You clearly don't believe me, my lord. Perhaps you'd like to join one of my séances," Mrs. Lysander suggested. She showed no sign of annoyance or anger. "There are those who wish to connect with you."

"Thank you, but no. I have no desire to commune with the dead."

"Not even to say goodbye to your parents?" she asked, a smile playing about her lips. "Tell them you love them?"

"My parents knew I loved them," Jason replied tersely. "They don't need to be reminded."

"I bow to your American pragmatism," Mrs. Lysander said. "But India is a very spiritual country, and I have great respect for the dead and their wishes."

"Mrs. Lysander, I'm sure we could debate the merits of spiritualism until dawn, but let's concentrate on the here and now, shall we?" Daniel suggested. "Had you ever met Mr. Stillman before tonight?"

"I had not."

"Had you heard about him?" Daniel continued.

"No. When I arrive at a séance, all the guests are strangers to me."

"Except for your hostess, who made the arrangements," Jason pointed out.

"I had not met Mrs. Tarrant before tonight. She made the arrangements through my assistant."

"And how do you obtain your clients, Mrs. Lysander? Do you advertise in the papers?" Daniel asked.

"No. My clients come to me based on recommendations from others. I refer all inquiries to my assistant, so that I know nothing of the participants when I meet them on the day of the séance."

"Is there a reason your assistant doesn't accompany you inside?" Daniel asked.

"Mr. Moore's function is to deliver me safely and take me to my lodgings once I'm done. Rather than wait in the servants' hall, he prefers to take himself to a nearby tavern and have his supper. He's due to collect me at ten o'clock." She glanced at the clock on the mantelpiece pointedly. It was nearly ten.

"Did you see or hear anything out of the ordinary tonight?" Daniel asked. "Did you sense the impending death of Mr. Stillman?"

"I did not. I did, however, notice that he was unwell. I thought he had indigestion, but then again, I'm not a physician, only a medium."

"Do you know whom Mr. Stillman wished to contact tonight?" Jason asked.

"No. We were only a few minutes into the séance."

"Did you feel any spirits hovering nearby as Mr. Stillman breathed his last?" Daniel asked, a tad sarcastically.

"I did, as it happens. It was the spirit of a little boy. His name began with the letter F, and he was desperate to contact his mother."

Daniel blanched and looked away, but not before Jason saw tears in his eyes.

"That was unnecessarily cruel, Mrs. Lysander," Jason pointed out.

"I meant no offense. I simply answered the Inspector's question truthfully," Mrs. Lysander said. Given the look in her eyes, Jason was sure she had meant to cause offense, or more likely pain.

"That will be all for now, Mrs. Lysander. If you will provide us with an address where you can be reached, you are free to leave," Daniel said, clearly desperate to be as far from her as possible.

"I'm staying with Mrs. Evans at Bluebell Cottage near Elsmere. I will be there for three more days, as I have several engagements in Brentwood."

"And then?" Jason asked.

"And then I will leave for Colchester. Good evening, Inspector Haze. Lord Redmond."

Mrs. Lysander seemingly levitated from the chair and floated out of the library.

Made in the USA
Middletown, DE
21 January 2025

69845654R00142